I am a member of the Romantic Novelists' Association, having c... of the ... through the N... I a... is a m... of th... ... ...ne Writers' Association.

Lover of cake, dragonflies and France. Hater of calories, maths and snakes. I was born in Hertfordshire but had a nomadic childhood, moving often with my family, before eventually settling in West Sussex.

I am married with four children, all of whom patiently give me time to write but, when not behind the keyboard, I like to spend time with them, enjoying both the coast and the South Downs between which we are nestled.

www.suefortin.co.uk

@suefortin1

The Half Truth

SUE FORTIN

Harper*Impulse* an imprint of
HarperCollins*Publishers* Ltd
1 London Bridge Street
London SE1 9GF

www.harpercollins.co.uk

A Paperback Original 2015

First published in Great Britain in ebook format by Harper*Impulse* 2015

A catalogue record for this book is
available from the British Library

ISBN: 9780008136505

Automatically produced by Atomik ePublisher from Easypress

Printed and bound in Great Britain

Special dedication, thanks and love to my husband, Ged, for his constant encouragement and support, for believing I could finish writing this story when I doubted it myself and for tirelessly occupying our youngest so I could write. Much love to my older children Liam, Hayley & Ross for their moral support and independence and to Esther for patiently sharing mummy with the keyboard.

Many people have helped me to write The Half Truth but particular thanks to Julie Cohen and the day spent at her writing workshop. More gratitude to the HarperImpulse team for their invaluable input and support. To The Romaniacs for being the best cheerleaders. To my sister, Jacqueline, for telling me to write the Tina story and to Laura E. James who urged me to complete the Russian one, the end result of both being The Half Truth.

Finally, a big thank you to all my readers whose support makes writing so rewarding.

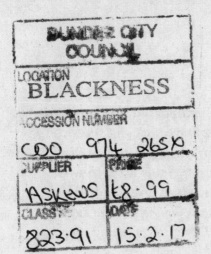

Chapter 1

Tina spun around, her eyes scanning the play area and beyond. She turned to her left and then her right, the sensation of being watched searing through her like a hot poker. The park was busy, but no one seemed to be paying her any attention. She was simply another mum entertaining her child on a warm Sunday afternoon. She physically shrugged in a bid to relieve herself of the hunted feeling, her eyes now seeking out her five-year-old son, Dimitri.

'Mummy!' he called, appearing at the top of the climbing frame. Tina waved at him, smiling broadly, revelling in her son's delight as he whizzed down the slide, landing with a bump in the sand at the end. He scampered up and darted back round to the steps.

Despite this momentary distraction, the feeling of being watched remained with her. She waited for Dimitri to complete a second descent.

'Come on,' she said, scooping him up as he landed with a dull thud on the ground again. 'Time to go.'

As they left the play area, Tina took another glance around. Her heart gave a little skip and she drew breath. The figure of a man caught her attention, but before she could look more closely he had disappeared out of view behind the coffee stand.

She closed her eyes for a moment. It was no good. She had to stop this. She should be used to it by now. It wasn't him. It couldn't be Sasha. He wasn't coming back. Ever. A slither of pain spiked at her heart, not as sharp as it once had been, but still strong enough to make her flinch mentally. Five years as a widow had dulled the intensity, or had she simply got used to living with it? She wasn't sure and now wasn't the time to analyse the notion further. It never was. Relegating the thought of her husband to the back of her mind, Tina took Dimitri's hand and headed over towards the kiosk.

'Do you want an ice-cream?' She knew she really didn't need to ask, but it was lovely to see the excited, gleeful expression on her son's face at the prospect of the treat.

'Ice-cream! Ice-cream!' sang Dimitri as he danced along beside her.

Standing in the queue, Tina realised she was doing it again; checking for anyone who might be watching her. As she looked beyond the kiosk her heart threw in an extra beat. There, hurrying away in the distance, was the man who had caught her attention earlier. The logical side of her brain challenged what was rapidly becoming her irrational part. It couldn't be Sasha. He was dead. Killed in a car accident. Her mind was playing cruel tricks on her. Was it any wonder, though, she thought as the figure continued its hurried departure? He looked the same height and build as Sasha, even had the same gait, his long stride covering the ground with ease.

The tugging of her arm caused her to look away as Dimitri pointed animatedly at the ice-cream he wanted.

'This one, with sprinkles and chocolate sauce,' he beamed, tapping the picture.

'Okay, sprinkles and chocolate sauce it is,' replied Tina, returning the smile.

When she looked back across the park, the man had gone. However, the sadness in her heart was not so eager to leave.

The call he had been waiting for came in. It lasted two seconds. The words 'We're on' were the only ones necessary. DS John Nightingale dropped the phone back in its cradle, simultaneously standing up. Seven pairs of eyes focused on him.

'Here we go, lads,' he said, the calm air in his voice belying the adrenalin rush that kicked at his heart rate. 'And lasses,' he added noting the raised eyebrows of his female colleague, Jackie.

John hiked his gun harness onto his shoulders, clipping it in place. He gave the Glock 26 snuggled in the holster a reassuring pat. An action born of habit; a subconscious reassurance.

There was a scuffling of chairs and flurry of action as the specialist organised crime- fighting unit scrambled. Primed, eager and hyped for what could be a particularly nasty encounter with the gang of armed robbers they had been tracking for the past six months.

The black BMW and 4x4 Range Rover sped swiftly through the dusk of the London streets, leaving a deserted headquarters behind them. They wove their way through the rear lights of the bedraggled tail end of rush-hour traffic, homing in on their target with stealth- like silence. No roaring engines, no flashing blue lights, no sirens. Purely an assured confidence in their training, experience and trust of each other.

John had been handpicked to head up this elite unit that operated loosely within the boundaries of London City's Met. They had been working together as a team for six years now. Faces rarely changed. Once you were in, you stayed in. They likened themselves to a marriage, the unofficial motto between them of 'Until death us do part.' And in two cases, it had. John pushed the black-dog memory of Neil Edwards' death away. Another reaction that had become a habit. He needed to stay focused on the task in hand. He wasn't going to lose another member of his team.

John headed the unit in the BMW, his partner and close friend, Martin Caslake, at the wheel and two more officers in the back seat, another four in the vehicle behind.

A text message alert sounded from Martin's pocket. He shifted in his seat, pulling out the phone and glancing at the screen. Reading the message, he cursed quietly to himself before tapping in a reply, all the time keeping one eye on the road ahead.

'I don't know why these private banks can't keep normal hours like the British ones. It would make our hours much more civilised,' said Martin.

'It's ten minutes before closing, the bank staff will be relaxed, on the wind-down for the weekend. It's the best time for the gang to strike,' said John.

'They are a week early.'

'Do you want to mention that to them?' said John. True, the original intel had said next week, but the update when he had gone into work that morning was that it was all happening tonight. He looked over at Martin. 'You got trouble?'

'I promised Maxine I'd take her out for dinner this evening. I forgot to let her know I wouldn't be able to make it after all.'

This provoked some jibes from the lads in the car. Mentions of 'hen-pecked' and 'under the thumb' banded about.

'Fuck off, you lot,' said Martin. He jabbed at the keyboard with his thumb.

'That was a long text just to say you were working,' said John, fighting to keep the smile from his face. 'You're very conscientious all of a sudden.'

More ribbing from the lads ensued.

'Well, some girls are worth it,' said Martin. 'Not that any of you would know, with your chuck-away, disposable love lives.'

'Sounds serious,' said John.

Martin shrugged in response without commenting. John didn't push for an answer. Personal relationships in the police force were difficult enough to maintain. Relationships within this specialist unit even more so. Hence why most of them were either single or divorced, John falling into the latter category.

As a car in front of them unexpectedly made a sharp right turn, causing Martin to swerve violently to the left, a tirade of comments on the other driver's Highway Code knowledge, or lack of it, followed. Martin's love life quickly forgotten. Subject matter no longer of any consequence.

'How long?' said John, checking his watch. The traffic was heavier than expected into the City.

'Less than five,' said Martin.

'Make that less than three,' said John.

Martin's reply was to downshift the gears and accelerate, overtaking the cars queued at the lights. Flashing his headlights, he bullied his way through, ignoring the tooting car horns protesting at the move.

John took a look over his shoulder to check that the Range Rover was still with them. It was.

The ambush was quick and efficient. The tip-off had come at the eleventh hour, but John and his team were prepared. Each knew their role. Screeching to a halt outside the private bank in Knightsbridge, John was out of the car and exchanging shots with the getaway driver before Martin had even cut the engine.

John and his team rushed to the entrance to the bank, the armed robbers meeting them in the foyer. Rapid exchanges of fire rang out throughout the hallway. Bullets bounced off walls and took nips and chunks out of plasterwork.

One of the robbers was taken out almost instantly whilst another took cover behind the reception counter and a third raced back up the marble staircase. The sounds of screams coming from the upstairs banking room and a rapid tap, tap, tap of gunshots followed.

John was huddled behind a marble pillar, Martin on the opposite side in a doorway.

John indicated to Martin that he and two others would go upstairs whilst Martin and the others gave them cover and dealt with matey behind the counter.

Covering gunfire gave John the chance to race through the foyer and up the stairs. He recognised the sound of a semi-automatic going off. The armed robbers' weapon of choice. The bullets rattled over his head, embedding themselves in the plasterwork. Ducking low, John ascended the staircase with speed. He heard the yell and groan of one of his team.

Taking a quick glance behind him, he saw Jackie sprawled on the steps, her hand clasping her leg, blood seeping through her fingers already.

'I'm okay! Go!' she shouted.

Another cry and as John's eyes swivelled in the direction of the counter, he caught a glimpse of the robber stumbling out from behind the counter. His finger closed over the trigger, gunfire spraying the foyer like a water sprinkler.

The next second a bullet shot through his forehead, exploding the back of his skull open. He was dead before he hit the floor.

John didn't waste any time. He sprinted up the remainder of the stairs and into the banking hall, his gun sweeping the room. Staff and customers were huddled together in one corner. Someone gave a small scream of alarm. Another whimpered.

Standing in the middle of the hall, the third gunman held a young woman in front of him, a gun at her head.

'I'll shoot her!' The gunman yelled through his ski mask.

'No you won't,' said John, steadying the Glock. 'Put the gun down.'

'You're not going to shoot me.' It was a jeer.

John weighed up the situation. The hostage was a good three inches shorter than the robber. It gave him just enough clearance above her shoulder.

'Are you going to do what I think you are?' It was Martin's voice behind him.

'Yep,' said John, his eyes fixed firmly ahead. 'You going to do your bit?'

'Yep. Already clocked her name badge.'

'Well, do you want to get on with it?'

6

'Alisha,' said Martin, his voice calm and low. 'Listen very carefully. You are going to be okay. I promise. All you have to do is stay very still. Do you understand?'

Alisha gave a small sob and eked out a sound of acknowledgement.

'Shut the fuck up!' said the gunman. 'Don't talk to her.' He cocked his gun. 'I'm not messing.' John could see his opponent's forefinger begin to squeeze the trigger. John's training now automatic, he zoned out his surroundings, focusing only on the man in front of him. He breathed for the count of three and as he exhaled he fired off one clean shot.

The gunman cried out and spun backwards. Alisha screamed and fell to the other side.

John fired off another shot.

The first had hit the gunman in the shoulder, the second in the arm as he had tried to reach for the gun he had dropped. John raced over, kicking the gun away. Alisha was scrambling across the carpet, sobbing in relief, frightened but unharmed. John stood over the groaning gunman and placed a boot on his chest.

'To coin a phrase,' he said, pointing his gun at the robber's chest. 'You're nicked.'

Chapter 2

It was a couple of hours later that John and his team regrouped back at HQ. The statements and paperwork could wait until the next day. The one surviving robber was under armed guard at the local hospital for the night. Interviewing would also wait until the next day.

'Well done this evening, everybody,' said DI Brogan, John's boss, coming into the open- plan office. 'No civilian casualties, despite that stunt you pulled, John.'

John gave a slight nod of apology. 'How's Jackie, Sir?'

'Flesh wound. They've removed the bullet, fortunately no long-term damage. You're obviously going to be a man down for a while.'

'Don't let Jackie hear you say that,' said John. 'Person down. We're going to be a person down for a while.' He stood up. 'We're going for a drink, Sir. Are you coming?'

'Before you go,' said Brogan. 'CID sent over some photos. Wondered if you could translate them, given your expertise on gang tattoos.' He dropped the brown envelope he had been carrying onto John's desk.

John picked up the envelope and pulled the half a dozen or so black-and-white photos out. He gave them a cursory glance and slid them back inside. 'What's the history?'

'Unidentified. Found dead, at the docks, yesterday. No ID, only the body art.'

'Okay, I'll take them home and have a look at them tonight,' said John, pocketing the envelope.

'Right, well, I'll leave you all to it,' said Brogan, turning and walking out of the office. 'Well done again, everyone.'

'It doesn't look very nice out there now,' said Tina as she began clearing the last of the tables at the café. She looked out of the window at the slate-grey clouds hovering overhead.

'Looks like it's about to rain,' said Fay, following Tina's gaze. 'And I haven't got my umbrella with me.'

'Why don't you get off early? I can finish up here.' Tina carried the tray of dirty cups and saucers out to the kitchen. She came back out a moment later for the remaining crockery. 'We're not exactly going to have a big rush on in the last half an hour. And Old Grumpy has gone.' She grinned at her colleague. Old Grumpy was their nickname for their boss; one he had earned with ease.

Fay was already untying her apron. 'Only if you're sure.'

'Of course I'm sure. Now go on, otherwise you'll get soaked.'

'Thanks, hun,' said Fay. She paused. 'Don't look straight away, but there's a man standing across the road – in a baseball cap.'

Tina smiled to herself as she placed the teapot onto the tray. Was this another unsuspecting male to add to Fay's Lust List? Fay's recent fall into singleton territory had made her practically a predator to all men. Tina looked cautiously out of the window from under her fringe.

It took her a moment to spot the man in question, but when she did it forced a sharp in-take of breath. She raised her head some more and looked closer. The man's eyes were hidden underneath the peak of the cap and the collar on his leather box jacket was pulled up. Although she couldn't see his features, instinct told her the man had spotted her. For a moment they were both suspended in time as they appraised one another. Then the man stepped back into the shadows of the disused shop doorway behind him.

'You all right?' said Fay. 'Tina?'

It took a second for Tina to register Fay's voice. 'Oh, yes, sorry.'

'Creepy, isn't he?' said Fay. Tina nodded. She didn't share with Fay that the man had reminded her of her ex-brother-in-law, Pavel. She didn't know what it was. Maybe it was his build, his stance. Possibly even the clothing. Whatever it was, Pavel had come straight to the fore of her mind.

'Why did you say creepy?' asked Tina, unsure if she really wanted to know.

'He was hanging around the other day. In fact, this is the third time I've seen him.'

'Really? Perhaps he's waiting for someone.'

'Hmmm, then why does he keep staring in here?'

'Stop it, Fay,' said Tina, flicking her friend on the arm and feigning a grin. 'I thought you were going anyway?'

Tina couldn't deny the uneasy feeling resurrecting itself again, her moment of generosity in telling Fay to go home, now a regret.

'I'll see you in the morning, then,' said Fay as she picked her jacket from the coat peg and hooked her arm through the handle of her bag.

Tina watched Fay disappear out the door and hurry off in the direction of the bus stop. She shivered at the rush of cold air, which had streaked in and was now winding itself around her body. She took another look across the road, the passing traffic partially obscuring her view.

There was movement in the darkened doorway. Tina narrowed her eyes, trying to get a clear view, but the traffic building up in the road was against her, the arrival of a bus making it impossible.

Drops of raining began to splatter against the glass and speckle the pavement. Within seconds the rain was pounding down, long stair rods of water hitting the tarmac and bouncing back up. Still the bus blocked a clear line of sight to the doorway opposite.

Tina checked her watch. Technically, it was still too early to close, but despite this she found herself walking towards the door, flipping the CLOSED sign around and sliding the bolts into their sockets at the top and bottom of the double glass doors.

As she busied herself with the final clean and tidy-up of the café, Tina couldn't help glancing across the road. It was if something was drawing her eyes there, something out of her control. It was setting her nerves on edge. She fumbled with a cup – it slid between her fingers and smashed onto the floor.

'Shit.' Tina took a moment to calm herself. She silently cursed Fay for pointing out the man across the road, but then almost instantly berated herself for over-reacting. 'It's just a man waiting for someone,' she said out loud.

With a renewed feeling of strength, Tina marched over to the door and, with her hands on her hips, looked across the road. Peering through the rain and gaps in the traffic, Tina studied the doorway. Empty.

'There, he's gone,' she said.

As she left the café, locking up behind her, Tina forced herself to look once more across to the doorway. It was definitely empty. What made her cross the road, she didn't know, but she found herself standing there. The rain was coming down harder now and people were rushing past her in the street, hurrying to get home or to their cars.

Tina stepped closer. The acrid smell of urine rose from the corner, the black-and-white- tiled doorway grubby and unloved. Four squashed cigarette ends lay next to a crumpled cigarette packet.

Tina's mouth dried as she looked at the white box. She crouched down and picked it up. The word 'Sobranie' and the logo of the Russian imperial eagle emblazoned on the front made her drop the box as if her fingers had been burned.

Tina stood up, swinging around to face the street, her eyes frantically searching the pavement from left to right. Her stomach lurched and her heart pounded. The faces of the passers-by, strangers. She recognised no one.

Rain dripped from her now-soaked hair, streaking down her face. She ignored it. Thoughts of Dimitri rushed to the front of her mind. The maternal instinct to gather her child, take him home and keep him safe was overpowering. It was the stimulus she needed. Her feet responded. Only her first few steps were at a walk before she broke into a run. The urgency fuelled her.

Chapter 3

Twenty minutes later, Tina burst through the kitchen door to her parents' home.

'Mum! Dad! Dimitri!' she called, letting the door slam behind her.

'In the living room,' came back her mother's voice from beyond.

Tina controlled her breathing. The casualness of her mother's voice was an instant tonic to her panic. Pam met her in the hallway. 'You all right, love?'

Tina forced a smile. 'Yes, I'm fine. Just pleased to finish work today and get home.' She gave her mum a peck on the cheek. 'Where's Dimitri?'

'He's in the greenhouse with your father. They were going to do a bit of gardening, but then the rain started. I think they are sowing seeds in the seed trays now.'

Tina went to the back door and looked out at the greenhouse. There they were, standing at the bench, carefully drilling small holes and dropping seeds into each one. It was a comforting sight and brought back childhood memories to Tina of her and her dad doing exactly the same. Memories that warmed her as an adult and as a child had made her feel loved and safe. The lump that rose to her throat took her by surprise.

'Are you sure you're okay?' asked Pam, putting a comforting

arm around her daughter's shoulder.

Tina nodded, blinking away unwanted tears. 'Dimitri is so lucky to have such a wonderful granddad. He really is. I just wish …' She couldn't finish her sentence.

Pam squeezed her daughter tightly. 'You just wish that Sasha was here to give his son these memories instead.'

'Something like that.' This time she didn't blink back the tears. Her mum ushered her to the kitchen table and sat her down.

'I hate to see you upset. I know you still miss Sasha.'

Tina took the sheet of kitchen roll her mother offered and dabbed at her eyes. Black streaks of mascara transferred onto the tissue. 'I miss him on behalf of Dimitri, if that makes sense.' She blew her nose and took a deep breath before continuing. 'Dimitri doesn't know any different and, in a way, that's a relief. I wouldn't want him to know the pain of losing his father.'

'It won't always be like this,' said Pam. 'One day there will be someone for Dimitri. And for you.'

'Maybe.' Tina knew they were on the brink of a familiar conversation. One where her mother would tell her she should get out and meet more people.

Her latest idea was Tina joining one of those online dating sites. So far Tina was resisting. She had been to a few dinner parties where match-making was definitely on the agenda. The last one had been a dinner party Fay had organised and Tina had accepted the invitation of a second date as a result. However, it hadn't gone beyond that. Tina had made it as far as a kiss goodnight. It seemed so awkward and unnatural, not only because it wasn't Sasha, but she was out of practice with the whole intimate kissing thing. The poor bloke must have thought he had eaten something nasty. She had muttered her apologies and practically fled into the waiting taxi.

'Are you staying for tea?' asked Pam, turning her attention to the oven. She opened the door and the smell of chicken casserole drifted out. Another comforting memory from Tina's childhood.

Another memory to chase away the demons of today.

'How could I resist?' said Tina. 'I'll set the table.' She stood up, relieved that the earlier disquiet she had felt was slipping away. She was safe. Dimitri was safe. They were loved. All was well in the world.

John woke the next morning and for a moment couldn't work out why it felt as if his head was being compressed from all sides. He groaned as he sat up. Sitting on the edge of the bed, he planted his feet on the floor.

Ah, now he remembered. The celebratory drink last night had been overdone. Still, they had good cause to celebrate.

The shower refreshed him, the coffee kick started his brain, the toast tamped down the queasiness and the Anadin relieved the pressure in his head. As he picked up his car keys from the sideboard, he noticed the brown envelope Brogan had given him the night before. He scooped it up; something to look over while he had his third coffee of the day at HQ.

The rest of the team seemed to be suffering slightly from the previous evening's excesses too. A day of paperwork and no running around catching the bad guys wouldn't go amiss. John settled at his desk.

'Did you sort it with Maxine?' he asked as Martin slid into his seat opposite him.

'Yeah, all good,' said Martin. He nodded at the photos in John's hand. 'Anything of interest.'

John studied the first one. It was a close-up of a man's shoulders and top half of his torso. The victim's throat had been cut. John passed it over to Martin.

'It appears he didn't die from natural causes,' he said. 'Slashed throat. Jagged edges to the wound, cut from right to left, I'd say.'

'From someone facing him, as opposed to behind him – assuming they are right-handed,' said Martin.

'Yep, the jagged skin means the neck was loose as opposed to

15

being taut when someone's head is pulled from behind.'

'Asleep?'

'Probably. Unless there are other signs of injury, meaning he put up a fight. Probably didn't know a thing about it.' John passed over another photograph. '*Otritsala*.'

Martin shrugged. 'You what?'

'The eight-pointed stars, tattooed on each collar bone,' said John. 'A sign of defiance. Medals that existed before the Russian revolution and used now to signify defiance to the Soviet regime.'

'So this is a Russian?'

'Yep. Prison tattoos mostly.' John slid another photograph over. 'Dagger with three drops of blood. That's typical of a murderer, the drops of blood reflecting the number of killings he's carried out. Could be that this fella was a hired assassin.'

'He's got a Swastika too,' said Martin, looking more closely at the photo.

'Doesn't mean he's a right-wing sympathiser or a Nazi. It's used as a sign of rebellion to authority. Some prisons have had these tattoos forcibly removed from their inmates.'

'And I suppose the SOS on his forearm doesn't mean Save Our Souls either,' said Martin.

'*Spasite Ot Syda*. Save me from judgement. Amongst other things.' John stopped. The next picture knocked the air from his lungs.

'You all right?' said Martin.

John looked slowly up at his colleague. 'This Russian was part of the Porboski gang.'

Martin sat up in his seat, his face alert. 'You sure?'

'See that tattoo on the inside of the upper arm. A dollar sign and that elaborate letter, which looks like a squared-off "n"? The dollar sign means he's a safe-cracker. That letter in Russian is a "P" and stands for the gang he's affiliated to.'

'Where did these photos come from? Have you got one of the face?'

John looked at the final photo. Another close-up of the chest. 'No. Just the arms and torso.'

'What are the Porboski gang doing back in the UK?' said Martin.

'No idea, but whatever it is, you know it's not good.' John took a moment to compose himself. The usual rush of guilt and anger swept over him. Images of his ex-partner, Neil, fought their way to the front of his mind. Images he usually managed to keep filed away in a drawer marked 'too close to home to think about', this time refused to be catalogued and archived so readily.

John could feel a dark cloud forming around him, waiting to smother him, to suck away the oxygen, leaving him gasping for breath. John's hand closed in a fist as the mental battle threatened to erupt. He was a good fighter. He could see off the attack. It seemed like minutes, but John knew from past experience it was merely one or two seconds. He breathed in through his nose and out through his mouth. Today's battle won. John looked down at his clenched fist and unfurled his fingers. The photograph now crumpled and scrunched.

John eyed his partner of five years across the desk. Martin understood. He had seen this happen before. He knew the reasons. John looked for accusation in the other man's eyes. There was none, although he felt sure his own screamed with guilt.

John stood up, gathering the photos together. 'Where's Brogan? We need to speak to CID. They seem to have found one of our Most Wanted. Just got to work out which one.'

CID couldn't shed much light on the identity of the Russian. He had been found down by the docks in a disused warehouse.

'Looks like he had been camping out. Used one of the old offices. Had a camp bed and camping stove. Nothing in the way of personal belongings,' said the CID Officer, Carter. 'Someone had tried to set fire to his stuff. Did a good job, mostly. There were a few charred remains left.'

'Can I have a look at his clothing?' said John. 'And have you got a photograph of his face?'

Carter went off to collect the evidence bag.

'It's only clothes. The clothes he was wearing.'

'Is it okay to take these out?' asked John.

'Yeah, go ahead. Forensics have been all over them.'

John inspected the clothing. 'All labels have been cut out,' he said. 'But this leather jacket is quite distinctive. Have you had any luck identifying its origin?'

'Not yet.'

The jacket was heavy in John's hands, a black, padded three-quarter-length garment. Lined with heavy checked fabric – certainly one to keep the Russian winter at bay. John laid it out on the table and poked around in the pockets.

'There's nothing there,' said Carter.

John felt the collar and gave the seam between the collar and lining a closer inspection. 'Got a knife or pair of scissors?'

A pair of scissors was obtained and handed to John. He began snipping at the seam of the collar until an opening of about three inches had been achieved. John wriggled his fingers in, feeling from one side to the next.

'Aha! Gotcha.' he said. He pulled out a small grip-sealed bag, about two by five inches.

'How did we miss that?' said the CID officer.

'Probably because you weren't looking for it,' said John opening the bag. He removed five folded twenty-pound notes and five ten-pound notes, together with three Russian notes of 5,000 roubles each. John did a quick calculation. 'About the same worth. A little under one fifty pounds.'

'Emergency funds,' said Martin picking up one of the notes by the corner. 'Don't suppose we will get any decent prints off them. Been handled too many times.'

Carter slid over a box containing several clear-plastic evidence bags. John looked through them. The victim travelled light. Three bags with fabric remnants, a London Tube map – the kind you pick up from any underground station.

'This looks a bit more interesting,' said John looking at a bag containing the strap from the victim's holdall with a flight tag still attached. Unfortunately, only a part of the digital flight code was left. 'Have you checked this out?'

'We think it's a flight in from Stockholm. There's only a partial barcode.'

'Have you checked recent flights in?' asked John.

'Needle in a haystack,' came the reply, accompanied by a shrug.

'Who found him?' asked John. 'Has he been cleared of any involvement?'

'A dock-worker. Had gone in for a crafty shut-eye. He was pretty shook up. Don't think he had the guts for it.'

'Did you get a photo of the victim?' asked Martin.

Carter passed it over. 'Recognise him?'

John and Martin both studied the face. A rounded thick-set face. Shaven head. An old scar above his left eye. A gold stud in the right ear. He didn't look familiar to either of them.

'Mind if we keep this?' said John.

'Go ahead.'

'Right, what else have we got here?' said John. He pulled out another bag containing the remains of a photograph.

'Shit.'

Martin let out a long, low whistle. 'Is that who I think it is?'

John took out the photograph, not worrying about holding the edges. Fingerprints were no longer a priority. A cold bead of sweat began its slow descent down his spine, undulating over every vertebrae. 'Pavel Bolotnikov,' he said, confirming Martin's thoughts. 'And who else was in the photograph?' Draped over Pavel's left shoulder was someone's arm, the owner's identity burned away.

'What the fuck is that doing in there?' said Martin.

Chapter 4

Back at HQ, John pinned the burnt photograph onto the evidence board. Underneath he pinned photographs of two men and a woman. He pointed to the first photograph and addressed his team.

'Sasha Bolotnikov, wanted for money-laundering. Fled to Russia soon after the Moorgate robbery. Killed in a car crash within weeks of arriving.' His team listened as he continued his commentary. 'Pavel Bolotnikov, part of the Porboski gang, involved in the Moorgate robbery where Neil Edwards was killed. Wanted for Neil's murder.' He paused as he wrote on the board. 'He too fled back to Russia afterwards.' He moved on to the third picture. 'Tina Bolotnikov. British passport-holder. Married Sasha Bolotnikov. Still in the UK. Living in West Sussex. And this,' he said pointing to the photograph of the dead Russian, 'is our unknown. A Russian gang member – Porboski gang, by the look of it, found murdered down at the docks. And this is a baggage tag, possibly from a Stockholm flight.'

'He doesn't look very Swedish to me,' said Adam, one of John's team.

'It's just a theory at present, but we think he may have caught a connecting flight to Stockholm from Tallinn. That's Estonia,' said John. 'It's a route favoured in the past by some of the Porboski gang.'

'What's he doing over here?' asked one of the team.

'We're not sure. Obviously a connection to the Bolotnikovs. I want all the flights in from Stockholm over the past week checked for facial recognition against this photo.' He tapped at the board. 'Clearly there's some connection with the Bolotnikovs, but what that is, I've no idea. Yet.'

'Wading through CCTV and facial recognition is going to take forever, especially if we don't know when he came into the UK,' said Adam.

'Have you got any better suggestions?' said John. His colleague shrunk back in his seat. 'We're also checking for Pavel Bolotnikov. Our unknown hasn't come over for a sightseeing trip. It could be that Pavel is in the country and that means trouble.'

'I want three of you to go and check out all the old stomping grounds of the Bolotnikovs and the Porboskis. The gang moved out of the UK after the Moorgate job, but they will still have contacts. People will know. Get some tongues wagging. We're playing catch-up now and I don't like it.'

John took a sip of his coffee as he let the information settle with his team. The Moorgate robbery was a tough subject for them all. It had been a bad day for the team.

'What about the wife?' asked someone.

'Martin and I are going down to West Sussex to check things out.' John put his cup down on the table in front of him. 'I'm waiting for the local police to run a few checks, see what she's been up to lately. I don't want to scare her off if she's got info. She may even be harbouring Pavel for all we know.'

A gentle murmur rippled out amongst his colleagues as more speculation was bounced around.

'No one wants Pavel Bolotnikov brought to justice more than I do,' said John picking up on the conversation. 'If he's here, we're going to nail him.'

John left work early. There was someone he needed to see. Neil

Edwards' widow, Hannah. Although Neil's murder case had never officially been closed, all leads had dried up as to where Pavel Bolotnikov was. Reports had come back from Russia that after his brother's funeral, Pavel had disappeared off the radar. If anyone knew where he was, they weren't talking. With no bilateral extradition treaty between the UK and Russia, any hope of co-operation from the authorities to hand Pavel over, were non-existent. Hannah Edwards needed to hear it from him himself that there had been some development in the case. John didn't want her switching on the news and finding out or some journalist turning up on her doorstep.

John parked across the road from the village school. He watched the parents arriving and lining up outside the gates, waiting for home time. He scanned the queue, looking for the familiar fair hair of his partner's widow.

He spotted her halfway down the line, head bent looking at her phone. Her hair was tied back in a ponytail and she had her gym wear on. She looked in good shape. John was pleased she seemed to be taking care of herself. There had been a time when he was worried she wasn't bothering. After Neil's death, her world had come to a standstill and John hadn't been sure if it would ever start up again.

The guilt within surged, as it always did, when he saw her, but this time it receded with more ease than before. He hoped she was turning things around.

The gates opened and the parents filed into the playground. John got out of his car and leaned against the bonnet while he waited for Hannah to come back out with Ella; her and Neil's eight-year-old daughter.

He didn't have to wait long. As mother and daughter emerged from the crowd of navy and grey uniforms, Hannah looked up and met John's gaze. She smiled and waved, said something to Ella, who looked over and waved too. Then they made their way across the road to John.

John kissed her on the cheek. 'Hi, Hannah, good to see you.' He leaned down and gave Ella a quick peck on the top of her head. 'Hiya, Ella. How are you? That's a nice school bag you've got there, is it new?'

'Hi, John. It's a High School Musical one.' Proudly she held it up for John to see the picture. 'It was a present.'

'Wow! That looks nice. Who got you that?'

Hannah interrupted before Ella could reply. 'You'll have to explain to John about High School Musical and your bag some other time. I'm sure he's really busy.' She looked up at him. 'Everything okay with you?'

'Yeah, fine. Look, can I give you a lift home?'

Hannah looked uncertain. 'It's okay, we're fine walking.' She hesitated. 'Is everything really okay?'

'Let me take you home,' said John. 'I do need to speak to you, but not here.'

'Not at the house. Let's walk. We can go via the park.' She didn't wait for John to agree, but took Ella's hand and began walking. John had no choice but to follow.

The walk to the park took only five minutes but each second lay heavier than the previous. Tension swirled around them. Only Ella was oblivious to it as she proceeded to tell John all about High School Musical. Hannah didn't speak and as John stole a glance at her from the corner of his eye, he could see the stiffness in her face, neck and shoulders.

Once at the park, Ella happily went off on the climbing frame and slide. John and Hannah sat on the bench watching but not really looking.

'What is it you need to tell me?' said Hannah. Straight to the point, no messing around.

'Just to forewarn you that there's been some development in the Porboski case.'

'You mean in the murder case? Neil's murder case.' Her voice was sharp. 'You can say it, John. There's no point pretending it's just the Porboski case. At the heart of it and the all-important part is the murder of Neil. It won't break me if you say it. I'm not going to collapse in a heap simply because you've mentioned his name. Or what happened to him.'

John sat forward on the bench, resting his arms on his knees, bringing his hands together. 'Yes, you're right. Sorry.'

'What's happened, then? I'm guessing you didn't come and see me personally purely to tell me that.'

'Off the record, we think there's a strong possibility Pavel Bolotnikov is back in the UK. We don't know why but I wanted to give you the heads up, just in case.'

Now she looked at him. 'Just in case what? Are we in some sort of danger?' Her eyes flitted to Hannah and back to John.

John placed a hand over hers. 'No, I don't think that at all. We're working on tracking him down right now, but I didn't want you to hear it from somewhere else, especially if the press get hold of it.'

'You could have just phoned. You didn't need to make a special trip out to the backwater of Berkshire.'

'I wanted to see you both. See how you were doing. Do you need anything? What about Ella? Is she okay for everything?'

Hannah moved her hand away. 'You don't have to do this, you know.'

'Do what?'

'Protect me. Look out for me. For Ella.' She turned to face him now. 'We're not your responsibility. No. Don't say anything. Listen, you were Neil's partner. I was his wife. Ella his daughter. The most awful thing happened. Neil was killed. You've been great to us, John, you really have and the first few months, I'm sure I would have died myself had it not been for you. And for that I am truly grateful. But, you know what? We've come out the other side and Ella and I are doing great. You need to look after yourself, so you can come out the other side too.'

At that point Ella skipped over. 'Can we go home, mummy? I'm hungry.'

24

'Yes, come on, let's go.' Hannah rose from the bench and took her daughter's hand.

'Is John coming?' said Ella. 'He can meet Dan.'

John's eyes snapped up to look at Hannah. A look of unease swept over her face. 'Who's Dan?' said John.

'Mummy's friend. He bought me the bag,' said Ella, running her finger and thumb up and down the strap.

John stood up. 'Why didn't you just say?' His voice was cold despite the hot ember of anger igniting inside. Was he angry that she hadn't told him about another bloke or was he angry because she was no longer the proverbial grieving widow, which ultimately meant she didn't need him?

'It's none of your business, really,' said Hannah, she raised her eyebrows. 'The Met, the unit, my life as a widow are in the past, John. It's been five years now. I can't pause time any longer. If there's something good that's come from Neil's death, it's that more than ever I value my future, Ella's future.'

'With this … Dan.'

'Maybe. Who knows? But I deserve some happiness and so does Ella.' Hannah began walking away, she paused and looked over her shoulder. 'You should be happy for us. Neil would want us to be happy.'

John didn't say anything. He stood and watched Hannah and Ella walk away. What was there to say? He didn't want the burden of Neil's memory to carry on his own. He thought it was a load he shared with Hannah. How could he have closure and move on when Neil's killer was still out there? When John's own guilt ravaged his mind and conscience both day and night.

Chapter 5

John had been parked up outside Tina Bolotnikov's house for about an hour. He looked through his notes once more, impatient for the return of their target.

He wondered what she would look like after all this time. He picked up an old surveillance photo from when they were watching Sasha. A young couple, not been married very long, about eighteen months, if he remembered rightly. At the time he had been struck by their happiness; it had radiated off them. They had shared lots of happy times.

John felt as if he had lived them too, although it had been from the other side of the camera. He was the third person in their marriage; unseen, unheard, unknown, but definitely there. He knew with certainty he would be able to talk to Tina about things that had happened as if he had been part of it. Like the time Sasha and Tina went to Hyde Park and got caught in a sudden rain storm. He knew they took cover under a large tree. He knew the lightning frightened her. He knew they ran to the café at the Serpentine. He knew they had hot chocolate. Tina had marshmallows. Sasha didn't. He knew more details about their married life than a third party should.

'Eyes up,' said Martin. 'Here comes the lovely Mrs B.' Martin shoved his newspaper into the foot-well and focused on the mother and child walking towards him. 'That's her, isn't it?'

Picking up the camera, John zoomed in on Tina Bolotnikov. For a moment he was stilled by the sight of her. She was as beautiful as she was five years ago. She had the same elegance about her. Head held high, shoulders back. Her hair, the colour of cocoa beans, bounced on her shoulders as the late-afternoon sun highlighted the milk-chocolate tones running through it. But there was something in her eyes that he couldn't remember seeing before. A wariness. Her blue eyes darted around all over the place.

Martin punched his shoulder. 'You going to take some photos or what?'

John began taking some snaps, distance ones and close-up ones.

'Take some of the boy as well,' said Martin. 'Do you think it's hers?'

John focused the camera on the dark-headed boy and took some more shots. Adjusting the lens, he took a close-up as the lad looked up. In that instant, he could see it by the eyes. He knew exactly who the father was. 'That's Sasha Bolotnikov's son.'

'How do you know that?'

John lowered the camera from his face and watched through the car window. He knew Tina was pregnant when they had been under surveillance. He had been in their flat, poking around, looking for evidence one morning when they had both left to work in the deli. He hadn't found anything, only a pregnancy test stick. Tina had left it sitting on the bedside table where she must have told Sasha that morning. Funny, he remembered, he had noticed how happy they were opening up the shop and going about their business. They had a secret; one which John now shared with them.

A small flicker of guilt wavered within John. He had used the new-found knowledge to his advantage. At the time it was a case of a means to an end; there was no guilt attached. He was simply doing his job, using this intel to his advantage in the war against crime.

He had managed to convince himself for a long time after the

27

botched Moorgate takedown that it was all part of the job, but as time wore on, guilt had come knocking. A gentle tap at first, one he could ignore. Now, however, it was practically hammering at the door but John wasn't answering.

'Work it out, dummy. The boy's about five years old. She was pregnant around when we had Sasha and the gang under surveillance. Anyway, you only have to look at him to know he's a Bolotnikov.' For a fleeting moment he felt a wave of sympathy for Sasha Bolotnikov. He must never have seen his son.

John took the final snaps as she opened the gate and walked up the path with her son, before letting them in and closing the door behind her.

John put the camera down and settled back in his seat. 'Let's sit and watch for a while. I don't want to speak to her yet. Someone might come a-calling.'

John settled back in his seat. This could be a long wait.

That night Tina sat on the edge of Dimitri's bed, watching until he had drifted off to sleep. She had read a story to him, as she usually did, but instead of leaving him to settle on his own, she had stayed.

Tea at her parents' house had been an enjoyable occasion, her earlier sense of unease having all but disappeared. She watched his eyes flutter open and then close, gradually becoming defeated by the heaviness of sleep. Listening to the gentle rhythm of his breathing gave Tina a sense of calm. It soothed her soul.

It was somewhat reluctantly that she left his room to go and tidy up the kitchen and settle herself in front of the TV. She hoped that catching the cooking programme showing on BBC2 would take her mind off recent events, enough that she could get a good night's sleep herself.

Tina went downstairs and through to the back of the house, into the kitchen. It was dark outside now and her reflection against the glass made her jump. She let out a startled cry.

'For goodness sake!' she admonished herself.

The air in the kitchen seemed cold. Tina shivered, her eyes immediately scoped the windows. They were all closed to keep the cool night air out. Something made her look beyond her reflection in the glass.

Her small garden backed onto an alleyway used as access for the middle terraced houses. A movement caught her eye behind the brick wall. This time she screamed. Without looking closer, she rushed to the windows and yanked the roller blinds down, shutting out the danger.

The door. Was it locked? Tina rattled the handled and pulled against it. It was definitely locked.

Someone was out there, watching her. She hadn't imagined it this time. Her heart pumped wildly as she dialled 999.

Chapter 6

'Sorry, Mrs Bolotnikov, but we can't find anything or anyone suspicious out there,' said the police officer as he came into the kitchen from the garden. 'Are you certain you saw someone?

Tina shifted uncomfortably in her seat, reluctant to speak. It sounded so stupid now. She caught a look pass between the police officer and his female colleague, who was sitting at the table with her, drinking a cup of tea. They clearly didn't believe Tina had seen anyone.

'I definitely saw someone looking over the garden wall,' she said, with as much confidence as she could muster. 'As I came into the kitchen, I had that feeling of being watched. That's what made me look up.'

'It was getting dark. Could it have maybe been a shadow from the trees at the back? Or a cat on the wall?' suggested the other officer.

Tina considered this idea for a moment, although she was in no doubt herself, she at least wanted the police to believe she was being rational. She shook her head. 'No, it wasn't a cat or a shadow. It was definitely a person.' Tina got up and put her cup on the worktop.

'What about someone next door? Do they use the back gate at all? Kids maybe?' The female officer enquired. Tina could sense her frustration rising. They didn't believe her. She graced them with an answer all the same.

'No one really uses the alleyway. It's only access for the middle terraces. Mr Cooper lives next door. Some days, not every day, I pop round there with a bit of dinner for him if I've made too much. I use the back gates then. He's in his eighties and lives alone. It wouldn't have been anything to do with him.'

The police officers gave another cursory look around the garden and into the alleyway, reporting back that if there had been anyone here, they were long gone.

Tina sighed as she closed the door on the departing officers. She turned the key in the lock and slid the bolts across at both the bottom and top. She yanked on the door handle and tried to open the door, just to check that there was no way anyone could get in. She repeated the procedure with the back door. The excitement of all the police activity had woken Dimitri, but Tina had managed to distract him with a Spiderman video in the living room. She poked her head around the door.

'Come on then, Dimitri,' she smiled at him. 'Excitement's all over. Best get you back to bed.'

'Did the police catch the bad man?'

'There wasn't a bad man, darling. Mummy made a mistake.' She scooped her son up from the sofa, groaning slightly at the weight of him. He'd soon be getting too old and big for carries. 'You will never guess what it was.'

Dimitri shook his head, returning her smile before snuggling his chin onto her shoulder.

'What was it?'

'Turned out it was the cat, that's all.' Tina made her way upstairs to Dimitri's room.

'Our cat, Rascal?'

Yes, Rascal. Silly old mummy.' She hoped she sounded convincing.

31

Tina didn't sleep well at all that night. She'd welcomed the dawn with bleary eyes and a hard day at work had done nothing to make her face seem any fresher. Fay had commented on how tired she looked, but Tina passed it off as staying up late to watch a DVD.

Dimitri seemed to be suffering too. The walk home from school that was usually filled with chatter of how the day had gone was today a rather silent affair. An early night for both of them, Tina decided, pushing down the uneasy feeling that nightfall would soon be upon them. She'd draw her curtains early tonight, before it even got dark. She would be safer then. Cocooned.

As she stepped in through the front door, Tina was immediately greeted by Rascal, mewing at her ankles, winding his polar-white body around Tina's legs.

'Rascal! What are you doing here?' said Tina stooping to pick the cat up. She nuzzled her face against the animal's neck. 'How did you get out of the kitchen?' As Tina walked down the hallway to the kitchen her mind went over the routine of that morning. Rascal was always confined to the kitchen during the day when Tina was at work. His passion for bringing his kill into the house and dropping it on the floor had meant his days of having access to all areas were gone. The live mouse had been the prize too far.

Tina remembered closing the door so the cat couldn't venture anywhere else in the house. It was always the last thing she did before going out. She wondered if perhaps today she had forgotten to do it, what with all the upset of the night before. To be honest, she couldn't remember. It was something she did every day: a matter of habit. She couldn't recall doing it or not doing it. Maybe Dimitri had gone back into the kitchen for something. But she didn't think so.

Tina felt her mouth dry and the reflex action to swallow stilted. Did that mean someone had been in the house today? Other than her leaving the kitchen door open, it was the only other explanation. They certainly wouldn't have been able to come through the front door, but she would check with Mr Cooper anyway, just in case he had seen something. The windows were all double-glazed units and all were locked closed. There was no way anyone could have got in through a window. That left only the back door.

Striding into the kitchen and over to the half-glazed UPVC door, Tina rattled the handle. Locked. Definitely locked. No, she must have forgotten about the internal door and left it open or not shut it properly. Was it any wonder she wasn't thinking straight after the night she'd had.

Later that evening, plating an extra dinner up, Tina popped next door to Mr Cooper. As was customary, she knocked on the back door and then let herself in. Tina had long given up telling him to keep the door locked. He was stuck in his ways, had never locked the door in all the time he had been there, in excess of fifty years – as he liked to remind her – so he didn't see why he should now. Of course, he would lock it at night time, but not during the day. He wasn't going to let society turn him into a jibbering wreck, afraid of his own shadow.

'Mr Cooper!' Tina called out, knowing full well he'd be sitting in the living room with the telly on loud. She could hear it blaring out now. She was thankful, as ever, that their dividing wall separated her living room from his staircase. She pitied the neighbours on the other side of him whose living room was back to back with Mr Cooper's. Tina placed the dinner plate on the kitchen table and went further into the house.

The usual smell of mustiness, rather like a charity shop, assailed her nostrils, as did the smell of the downstairs toilet. Mr Cooper lived on the ground floor now, the dining room converted into a bedroom and what once would have been the scullery now a wet room.

Tina knocked loudly on the living-room door and pushed it open. 'Hello, Mr Cooper.'

He looked up from his winged back chair and smiled a tooth-less mouth to her.

'Hello, love. You all right?' Mr Cooper smoothed his hand

over his head, a mixture of grey wispy hairs and a balding patch, speckled with age spots. Ever the gentleman, he made to stand up, one hand grasping his walking stick and the other trying to gain leverage from the arm of the chair.

Tina waited until he had risen slightly and indicated to the other chair for her to sit. He really didn't need to, but it was an old habit he clearly had no intention of breaking, despite her protests not to get up in the early days of her visits. She duly took her seat next to the fireplace.

'I've put a dinner out on the kitchen table for you. Chicken pie and veg. Hope that's okay.' She smiled as he nodded.

'Thank you. I'll look forward to that for my lunch tomorrow.' He settled himself back in his chair again. 'How's Dimitri? School okay, is it?'

The usual questions. It was comforting. However, Tina wanted to ask him about last night, but not in a way that would alarm him. 'Did you sleep all right last night?' she ventured.

'Not too bad, love. Not too bad at all.'

'You didn't hear anything, then?' She toyed with the idea of not mentioning the police, but then thought better of it. If one of the other neighbours spoke to him they might tell him. 'I thought I saw someone in the alley last night. I was a bit frightened and got the police to come round. Just to check it out. Everything was okay, though. I must have imagined it.' She added the last bit hurriedly to allay any fears.

'Really? Well, no, I didn't hear a thing. But then you know me, deaf as a post.' He chuckled and tapped his ear. 'I suppose you've come round to tell me to lock my back door.' He looked good-humouredly over his glasses at her.

'You know my feelings on that,' Tina replied with warmth in her voice.

'And you know mine, love.'

She let it drop. It was pointless trying to convince him other-wise. 'Do you want me to make you a Horlicks before I go?' Tina asked standing up.

'That'll be nice, thanks, love.'

Opening the fridge for the milk, Tina tutted to herself. Mr Cooper was low on milk. She'd have to nip back home and get some. She popped her head back round the living-room door. 'You haven't got enough milk, Mr Cooper. I'll quickly nip next door and get some. Won't be a minute.'

'Wait, love. There's plenty of milk there. Should be at least a pint.'

'You've got enough for a couple of cups of tea, but that's about it.'

A look of concern settled in the creases of Mr Cooper's weathered skin, accompanied by a deep sigh. 'I must be losing my marbles. I could have sworn there was a pint there. Look, don't worry, love. I'll be okay tonight.'

'I'll bring you some first thing in the morning,' said Tina. 'I'll see you then, okay?'

'Yes, okay, pet. See you in the morning.'

Tina smiled as she left. In all the time she had lived here, Mr Cooper had never once called her by her name. It was always some term of endearment or another. She wondered if he actually could remember her name. Poor thing! Maybe he was getting a bit forgetful. Looking in the breadbin, she saw that there were only a couple of slices left. She'd get him some bread as well. She paused before opening the back door and called out loudly. 'And don't forget to lock the door!'

John flexed his shoulders and rotated his neck. It had been a long night sitting in the BMW with Martin. The September weather was still warm in the day, but dipped into autumn during the night. The coffee in his flask long gone, as were the sandwiches they had bought from the garage the day before.

They had watched the police activity at Tina Bolotnikov's house the night before. A quick call to the local police station had told them what was going on. John had decided not to go in with all guns blazing at that point. The local police seemed to have it under control and there was definitely no one about. John had decided to sit it out. He didn't want to spook their target straight away.

'I'll phone in to the office,' said John. 'See if they've had any reports back from the local police or any luck on the facial recognition.'

'It's all right, that facial recognition, if the person looks straight on at the camera,' said Martin. 'Not so good on profiles.'

'I know,' said John. 'But it's our only lead at the moment. You never know, we might get lucky. It's not as if they are going to come through passport control with a hat and glasses on. Have a bit of faith.'

John got through to the office.

'We're still looking through CCTV of Heathrow,' said Adam. 'Have you any idea how many flights come through that airport every day, not to mention passengers?'

'Keep looking. We need to find him.' John ignored the deep sigh from Adam. He knew it was a shit of a job, but it needed doing. John needed to know who the dead Russian was, when he came into the UK and if Pavel Bolotnikov was back as well. If he had come in, John needed to track Pavel down – and fast. The Russian had slipped through his fingers once before. John wasn't about to let it happen again. This wasn't simply professional. This was personal.

'Before you go, the Boss wants a word with you,' said Adam. 'Hold on, I'll put you through.'

Brogan's voice came on the line.

'Anything to report?' he asked.

'Nothing as yet, Sir,' said John. 'There was a bit of activity here last night. I spoke to the local nick and apparently she reported a Peeping Tom in the alleyway behind her house.'

'And was there?'

'The local police didn't find anyone.'

'What do you think?'

'Hard to say. Could be a coincidence. Adam is working on

the CCTV at Heathrow now, but it could be a long and, possibly fruitless, task.'

'Mmm, I know,' said Brogan. 'Man-hours wasted that could be put to better use elsewhere.'

'Give him a bit longer, Guv,' said John. 'Whether it was Pavel here last night or not, doesn't really matter now. If it was, after the police activity last night, he's hardly like to come strolling down the road.'

'What did you have in mind?'

'Direct approach. I'll go and speak to Tina Bolotnikov. If Pavel's back and she knows, she's hardly likely to be reporting intruders. My guess is she doesn't know anything. Her and Pavel were never great friends when they all lived in London, so I can't imagine anything has changed since then. I want to persuade her to call us if he turns up.'

'Just go easy, though, John,' said Brogan. 'Don't overdo the Pavel bit, not until we know if he's here and why.'

'Sir.'

Chapter 7

Straightening the tie he was unaccustomed to wearing these days, John knocked on the door of 17 Balfour Avenue. He had gone to the local supermarket washrooms to freshen himself up after a night spent sitting in the car.

John had waited for her to return home from dropping her son at school. She was wearing jeans, so he had assumed she wasn't at work today.

Through the two narrow slits of obscure glass in the front door, John could see her silhouette, approach and hear the locks being turned. The door opened a couple of inches, the security chain doing its job.

'Yes?' Her voice had a wary tone to it.

John held up his police identity badge.

'Hello, Mrs Bolotnikov?' She nodded, her eyes scanning the ID card. 'I'm DS Nightingale from London's Metropolitan police force. Would it be possible to come in and have a chat with you?'

'The Met?' She reached her hand through and took the card. 'I'll need to confirm your ID, if it's all the same to you.'

'Of course. I'll wait here.' She closed the door and again he heard the locks turning. She certainly wasn't taking anything at face value.

John turned to face the road. Martin had moved the car, parking outside Tina's property. John mouthed the words 'checking badge' at his partner, who nodded his understanding. Eventually, John heard the sound of the bolts being drawn back on the door. Tina opened the door, this time there was no security chain.

'Come in Detective Sergeant,' she said and offered a small smile.

John followed her into the living room. Neat and tidy but with a warm, lived-in feel to it.

'Would you like a tea or a coffee?' said Tina. John took her up on the offer of coffee. 'Please take a seat. I won't be a moment.'

John wandered over to the fireplace and looked at the photo of Tina and Sasha. A couple very much in love. Next to the fireplace, the alcove had been fitted with shelves, which contained more knick-knacks and a selection of books.

'Do you take sugar?' Tina called out from the kitchen.

'Two, please.' John inspected the books. You could tell a lot about someone by their book shelf. They ranged from hardbacks to paperbacks, pink covers with bubble writing to more sinister-looking ones with a bold font. She certainly had a broad taste in reading material. Tina came back into the room. 'I was looking at your books,' said John turning to her.

She raised her eyebrows, a small smile tugged at the corners of her mouth. A smile John had seen before but not up close, always from behind a long-distance camera lens. John averted his eyes, looking back towards the books.

'You fancy a bit of Jilly Cooper, then?' Tina said, passing John a cup before sitting down on the sofa.

He took a sip of the rich, dark coffee. The supermarket coffee didn't compare. 'Not my cup of tea,' he said.

'Oh, I thought you said coffee,' said Tina.

This time it was John's turn to look amused. He chuckled. 'No, I meant Jilly Cooper is not my thing.' He raised his cup a fraction. 'This *is* my cup of tea, though … well, coffee.'

He watched the thought trace across her face and then she broke into an embarrassed smile. She took a sip of tea, her hands clasped around the mug. John noticed her long, slender fingers, which matched the rest of her.

John couldn't help but feel he was seeing her for the first time, despite the fact that he had watched her for months and months. Before it was as if he was watching her on TV, continually through the lens of a camera, now today he was in the same room as her, he was seeing her up close and in the flesh for real. This time he was actually talking to her.

'So, what can I do for you?' Tina said, breaking the small silence that had descended. 'I'm guessing it's nothing to do with the report I made of being followed and watched, not if you're from the Met.'

'Well, yes and no,' said John. He sat down in the wing-backed armchair beside the fireplace. The bold geometric pattern gave the old-fashioned furniture a modern twist. 'We are currently investigating the possibility that Pavel Bolotnikov is in the UK.' He watched her face. Her pallid face turned the colour of dishwater. She hadn't been expecting that, he was sure.

'Pavel?'

'Yes, your brother-in-law.'

'I know who he is.' There was a slight snap to her voice. She sat up straight and let out a controlled breath. When she spoke, her voice was calm. 'What has this to do with me?'

'We would very much like to speak to Pavel about an incident that happened five years ago. We thought he might be in touch with you. Perhaps needing somewhere to stay.'

'I haven't heard from him. In fact, I haven't heard from him since … '

'Since when, Mrs Bolotnikov?'

She dropped her gaze to her hands. Her thumb kneaded the china cup handle. 'Since my husband died.'

'My condolences, Mrs Bolotnikov,' said John.

'Thank you. And it's Tina. Much easier and quicker than Bolotnikov.' John gave a small nod of acknowledgement before continuing.

'So, you haven't heard from Pavel?'

'No.'

'You don't keep in touch?'

Tina put the cup on the coffee table and stood up. She walked over to the mantelpiece and picked up the photograph of herself and her husband.

'Pavel and I, we didn't get on that well.'

'Why's that?'

'You're the police officer and you're here asking about Pavel? I expect you can work it out.' She replaced the photograph. 'I didn't like his career choice. I don't know exactly what he was involved in, but I knew it wasn't on the right side of the law.'

'Didn't your husband ever say anything?'

'No. Pavel was his brother. My husband still felt loyal to him. It was a moot point. We ceased discussing it as it caused too many arguments between us.'

'Does the name Porboski mean anything to you?' This time the physical jolt was apparent.

'Then. But not now.' John waited for her to continue. 'Everyone in the Russian community knew the Porboskis were involved in all sorts of criminal activity. Is that the right phrase?'

'It's as good as any,' said John. He gave a small smile to reassure her. 'Did your husband ever mention the Porboski gang?'

'No. Well, maybe. Only in passing. It was a long time ago. As I said, everyone knew who they were. You didn't mess with them.'

John allowed for another pause. He needed to tread carefully and decide where to take the conversation.

'Just going back to Pavel. You've not heard from him since your husband's death?'

'That's right.'

'By that I take it you mean the funeral?'

Tina looked at him for a moment. She appeared to be coming to some sort of decision. He allowed her time to wrestle with whatever it was. If he was too keen to encourage her, she might

41

clam up. His patience won out.

'I didn't go to the funeral. It was in Russia. It was organised and carried out within a matter of days. I was told not to come.'

John knew this. It was in the file. After the Moorgate robbery, Tina had been kept under surveillance for another two weeks in the hope she would lead them to Sasha. When the reports of his death came in and still she didn't make any attempt to go, the trail had gone cold. John had been convinced at the time she was in on it and would fly out to Russia sooner or later. He was wrong on that occasion. He had never understood why she hadn't gone though.

'And you accepted that?' he said.

'What choice did I have? I didn't know where or when the funeral would take place. I didn't speak Russian. There was no one to ask. Pavel wouldn't tell me. I tried asking his wife, but she refused to take my calls. Under his instructions, no doubt.' She sat down on the sofa. Her shoulders dropped. 'All I wanted was to say goodbye. It was hard to accept my husband had died when I had no funeral, nothing solid to help me come to terms with losing him.'

'Why didn't you go to Russia with him?'

'It was a sudden decision. It wasn't planned. He came home, said his grandfather was unwell and he had to travel to Russia that night.'

'I still don't understand why you didn't go.'

'I was pregnant. Early stages. I was very ill with morning sickness. Sasha didn't want me to travel that far and be in a foreign country. He insisted I stay here.' She twisted a silver band on the ring finger of her right hand. The usual hand for Russians to wear a wedding ring. 'If I had known it was the last time I would see him, I wouldn't have agreed to stay.'

'But you could have been in the car with him.' John's reply was gentle. He could see the angst in her whole body language.

'I've thought about that and in those early days it made me wish it even more.' She looked him straight in the eye. 'But once I had my son, I knew I had everything to live for and I have never once revisited those dark thoughts.'

'Does Sasha's family know about your son?'

'I told Pavel, but he wasn't interested. All he said was that the life insurance would see me right. I wrote to Sasha's mother. I had an address in Russia for her. Not that she would be able to read it, but I thought maybe someone would translate it for her. It was a long shot, but I thought she had a right to know she was to become a grandmother. I never received a reply. I didn't have their phone number and, besides, what use would phoning have been? I can't speak Russian and she can't speak English.' She let out a frustrated sigh. 'I've never heard from a single member of that family since Sasha's death.'

John didn't know why, call it intuition and years in the force, but he believed her. He was sure she hadn't spoken or had any contact with any of them since that day.

'Can I ask one thing?' said John.

'Sure.'

'Did you ever get proof of your husband's death?'

'Like a death certificate? Yes, I did actually. Pavel sent it to me, said I would need it for insurance claims. Actually, he sent it to his solicitor here in the UK who translated it and signed it as an authentic copy and translation.'

'Okay, thank you, Tina,' he said standing up. 'Can I leave you my number in case you think of anything or if, indeed, Pavel does get in touch?'

Tina took the card John proffered. 'I don't think he will, but if he does …'

John followed her out to the hallway. 'If I find anything else out about Pavel, I'll let you know,' he said. 'Please don't worry, though.' For some unexplained reason, he rested his hand on her arm reassuringly and allowed it to linger, probably longer than it should.

'Thank you Detective Sergeant,' she said.

'John. Call me John, it's much easier.' He smiled into her

forget-me-not blue eyes and saw nothing but trust.

She trusted him.

The satisfaction that this had been gained sat uncomfortably alongside his betrayal of her five years ago. He was responsible for Sasha leaving. He was responsible for the pain widowhood brought her. Blood had stained his hands then: blood that was washed away with soap and water. The moral stains, however, weren't so easily removed.

His job sucked at times. John walked down the path feeling a complete and utter shit.

Chapter 8

John threw the manila file onto his desk and sighed. It was no good, he couldn't make any headway into Sasha Bolotnikov's death. All lines of enquiries led to dead ends. Sasha Bolotnikov had been killed in a road accident within weeks of returning to Russia. It was a convenient death, if nothing else. John wondered whether it had indeed been an accident.

At the time, John had been incapacitated, recovering from surgery to remove a bullet from his shoulder. He had wanted to come back to work but was overruled by both doctors and his superiors. When he did return to work, Sasha's death had been investigated and no further questions asked.

He looked up as Martin came and sat at the desk. 'Any luck?'

Martin shook his head. 'Nope. The Russians aren't playing ball. No one is talking. The official line is they can't release any more information about Sasha's accident than is already in the public domain and, as for Pavel, they have no idea where he is and have no interest in finding him for us.'

John looked across the office at Adam. 'Anything with the facial recognition for the Russian or Pavel?'

'Not yet. We're going back another week now.'

'Okay, thanks.' John tapped his biro between his teeth and turned to Martin. 'We've tried all the official lines, let's try unofficial.'

'Anyone in mind?'

'Baz Fisher.'

John eyed Baz Fisher across the Formica table top of the Rosie Lea Café.

'Come on, Baz, you must know something,' he coaxed as he slowly stirred the teaspoon around in the dark-brown liquid.

'Look, John …' began Baz Fisher.

Martin cut him off. 'That's Detective Sergeant Nightingale to you, Baz. Don't forget your manners, now. There's nothing I hate more than disrespect.' He picked up his plastic teaspoon and snapped it in half between his fingers. 'It gets me agitated, see.'

John watched Baz Fisher, local 'fence', well known for being a mine of information. Through his café business and his rather unfavourable associations with a local gambling syndicate, Baz got to hear a lot of things. Baz flicked a glance in John's direction before nodding towards Martin. 'Put ya pet on a lead, will ya.'

'Come on, Baz.' John gave a faux reassuring smile. 'All you have to do is tell us what you know about Pavel Bolotnikov.'

'I dunno, John,' he threw Martin a defiant look. 'These Russians don't like people poking about in their business. It's dangerous, like. Know what I mean?'

'Baz, we can do this two ways,' said John. 'We can take you in for questioning, which will no doubt mean word will get out that you've been singing or we can do it nice and discreetly here, where no one gets to know.'

Baz eyed John and then Martin. 'I don't have much choice, do I?'

'I'm not asking much' said John. 'Just tell me if Pavel Bolotnikov is in the UK and where.'

A bead of sweat traced its way down the side of Baz's temple. He wiped at it with a paper serviette.

'You didn't hear from me. Got that?' conceded Baz after a few moments.

'When have we ever heard it from you?' said John. 'You know

we will look after you.'

Baz cleared his throat, looking around the café once more. John bit down the impatient breath that was threatening to escape,

'Pavel is not in London any more. I don't know exactly where he was staying, but I do know he's gone.'

'How did he get into London?'

'Flew.'

'From where and when?'

'Two weeks ago yesterday. I don't know where from. I'm not his travel agent.'

'And where is he now?'

'Like I said, I don't know.' Baz wiped at the newly formed sweat on his forehead. 'Come on, John, give us a break. I've said too much already.'

John exchanged a look with Martin before both men looked back at their informant. After a few moments' silence, John prompted him. 'Tell us where he is now and we're done.'

Baz went to protest, but must have thought better of it. He cursed quietly. 'I swear, John, this is all I know.' He leaned in and spoke in a hushed voice. 'Word has it, Pavel's gone to the seaside.'

'Seeing as the UK is an island, that gives a lot of scope as to where he could be,' snapped Martin.

'Okay, okay.' Baz held up his hands. 'West Sussex.'

'A lot of coastline in West Sussex,' replied John.

'Littlehampton. He's gone to Littlehampton.' Baz let out a sigh. 'Now that's got to be worth something.' He pointed towards the pocket that housed John's wallet.

John obliged and drew out a crisp twenty-pound note. He placed it slowly on the table before repeating the process with another one.

As Baz went to scoop the notes up, John laid his hand flat over them. 'Was he alone?'

Baz shrugged. 'Dunno.' He looked at John and then Martin. 'And that's straight up, I'm not his secretary.' He looked at the notes.

John lifted his hand and watched as Baz greedily shoved his

earnings into his trouser pocket. 'If that's all, gentlemen, I'll be on my way.'

As Baz went to leave, John stuck out his hand and caught the man's arm. 'Keep your ear to the ground and let me know if you hear anything. Anything at all. Got it?'

'Yeah, course,' muttered Baz before scurrying into the back of the café.

'You reckon he knows anything else?' queried Martin.

John shook his head. 'Don't think so.' He took a slurp of his tea before pushing it away. 'Jesus, that's disgusting. Come on.' He stood up. 'We can pin the facial recognition down to a date now. I want to see if Pavel came in alone or not.'

'Do you know something I don't?' asked Martin following John out of the café.

'Just a hunch. I want to see the CCTV first, though.'

John and Martin arrived back at the office to find Adam looking rather pleased with himself.

'I take it that's your good-news face,' said John.

'We've got a match for the dead Russian,' said Adam, tapping at the keys on his computer. The victim's face appeared on the screen next to his personal details. Adam gave a summary. 'Ivan Gromov. Porboski gang member. Lives in Russia. Was a regular visitor to the UK up until about five years ago. Not known to us. Has used various different aliases.' He scrolled down the screen for more information.

'Came into the UK via Stockholm ten days ago. Connecting flight from Tallinn,' said John.

Adam looked at his boss. 'You beat me to it.'

'Good stuff,' said John, conscious of not spoiling his junior colleague's moment. 'Can you look for Pavel Bolotnikov now? We're pretty sure he came into the country prior to Gromov. My guess is Gromov was sent to follow Pavel, either to find out what Pavel was up to or to stop him from doing it. Pavel turned the tables on him.'

'Pavel killed Gromov?' said Adam.

'Kill or be killed,' said John. He nodded at the computer. 'Get cracking, then, and see what you can find. I want to know if Pavel came in alone.'

Adam got to it straight away. Within an hour he was calling John over.

'Sir, you might want to come and look at this.' John came and looked at the monitor. There was Pavel Bolotnikov in full Technicolor.

'Was he alone?'

Adam flicked to another CCTV screen capture. 'It would appear not. Came through passport control and customs separately, but joined up in arrivals.' Adam zoomed in on Pavel and his accomplice.

Martin came and peered over his shoulder at the screen.

'Is that who I think it is?'

Chapter 9

Tina smiled as Dimitri danced in and out of the shade of the sycamore trees, the late afternoon sun stretching the shadows into long, narrow strips, which spread over the pavement and climbed the garden walls.

'The crocodiles can't get me when I'm on the black bits,' said Dimitri, as he hopped from one shaded patch to another.

The light breeze that tripped through the trees threw the edges of the shadows from side to side, making the jumping across the sea of crocodiles quite precarious.

'Ah! Your foot landed in the water,' said Tina as Dimitri performed a rather optimistic leap from one shadow to another. She chased after him, snapping her hands together. 'Snap! Snap! Snap! Here comes the crocodile!'

He squealed and laughed as he darted to the shade of another tree and leaned against the trunk. 'Not quick enough, Mr Crocodile.'

Dimitri looked on further down the avenue, assessing his next death-defying leap across crocodile-infested waters. He raised himself from the tree trunk and peered more closely at something ahead of him.

'There's a man outside our house,' he said.

Tina followed his gaze. Standing outside her front gate was John Nightingale. She was surprised to see him and found herself subconsciously running her hand across her hair, which was tied back in a ponytail. A fleeting thought, that she wished she had her hair loose today, whizzed through her mind. Swiftly followed by another that she was in her work uniform. However, these were soon overtaken by the idea that something might be wrong. She hadn't been expecting to see the police again, unless there had been some developments.

'Hello, Tina,' said John as she neared him.

'Hello,' said Tina. 'Is everything all right?' An uneasy sensation pitched up in her stomach and instinctively she took Dimitri by the hand, drawing him into her.

'Everything is fine,' replied John, he looked down at Dimitri and smiled. 'Hello, I'm John. You must be Dimitri.'

Dimitri turned into Tina's legs. 'Say hello to John,' she said. John crouched down and held out his hand.

'Hello,' said Dimitri. He looked at John's hand for a moment and then solemnly shook it.

'I wondered if we could have a word,' said John standing up. 'We?'

John motioned with his head to the other side of the road. Another man Tina didn't recognise lounged against the side of a black BMW. 'Martin, he's my partner.'

'Two of you. That sounds to me like everything is not fine.'

She watched John's face for any sign that she might be right. It was impassive. 'Can we come in?' he said after a moment.

'I suppose you had better.'

Tina hoped that the air of calm she was desperately trying to project was working. She didn't want to alarm Dimitri any more than he had already been the past few weeks. She was very much aware he was picking up on her anxieties. He had started having upsetting dreams about hearing footsteps in the night and being watched. A couple of nights ago, his whimpering had woken her, the result of a nightmare that someone was in his room.

Once inside she busied herself making tea for the adults and poured a glass of milk for her son. 'Why don't you pop the TV on?' she said to Dimitri as she took the drink and a biscuit through to the living room.

'TV? Now?' said Dimitri excitedly. 'I can watch it now?'

'Yes, just this once I'll make an exception to no TV immediately you get in. You can do your reading and writing later instead.'

Martin followed her into the living room. 'I'll watch TV with you, if you want. Haven't seen Tom and Jerry in years.'

'Tom and Jerry,' said Dimitri. 'I don't watch that, it's for babies. No, I'm going to watch Ben 10.'

'Ben what?'

'Sit down and you'll find out,' said Tina. She was grateful that Martin was acting as a distraction for Dimitri but, at the same time, apprehensive as to what John was about to spring on her.

'How's everything?' John asked her as she came back into the kitchen.

'Okay. Nothing I can really put my finger on,' said Tina, motioning towards the table. She took the two cups over. 'I've still got that *being watched* feeling, which I can't seem to shake off. I used to always leave the curtains and blinds open when it was dark, but I don't any more. I find myself double-checking doors are locked. That sort of thing.'

'You can call me if you're worried about anything,' said John.

'Thank you but I don't really think you want me to call you at every bump in the night.' She took a sip of her drink. 'Last night, I was lying in bed and I was sure I could hear floorboards creaking every now and then.'

'Really?'

She gave a small laugh at the look of concern on his face. 'You know what these old houses are like. I was just dropping off to sleep, so I wasn't really sure what it was. Probably the wind or something.'

'You weren't frightened?'

Tina dropped her eyes. She felt foolish, although at the time she had woken with a start and her heart had raced liked an F1 car off the starting grid. 'Just a bit unnerved. What with what's been going on recently. I think I've been overreacting. Anyway, what was it you wanted to talk to me about?'

'I don't want to alarm you any more, but things have moved on with our investigation and we know Pavel came into the country over a couple of weeks ago.'

Tina slowly put her cup of the table. 'Do you think it was him I saw in the garden?'

John shrugged. 'Honestly, I can't say. We don't know why he's here. Has he been in touch with you at all?'

'No. No, he hasn't. I don't really know what to make of it. What exactly do you think Pavel is involved in? Why do you need to speak to him?'

She watched John take a sip of his tea, clearly stalling for time as he weighed up her question and formulated his response. His eyes met hers. The evening light bounced off the flecks of gold that laced his green eyes. Troubled eyes. She braced herself for his response.

'And before you say "to help us with our enquiries" you need to come up with a better reason than that.' She felt agitated now. John was definitely holding back.

'I'd love to tell you everything, but at this stage in the investigation …'

She held up her hand to stop him continuing. 'Police bullshit. Waffle. Call it what you like, but it's not answering the question.' She saw the corners of his mouth twitch slightly, as if amused, before a frown settled on his face. He gently drummed his fingers on the table. Long, lean fingers that looked like they should be playing the piano. Fingernails clipped short. There was no wedding band or even a sign that he had ever worn a ring on his finger. She wondered briefly if there was a girlfriend on the scene.

'Okay, I'll be honest with you,' he said.

'Good. I don't like being taken for a fool and not told everything.'

'Pavel was involved in an organised money-laundering ring.'

'Money-laundering.' Tina couldn't help giving a small laugh. The serious look on John's face killed her laughter. 'That's a serious offence. Is there anything else?'

'Organised crime. Armed robbery and money-laundering. Yeah, you could say they are serious offences.'

'I knew he was involved with the Porboski gang, but I didn't think it was anything as serious as armed robbery and money-laundering,' said Tina. 'I thought it was more petty crime, a bit of smuggling in vodka or passing on stolen items – that sort of thing.'

'Much more serious,' said John. 'Murder.'

Tina balked. Murder? Pavel? No, that was way off.

'Are you sure?' she said. 'You think Pavel is involved with a murder? Who?'

'A police officer.'

'Oh God, that's serious.' Tina rested her head in her hands.

'All murder is serious,' said John.

There was an uneasy silence whilst Tina took in what she had just been told. Much as she disliked Pavel, she had never had him down as a hardened criminal – a murderer.

'I'm sorry,' she said at last. 'I'm finding this really hard to take in. Sasha never said a word. He couldn't have known.'

'Do you recognise this man?' said John. The change in direction was welcomed. Tina looked at the photograph John placed on the table in front of her.

'Is he dead?' She leaned back in her chair, averting her eyes from the image.

'Yes, he is,' said John. 'Found at some docks in London in the last few days. We believe he was looking for Pavel.'

'Pavel's very popular.' Her voice was dry. 'And no, I don't recognise him.'

'Are you sure? Perhaps he came into the deli your husband ran?'

Tina's eyes flipped to him. 'How did you know Sasha ran a deli?' She never referred to it as a deli, it was always 'the shop'.

'It's on record,' said John. He moved position in his seat. 'Intelligence-gathering.'

'Surveillance? Were you watching the shop? Have you been spying on us?'

'Gathering information on suspected criminals goes with the job. It says here that Pavel frequented a deli. You mentioned the shop before. I put two and two together. It's what I do. I'm a detective.' He gave a smile.

'Sorry, of course,' said Tina. 'I'm just a bit on edge, that's all.'

'It's okay,' said John. He picked the photo up of Ivan Gromov and slipped it back into his inside pocket. 'Did Sasha ever give you anything to look after? Did he ever say anything about what Pavel was up to?'

Tina thought back and shook her head. 'As I said before, we didn't talk about Pavel and as for giving me anything of significance, then, no. He didn't.'

'Okay, well thanks for your time again,' said John. He stood up. 'If you think of anything, let me know. In the meantime, we're going to keep a discreet eye out for Pavel. Surveillance. Don't look alarmed. There's nothing for you to worry about.'

'You think he will try and contact me?'

'It's one of our theories. We'll be parked up overnight, in case he does show.' He passed Tina his card. 'Here's my number, put it in your phone. If you think of anything, call me. If you're worried about anything, call me.'

'Thank you,' said Tina. She couldn't help feeling slightly unnerved again and that John was keeping something from her. 'Is there anything I should know?'

'Please don't worry,' said John. 'If there are any developments, I'll contact you straight away.'

'What did you tell her?' said Martin as John got into the passenger seat of the BMW.

'That Pavel was back in the UK. Kept it simple for now. I don't want her freaking out on us,' said John. 'We need her to draw Pavel out of the woodwork.'

'What's the plan now?'

'Back to the office. I want to check in with the team. See if anyone has got any info about the Porboski gang making a comeback. You have another chat with Baz Fisher. All this poking around is bound to have stirred up the locals. He might have heard some more by now.' John looked up at 17 Belfour Avenue. 'I'll come back later to see if Pavel turns up.'

'So, go on, admit it,' said Martin.

'Admit what?' said John. He had an idea what Martin was referring to, but he wasn't going to make it easy. The ribbing that would follow would be enough.

'You've got more than just a passing interest in Mrs B.' Martin pushed the keys into the ignition and fired up the engine.

'Of course I have. This case means a lot to me,' said John. He fastened his seat belt and looked straight ahead, purposefully avoiding any eye contact with his friend.

'You know what I mean,' said Martin as he pulled out onto Belfour Terrace. 'Just don't let Brogan get wind of it.'

'You worry about the driving and I'll worry about what Brogan knows, or thinks he knows,' said John. 'I'm not about to compromise the operation, despite my suspicions. I'm sure Tina is the link, even if she doesn't know it herself.'

'See! I told you.' A big grin swept across Martin's face.

'What?'

'It's Tina, now. Not Mrs Bolotnikov. Absolutely proves my point.'

John shook his head. 'You're a dick at times, you know that?'

'It might have been said once or twice before. Mostly by you, granted. But, I'm a dick who's right.' Martin laughed out loud, clearly delighted with himself.

Trouble was, John couldn't really deny it. He was very much taken with Tina. Despite thinking he knew her from the surveillance five years ago, he didn't know the woman she was now. She was something of an enigma, a woman who sparked his interest in more ways than one. However, he was painfully aware that she was, at best, a witness, at worst a suspect.

Chapter 10

Tina watched from her window as the BMW drew off down the road. She craned her neck until it had disappeared out of sight. A little feeling of unease snuck up on her and she glanced up and down the road, half expecting to see Pavel outside.

What exactly he was doing back in the UK, she had no idea. Had he really been spying on her? She wished she could have found out more about what he had been up to when he had lived in the UK, but John had been tight-lipped.

She wondered if Sasha had known anything. He had certainly never given her any indication that Pavel was mixed up in anything as serious as murder. Sasha would have told her. They shared everything. She turned away from the window and her eyes came to rest on the photo frame on the mantelpiece. She walked over and picked it up. A sparkly frame with bits of tiny mirror tiles, sparkly glass, a bric-a-brac home-crafted frame that Sasha had given her. Inside was a photograph of the two of them, taken on Brighton Pier.

She smiled. The frame really wasn't her style and didn't fit in with anything else in the house. She remembered how proud Sasha had been when he had presented it to her. She had wanted to laugh, but he had been deadly serious when he said how precious it was. A token of how precious she was and how precious their love was. How sad that they had so little time together. She replaced the frame.

'I'm going to pop upstairs to get changed,' she said to Dimitri. 'Then I'll go next door and see if Mr Cooper wants some tea. You okay there?'

A brief 'yes' in reply, which didn't even involve her son taking his eyes from the screen. Okay, the TV wasn't the ideal babysitter, but today she was grateful for it.

Tina sighed to herself as she climbed the stairs, picking up a couple of toys that Dimitri had discarded at some point that morning before school. All she ever seemed to do was tidy up after him. How was it possible a six-year-old could make so much mess? She reached the landing and, just to prove her point, there was a sprinkling of what looked like powder on the carpet.

She scuffed it with her foot in an attempt to rub it in. She paused. Not simply because she knew she was being lazy and should really get the Hoover out, but because the powder had a grey tinge to it. What on earth had he tipped out? She looked into his bedroom and noticed an old cardboard box in the corner that he had brought home from school. Well, he told her it was a robot, hence the silver foil stuck randomly all over it, together with milk-bottle lids. The dust and dirt had probably come from there. She went to call out his name and tell him to come and tidy up, but stopped herself.

Tina rubbed her face with her hands. All this business with being followed and now Pavel being in the UK, stirring up emotions about Sasha, was getting to her. She needed to stay rational and not let the stress take its effect on her and, as a result, on Dimitri. She couldn't tell him off for playing. She'd clear it up and say no more.

When she went next door to Mr Cooper's. It was no surprise that the back door was unlocked and he was dozing in his chair with classical music coming from the old radiogram beside him. Stepping into Mr Cooper's living room was like going back in time by about fifty years. Despite Tina enjoying the comforts of modern-day living, she always felt a comfort in Mr Cooper's home. It reminded her of her Nan's house and gave a reassuring warm, nostalgic feel.

Today, however, she didn't get that usual wrap of warmth. The house felt different. She couldn't put her finger on exactly what it was but there was an odd atmosphere. She gave herself a mental shake. Things were definitely getting to her.

She decided not to disturb Mr Cooper in his mid-afternoon nap, she would simply pop back later with a plate of dinner. Retracing her steps into the hall, Tina glanced towards the front door to see if there was any post. A collection of envelopes lay scattered on the doormat. They mostly looked like junk mail. Mr Cooper rarely got any personal post. All his bills were paid by direct debits and, apart from his daughter in Australia, there wasn't really anyone else in his life. Tina bent to collect the mail all the same and flicked through to make sure there wasn't anything important-looking. If not, she'd put it straight in the recycling, like she usually did.

The bang from upstairs made Tina jump. It sounded like a door. Tina stood still and listened, but all she could hear was her heart thumping inside her chest, as if trying to beat its way out. Then another bang, this one not quite so violent. Tina looked up the darkened staircase. Mr Cooper never went upstairs any more, his legs weren't up to it. Tina had only been up there once herself, when he had needed an extra blanket last winter. He had spilt tea on his usual one and she had offered to take it home and put it through her washing machine. Tina remembered from then that upstairs was like a museum, dark where the curtains were kept drawn, mainly to stop the wind blowing through the gaps in the wooden window frames. Mr Cooper had never seen the need to invest in the upkeep of his property, not one for double glazing or central heating. He had managed all his life without it and didn't see why he needed it in his senior years. Tina remembered how most of the bedroom furniture was covered with off-white dust sheets.

The door banged again from upstairs. Steeling herself, Tina acceded that she would have to go up and close it properly, although she did wonder why it had started banging now. The ascent of the staircase set her nerves jangling.

'This is so stupid,' she muttered to herself. 'What on earth am I afraid of? It's just a house. Exactly like mine.' She was now at the top of the stairs and she hastily located the light switch. The landing was immediately swathed in light and Tina was thankful that Mr Cooper had never felt the need to convert the landing light to one of those energy-saving bulbs that seemed to take an eternity to reach their full power.

Tina quickly identified the door that was responsible for banging. She went to poke her head round the doorway but stopped and switched on the light. Sadly, this one wasn't working at all.

All Tina's senses were telling her not to go into the room.

Her i-phone bursting into life from her pocket made her let out a startled scream. Her body jumped involuntarily and her breath caught in the back of her throat.

'Shit!' She held her hand to her racing heart and groped in her jeans pocket for her phone.

'John Police' flashed up across the screen.

Tina accepted the call. 'Hello.' She closed the bedroom door, giving it an extra tug, until she heard the click of the catch fitting into the lock.

'Hi, Tina. It's me, John. Everything okay?'

She pushed the bedroom door to ensure it wouldn't come open again. 'Hi, John. Yes, all okay. I'm at Mr Cooper's.'

'Just letting you know that I'll be parked up outside tonight.'

'Just you?'

'Yeah. Martin's follow up some leads. If you need me, shout.'

'Thanks, that's good to know.' Tina immediately felt herself relax.

'Have you eaten?'

'Yes, thanks. Don't worry about me, you carry on as normal.'

'Are you planning to be there all night?'

'Pretty much. Martin will be back down tomorrow.' He sounded casual, as if it was a regular thing.

'All night in the car? Will you be okay?'

She heard him laugh before he spoke. It was a gentle laugh, filled with warmth. 'I'll be fine. I've staked out in worse places, I can assure you. Now, don't forget, anything that's bothering you, call me. Anything at all.'

'Thank you. I'll try not to freak out, though, if there are any creepy crawlies about. I'm not sure spiders count as emergencies.'

She ended the call and was very aware of the smile that had, at some point, pasted itself on her face. It was still there as she left Mr Cooper, still dozing in his chair, and went back next door to get the tea ready.

Chapter 11

Tina wasn't sure what woke her first. The soft whimper of Dimitri crying or the unfamiliar creak of floorboards. Creaks that didn't happen as the house breathed in and out, slumbering its way through the night. No, those creaks were embedded in her subconscious, they didn't stir her. The creaks she heard tonight were different. They had a sense of rhythm and weight to them.

She was up and grabbing her dressing gown as these thoughts filtered their way through her sleep-muffled brain. Dimitri's whimper had turned into a cry.

'Mummy!'

'It's okay, darling. I'm coming.'

Tina pushed open her son's bedroom door. It was ajar. She had left it closed. She always closed his door. Perhaps he had been up in the night. That would explain the unusual groaning of the floorboards. She let out a deep breath and calmed herself as she entered the room.

Dimitri was lying in bed, the duvet pulled over his head. She could see his feet jiggling. He pulled the cover down and called out her name again, before hiding his face under the racing-car fabric.

'It's mummy,' said Tina rushing to the side of his bed. She pulled the cover back and stroked his head. 'Dimitri. Mummy's here.' Enveloping him into her arms, she held him tight, making reassuring soothing noises. His little body relaxed into her and his arms wrapped around her neck. Soon his crying eased.

'There was a monster in my room,' he said.

'It's all gone now. You must have been dreaming,' said Tina. She pulled away from her son and smiled, holding her hand to his rosy cheek. The shaft of light from the hall cast a shadow across the bed, leaving the rest of the room in darkness.

Tina turned to look across the room. Dark corners and unidentified black shapes invaded the room. By day the furniture and furnishing were comforting. By night menacing. Alien in the darkness.

Unable to rely on sight, she listened intently. The atmosphere was heavy. She felt Dimitri's body stiffen. Through the thin cotton of her nightshirt, his fingernails dug into her back. Tina wasn't sure what she was listening for. Anything that shouldn't be there. Footsteps. Breathing. Movement.

Nothing was out of place and yet, as her mind jumped back to what had woken her in the first place, she knew there had been a foreign noise, one that did not belong in the house. One that threatened her.

'Do you want to sleep in Mummy's bed tonight?' She didn't wait for Dimitri to say yes. Tina pulled back the duvet and picking him up, carried him through to her bedroom. 'There, we will look after each other.'

'Can I have a glass of water, please?' said Dimitri as Tina tucked the cover under his chin.

'Of course.'

The words came out rather more freely than she felt. Going out into the hall, she closed the bedroom door tight behind her, checking it was shut firmly. Tina hurried across the landing. Pausing at the top of the staircase, she looked down into a well of darkness. She looked back at the bedroom door. An irrational feeling of wanting to be on the other side of the door with Dimitri crawled over her. Goosebumps prickled her skin. She glanced at

Dimitri's bedroom door. The blackness seemed to be reaching out, stretching its way onto the landing, curling itself around her ankles.

Tina fumbled for the two-way light switch at the top of the stairs. Immediately the downstairs was illuminated. She ran down the staircase and flicked the living-room light on, then the dining-room light as she navigated the hallway towards the kitchen. She cursed the energy-saving light bulbs. She wanted instant brightness, not the soft glow that slowly stretched its way into the corners of the rooms.

Entering the kitchen, she was grateful that the spotlights were more forthcoming, immediately bathing the room in white light.

Rascal stirred in his basket, lifting his head to see who had interrupted his sleep.

'Sorry, fella,' said Tina as she filled a glass from the water-filter jug in the fridge. 'Go back to sleep now.'

She closed the kitchen door behind her. The next challenge was to make it up the stairs, switching the lights off and having the blackness follow her.

She ignored the slosh of water that spilled from the glass as she rounded the newel post and took the first stair. It was only water, it would dry and not stain. The sound of footsteps on the landing stopped her. Heavy footsteps. Too heavy to be Dimitri's. Long strides. Too long to be those of a child. She looked up.

Two black-booted feet stood at the top of the stairs. Before she could look any further, darkness descended all around her as the lights were turned off from the upstairs switch.

She screamed. Dropped the glass of water. Her first thought was Dimitri. Whoever was in the house stood between her and her son. There was no space in her head for any other thought. Dimitri and his safety were paramount.

The thundering of booted feet on the staircase penetrated her thoughts. They were coming towards her. An automatic reaction to protect herself kicked in, but before she could throw herself out of the way, two hands grabbed her shoulders, pushing her backwards off the first step. She fought to muffle her scream. She could hear Dimitri calling her.

Oh God, please don't let Dimitri come out. Please make him stay in the bedroom.

She stumbled backwards, hitting her head against the wall. The hands still held her. She felt the weight of his body against hers. One gloved hand came up and covered her mouth.

'Shhhhhh.' He hissed the noise in her ear. 'Shhhhhh.'

Tina nodded furiously, fighting back the whimper in her throat. His voice was deep and loud in her ear. His breath hot on her neck. It seemed an age before he released his hand from her mouth – just a fraction. Convinced she wasn't going to scream, he took it away completely.

In the darkness Tina couldn't see what he was doing, but she could hear him grappling with the coats on the pegs at the bottom of the stairs, finally finding what he needed.

'Mummy?' Dimitri's voice called out again.

The intruder gave Tina a nudge. She took her cue.

'Stay there, Dimitri,' she called out. 'Stay in the bedroom. Do NOT come out.'

The man bundled Tina down the hall and into the living room, pushing her into the armchair. He gagged her with a scarf he had taken from the coat pegs, then forced her to bend forwards before binding her hands and feet together.

No sooner had he done this than he was gone. Down the hall and into the kitchen. She heard him unlock the back door. She didn't wait to hear whether he shut it or not. She yanked and twisted her bound hands. Fortunately, there was enough stretch in the knitted scarf to pull her hands free. Some more fumbling and she released her feet. Pulling the scarf from her mouth she leapt out of the chair and ran upstairs.

She needed to get to Dimitri.

Tina burst into the bedroom. Dimitri was standing at the window. Tina ran over to him, sweeping her up into his arms.

Dimitri wriggled an arm free and pointed to the street below.

'Mummy, that man's coming,' said Dimitri.

Chapter 12

Tina's breath caught in her lungs. She grabbed at the venetian blinds with one hand, pulling the wooden slats apart.

There, striding down the path towards the front door, was John. Tina felt her knees buckle with relief. The hammering on the door was the sweetest sound to her ears. Putting Dimitri down and taking his hand, she hurried him downstairs.

'Thank God you're here!' she gasped, surprised by how relieved she felt to see John. He was in the hallway, closing the door behind him before she could catch her breath.

'What's happened? I saw Dimitri up at the window,' said John. 'The lights were going on and off downstairs so I thought I'd check it out. Are you both okay?'

Tina composed herself. She looked from John to Dimitri and back again, willing John to understand.

'I came down for some water, dropped the glass. You know what it's like, unexpected things going bump in the night.' Over the top of Dimitri's head she flicked her eyes towards the kitchen. 'I think the back door has been left open.'

She watched John take in the glass lying on the carpet, the coats on the floor and then search her face.

He reacted instantly, but with such an air of calm and authority that immediately Tina felt safe.

'You go back upstairs,' he said. Then he mouthed to her to lock the bedroom door. 'Wait there, I'll be back in a minute.'

John watched Tina and Dimitri go back upstairs. Once he heard the bedroom door shut and the key turn in the lock he withdrew his Glock from its holster. He was pretty certain that whoever had been in the house was long gone, but he wasn't taking any chances.

The kitchen was empty and the back door wide open. John opened the blinds to allow some light to seep across the garden. Cautiously he stepped out onto the patio, giving his eyes time to become accustomed to the dark. His instincts told him there was no one in the garden, but he checked anyway. The back gate was locked from the inside, so presumably the intruder hadn't left that way. Probably hopped over the wall. John looked up and down the access footpath at the rear.

Convinced that the intruder had gone, John went back indoors and up to Tina's bedroom. He tapped on the door.

'Tina, you okay? I'll put the kettle on,' he said softly, conscious that she was probably trying to settle her son. 'I'll be downstairs.'

Tina came into the kitchen some ten minutes later. She looked a mixture of relieved and upset.

Without thinking, John took her in his arms and held her for a moment until she pulled away.

'Thank you. I needed that,' she said.

'Are you hurt?'

'No, not really. Banged my head, but it's okay.'

John sat Tina at the table with a strong cup of tea and listened as she relayed to him what had happened.

'I can't understand how I didn't see him,' said John. 'You say, you heard him unlock the back door before he ran off?'

Tina nodded. 'Definitely. I was listening for him to go.'

'I doubt very much he came in that way and locked the door behind him,' said John. 'Locking your escape route is a schoolboy error. No one would do that.'

'And you didn't see him come through the front door?' said Tina.

John shook his head. His mind trawled through all the possibilities. He didn't want to make the next suggestion, but it seemed the only feasible scenario. 'Did you leave the house at all, even for a few minutes? Not even to go out into the garden, put something in the shed, bring the washing in? Anything like that?'

Tina thought for a moment. She closed her eyes and let out a small groan. 'I went next door to see Mr Cooper.'

When she looked at John, her eyes were filled with tears. 'The man must have come in then. Dimitri was in the house. Alone.' Two tears raced each other down her face. 'The man was in the house when Dimitri was here and I wasn't.'

'Hey, it's okay,' said John. He came round to her side of the table and pulled out the chair next to her. He put his arm around her shoulders. 'Don't upset yourself. Dimitri wasn't hurt. Nothing happened. Whoever it was, wasn't interested in Dimitri.'

'It makes me feel physically sick to think about it,' she said, brushing away more tears. 'Who do you think it was? Pavel?'

'It seems the most likely,' said John.

'Why the hell would he creep up on me like that? Why did he frighten me? I really don't understand.'

'Was there anything about him at all that seemed familiar?' said John. The question he really wanted to ask burned on his lips. He squeezed his finger and thumb across his mouth, swiping it away. She didn't need spooking any more tonight.

'It all happened so fast,' said Tina. 'I was thinking about Dimitri. I was terrified he would come down and I didn't know what the man would do to him.' She shivered. The shock was hitting her now. Time to end the questions.

John made Tina another drink and sat with her until she seemed calmer. The tears had stopped, as had the shivering.

'I think it would be a good idea if I stayed here the night,' said John. 'If that's okay with you.'

'Okay? Of course it is,' said Tina. 'In fact, I was hoping you would say that. I would be a lot happier knowing you were in the house rather than across the road.'

John looked at his watch. It was the early hours of the morning. He probably wouldn't sleep now. Not after what had gone on. He didn't think the intruder would be back tonight, but John wanted to be on the safe side.

'You go up to bed and I'll see you in the morning,' he said. He walked her to the bottom of the stairs. Her hand rested on the newel post and he covered it with his own. 'If you need me, just shout. I'm only down here.'

She turned her hand so their palms were touching and curled her fingers around his, squeezing it. John returned the gesture.

'Thank you,' she said. Her voice was soft. Her eyes full of gratitude and trust. 'I feel a lot safer knowing you're here.'

The night passed without any more activities. John dozed on and off on the sofa, assured that Pavel, if indeed that's who the intruder had been, wasn't coming back. As the morning sun broke, John went out into the back garden and phoned through to Martin to give him an update.

'It's safe to rule out Tina being involved in any of it, then,' said Martin.

'She was properly spooked last night,' said John. He turned to look back at the house. 'If she was acting, then she's missed her vocation.'

'And you think it was Pavel? No one else?'

'Put it this way, it wasn't anyone who particularly cared about her.' The blind went up at the kitchen window. Tina gave him a smile and, holding up a mug, pointed to it. John gave her the thumbs-up. As he did so, he became aware of the breadth of his smile. Unnecessarily wide. 'Anything from Baz Fisher?' he said to Martin. He noted the pause before his partner answered.

'We haven't been able to find Baz. No one's seen him for two days.'

John understood the significance of this information. 'You think he's hiding?'

'Could be one of two options.'

John swore under his breath. 'Keep looking.'

He ended the call. Baz Fisher unobtainable. This was not a good sign.

Chapter 13

'Morning,' said Tina. She sounded brighter although the heavy eyelids were traitor to her demeanour.

'Hey. How are you?' said John, taking the cup she held out to him.

'I've had better nights. What about you? Did you get any sleep?'

'Enough. How's Dimitri?'

'Still sleeping. He was okay, though. I don't think he realised anything happened last night. He just thinks he had a nightmare.'

They sat at the table. John sensed she wanted to say something but was choosing her words. He sipped at his tea, giving her time.

'Do you think Sasha was mixed up with the stuff Pavel was into?' Her voice had a sad edge to it and she kept her eyes firmly fixed on her cup.

'It's possible,' he said quietly.

'But you must have an idea. You must have considered this before. If you think his brother is, then it stands to reason that Sasha might be as well and you would have investigated it or it was on the agenda. I mean, I'm no detective, but even I've thought of that.' This time she did meet his eyes. There was that quiet strength in there he hadn't seen before.

He nodded to soften the blow of the words that followed. 'Yes, it's been considered.'

'And?'

'And … we never found anything to arrest him for.'

It was her turn to nod this time. 'But you looked.' She took a sip of her drink. 'How long will you be about? What if Pavel doesn't turn up?'

'It's indefinite, but subject to change at any time. We may get new information in that sends the investigation off in a totally different direction, a different location. It's really a fluid thing. Nothing is set in stone.'

'And I suppose it's all about funding and making the best of police resources.'

'Sadly, yes, funding and overtime do come into it.'

'What does your wife or girlfriend think to you being out all night? Does she mind?'

'I haven't got either of those.'

'Oh, sorry. I didn't mean to assume … of course, your partner. What do they think?'

For a moment John was confused. She looked embarrassed, as a flush of red crept its way up her neck. Suddenly it dawned on him what she had meant. He laughed out loud. She looked at him, a look somewhere between bewilderment and embarrassment. He reined his laughter in. 'I don't have a partner either. For the record, I'm SAS.'

'SAS? I thought you were in the police. Wait, are we having two different conversations? I'm so confused.'

'Straight and single.' He grinned at her.

Tina threw her head back, covering her face with her hands. 'Oh, my God! I'm making such a fool of myself.' She took her hands down and laughed. Her eyes sparkled like fairy lights. For a moment the tension and unease had been eradicated. It was good to see her relax.

'And something else, for the record,' said John. 'I'm divorced after a very brief marriage.'

'I'm sorry.'

'Don't be. I'm not. We were young. And, if I'm honest, I put my job first.'

'You don't sound like you have any regrets.'

'No. It was a mutual agreement to separate. We didn't have any children, so it was pretty painless.'

They chatted some more, both aware that it was a distraction from real life: time out from the unsettling events of the last few hours. Besides, it was nice getting to know her through his own eyes and not through the lens of his camera or police files. The conversation poignantly avoided Pavel and Sasha. They talked of only superficial things; films they liked, tastes in music, favourite food. Safe topics, but ones John found they had a lot in common with. It was enjoyable getting to know her this way. Not a trial, like it sometimes was when he was undercover or fishing for information. This felt, somehow, real and genuine. He was glad she hadn't pushed him any further about Sasha's role in the investigation. He wasn't in a position to divulge any information to her and that would, he guessed, irritate her. He needed to keep her on-side so she trusted him and, in turn, would feel able to confide in him. He also needed to play the long game, but he was aware that time wasn't his friend. Any time now Brogan could take him off surveillance if he didn't get any results. The impatience in his personal desire to get to know Tina better was also hot on his heels.

Tina got up and put the cups in the dishwasher. 'I was wondering if I could ask you a question? Well, it's more of a favour.' She turned to look at him and twiddled the heart- shaped pendant on her necklace.

'Fire away.'

'It's a bit awkward, so feel free to say no.'

'Okay, but I need to know what you want to ask,' he said, tacking a smile onto the end, which hid the apprehension he was feeling.

'I'm supposed to be attending a fortieth birthday party on Friday evening. My boss's wife. I have said I would go, but what with everything I was going to make an excuse.'

'You shouldn't let the events take over your whole life,' said John. 'Don't stop doing things, otherwise you'll become a prisoner in your own home.'

'I know. That's the thing that is bothering me the most. I hate the thought that it has the potential to control me like this.' She continued to run the pendant back and forth along the chain.

'So where do I fit into all this?' said John, although he had an inkling what was coming next. The thought warmed him.

'Would you consider coming with me as my plus one? Not in a boyfriend capacity,' she added hastily, her cheeks once again tinged with a blush of pink. 'Just as a friend. I figured you would be sitting outside anyway, you know, following me, so you might as well come in and socialise a bit. That's if you want to. I mean – you don't have to, not if you would rather not. I don't want to get you into trouble, or anything …'

John couldn't help smiling. She was gabbling and the pink flush had turned a deeper rose colour. He held up his hand to put her out of her misery.

'Yes,' he said. 'Yes, I'll come as your plus one.' The relief on her face was clear. Again, a warmth swept through him.

'Oh, thank you. I do appreciate it,' said Tina. She grinned at him. 'I promise we won't have to stay very long and I won't leave you to fend for yourself.'

'So, you'll be protecting me?' The thought amused him.

'Most certainly! Jessica will probably be there. She's my boss's sister. She's works in the café sometimes when we are short-staffed. She's, how shall we say, a rather desperate man-eater. Jessica is to men what heat-seeking missiles are to tanks.'

'Then I'm totally depending on you.'

'Will it be okay with your boss?'

'He'll be absolutely fine. I'm lucky when I'm out in the field like this, I have the autonomy to make my own decisions. Working undercover, you can't just tell the bad guys to hang on a moment while you check with your guvnor.'

76

Okay, he was bending the rules slightly and John was pretty sure Brogan wouldn't be too impressed. He'd cross that bridge if, and when, he got to it.

'Thanks so much,' she said. 'Dimitri is staying with my parents. He goes to stay with them most Friday nights. They love having him and he really loves being there too.'

'Gives you a break as well,' said John.

'Not that I do anything, but it's nice to know I can, should I want to.' Tina looked at her watch. 'Eeek, I didn't realise that was the time. I'd better get Dimitri up. I did wonder about keeping him out of school, but I don't want to worry him.'

'No, keep to your usual routine. I'm sure Dimitri will be safe. Have you got work today?'

She nodded. 'I think sticking to my routine will do me good too.'

'I'll drop you both off,' said John, acknowledging the slight feeling of disappointment ebbing through him at the thought of Tina not being about that day. He took his cup over to the sink, where she was standing. She didn't move out of his way and as he reached around to place the cup in the sink, he was very aware of the closeness of her body to his. The ever-so- faint smell of perfume teased his nostrils, a delicate flowery fragrance. It was at odds with the strong young woman he was only really getting to know. His perception of her five years ago, as a delicate, fragile widow, was slipping and making way for someone who had weathered a fierce storm of grief and was heading towards calmer waters, full of a quiet confidence that he hadn't noticed before.

'Thank you,' she said. An awkward silence settled between them. Tina broke first. 'I'd better get Dimitri up.' A small look of embarrassment caressed her face. As she side-stepped away, John concentrated on looking out of the window, ahead of him.

What the hell was he getting himself into? Agreeing to all but go on a date with her, thinly disguised as police protection. *Shit*. This simply wasn't like him. He hadn't planned this at all.

Tina's cat wound its way around his legs, arching its back

slightly. It let out a small purr. He bent down and picked it up. 'We seem to have strayed from the script, kitty. Let's hope your mistress is worth it.'

Chapter 14

For the first time in several weeks, Tina felt relaxed going up to bed. It was reassuring having John in the house. Much as she hated to admit it, things had started getting to her. She had always prided herself on being able to cope on her own. But having John there tonight, in the house, gave her a sense that she wasn't alone in this world. At night times the loneliness and grief of not having her husband haunted her the most. It wasn't that she couldn't cope alone, it was simply that she didn't want to be alone. She hadn't chosen to be a single mother, a working woman, juggling motherhood with day care and work life. It had been enforced on her and whilst some women extolled the virtues and revelled in the freedom this brought them, most of the time they had chosen that life. She hadn't. She hadn't chosen to be alone.

Thoughts of Sasha pushed their way to the fore. Not for the first time in the past five years, she wondered what her life would be like if he was still with her. Probably not very different. Or maybe it would be. What if he was mixed up in whatever business Pavel had been mixed up in?

She made a conscious effort to consign these thoughts to the depth of her mind. Now wasn't the time to go over it all. She stopped outside Dimitri's door and poked her head round. The landing light seeped across his bedroom, casting a gentle haze of soft yellow into the room. She paused and listened to his rhythmic breathing. Calm and peaceful. Oblivious to the storms brewing in a life he had so many connections with, yet no connection at all.

A muffled bang brought Tina out of her thoughts. She stood still. Alert. Listening for it again. Silence. She pulled the door to Dimitri's bedroom closed and stepped across the landing to her own. There was the noise again. Not an acute, sharp sound right by her, but close enough to break through the stillness of the night.

She realised it was coming from Mr Cooper's. It must be that door again. She would have to get someone to have a look at the catch. The last thing she wanted was to be kept awake by the thud of the door every so often. She was unsettled enough as it was. She made a mental note to check the window in the room too. Maybe it had been left open and the draught was causing the door to bang. She had meant to do it before but had got distracted when her phone had rung.

As Tina crossed the landing and went into her bedroom, her feet bare, she felt something sharp dig into her big toe. She stifled a whimper as she inspected the carpet and stumbled, landing on her bed. She inspected her toe and picked out a small whitish piece of plaster, about the size of a garden pea.

The sound of footsteps, light but hurried, taking the stairs two at a time, made her turn towards the bedroom door. A small tap followed.

'Tina? You okay?'

It was John. She got up and, avoiding the dust patch on the carpet, padded over to open the bedroom door.

'Yes, I'm fine,' she said.

'I heard you cry out and then a bang,' he said, looking beyond her shoulder into the room.

'I trod on something and stumbled. I'm fine, honest.' She turned to look back at the offending dust pile. 'Dimitri's been leaving a trail of dust and dirt for me to clear up. He had an old cardboard box earlier.'

John followed her gaze. 'Oh, sorry! A bit of overkill on my part.'

'Possibly. I think I'll be safe now. As far as I can see, no more booby traps for me to avoid.'

She met his look, suddenly very conscious of how close they were to each other.

'Right. Okay.' For the first time he didn't sound so in control. He backed away a few steps. 'I'll … er … leave you to get some rest. Goodnight, Tina.' He turned and she could hear him taking the stairs nearly as quickly as he had come up them.

She closed the bedroom door and sat down on her bed. What happened there? She wasn't quite sure. In the briefest of moments an unspoken sense of mutual awareness had passed between them. A depth of awareness she hadn't experienced for a long time.

Tina closed her eyes. So much was happening right now, maybe her senses were simply heightened, feeding her imagination.

John eyed Martin across the table of the café they had met in to discuss the Porboski case. He didn't like what Martin was saying, but knew it had been coming. Martin leaned in closer.

'Look, John, the bottom line is, if Pavel fails to turn up this weekend and we don't get any further intel on where he is, then Brogan will be calling you back to HQ. He's griping about man-hours on searching through CCTV and enquiries that are leading nowhere. At the moment, our only saving grace is that we have definite ID on our guests from Stockholm and that Baz Fisher is still missing.'

'Where the hell could he have gone?' said John.

'No one is talking. It's not looking good.' Martin took a mouthful of coffee. 'Apparently, there's some movement on another case that Brogan wants to follow up and, as far as he's concerned, he's paying you to do nothing more than babysit,'

'Bollocks,' muttered John, his frustration simmering.

'Brogan's getting stick from above. The recent robberies on the post offices in the Hackney area is attracting attention. The local media has been full of it this week.'

'The post office is well insured,' said John. 'Does Brogan want to tell that to Neil's widow that despite reliable intel, we're not going to bother too much about catching the killers?'

'Listen, mate,' said Martin. 'This is me talking to you as a friend. Off the record.'

'Why do I get the impression I'm not going to like what's coming?'

Martin ignored John's comment.

'I know how much this case means to you. We all do. But, mate, this guilt that you carry around with you the whole time, it's not doing you any favours. Some things you have to let go.'

'And some things you can't.'

'You're not responsible for what happened at the Moorgate robbery.'

John looked out of the window. Martin had no idea what he was talking about. This was a conversation John didn't want to have. 'Thanks for the advice, but let's just drop it now.'

Martin let out a defeated sigh. 'That counselling you had worked, then.'

It was John's turn to ignore the remark. He rubbed at his scarred shoulder.

The counselling – it had been part of his rehabilitation back to work after the shooting. A condition that he had begrudgingly adhered to. He knew the game and played by the rules. He had made all the right comments, said all the right things. He hid his guilt. He hid his need for justice. It paid off and he had been declared fit to return to work, but he had never once lost sight of what he needed: atonement.

Chapter 15

Tina sat on the edge of her bed to fasten the strap of her shoe. Black, strappy sandals to go with the black, strappy dress she had picked to wear for the work's do. It was a simple shift dress with a few beads embroidered around the neckline to add a bit of sparkle. She hadn't worn it for several years; it was sitting in the back of her wardrobe. She remembered the last time she had worn it, on a night out with Sasha. It was his birthday. It was the last birthday they were to spend together. Guilt brushed the back of her neck, sending a small shiver down her spine.

She took a deep breath, expelling the emotion. She didn't want to feel guilty for going out or to feel guilty that John was accompanying her. She reminded herself that he was merely doing his job, keeping her safe in case Pavel turned up.

Tina poked the end of the strap through the buckle and stood up, facing herself in the mirror. The dress, if anything, was slightly baggy in places it probably hadn't been baggy before. She didn't possess a set of bathroom scales – she had never been one for weighing herself. Of a naturally slim build, she used the tightness of her clothes to determine whether she had gained or lost weight. The past five years had taken their toll on her and she had been aware at one point that her weight was plummeting, hitting rock bottom along with her grief. If it hadn't been for Dimitri, his mere existence giving her strength to pick herself up, Tina wasn't sure where she would be now. She had put the weight back on, but not to the comfortable size twelve she had previously been. These days a size ten gave her plenty of room, it wasn't a great look for someone so tall, but she usually managed to get away with loose-fitting clothes to disguise the bony skeleton underneath.

However, she had felt in the last 18 months or so she was getting something of a figure back, but the last few weeks her nervous energy seemed to be having an adverse effect.

When she had dropped Dimitri off at her parents' house that evening, her mum had commented on her appearance.

'Is everything all right, darling?' said Pam. 'Only I noticed during the last week or so you were looking very tired and a bit drawn and sallow.'

Tina had laughed it off. 'Oh, mum, you know how to make a girl feel good about herself, especially when she's just off on a night out.'

Tina had kissed her mum and told her not to worry, that everything was fine. It was probably due to being busy at work. She wasn't sure her mother had been convinced, but the older woman had said no more of it. The last thing Tina wanted was for her mum to start worrying about her. Any mention of Pavel was strictly off the agenda. Her parents had been most disgusted that none of the Bolotnikov family had kept in touch with Tina after the death of their son-in-law and were even more anti the Russian contingent once they learned that Tina was pregnant. No, mentioning Pavel would certainly be a bad move.

Tina squirted a dash of perfume on her wrists and rubbed them together before gathering her small shoulder bag and going downstairs.

John was waiting in the living room. As she walked in, Tina was aware she had taken a large and loud intake of breath. She was also aware John had done the exact same thing. They looked at each other and laughed.

'Well, don't you scrub up well?' she said casting an approving eye over his grey chinos and pale-blue shirt.

'You don't look so bad yourself,' he replied. He looked down at himself. 'I hope it's okay, only I haven't got a great selection with me in my travelling wardrobe.'

Tina looked over at his holdall on the sofa. 'I think you've done very well, considering.'

John held out his arm. 'Shall we?'

Tina hooked her arm through his. 'Yes, let's.'

The birthday party was a bit starchy at first and after thirty minutes of circulating amongst other guests and explaining that John was 'just a friend', Tina was regretting her decision to invite him along. Fay had bailed out at the last moment, citing a headache. Tina wished she had had the foresight to do the same.

'I'm so sorry,' she said after her boss' sister had subjected her to a particularly long interrogation. 'I wouldn't be surprised if Jessica came back with her clipboard and a whole survey for you to complete.'

'Don't worry about it,' said John.

'Although, I must compliment you on your new identity,' said Tina. 'You've got a great imagination. I mean, who would have thought I'd be bringing along John, an accountant from London who I met through a friend at a party. That's John who also has his own pad in Fulham and left school and worked his way up through the firm of accountants. It's like you're a professional at this. The original hustler.'

John shrugged and grinned, but didn't mask the uncomfortable look that lingered behind his eyes. A moment of awkward silence sliced between them before John spoke. 'I had to come up with something. It was the first thing that came to mind.'

'And how much of that was the truth and how much fabrication?' said Tina. She injected a light-hearted tone to her voice. John was, no doubt, just uncomfortable having to lie about himself to her boss and his wife. After all, he was a policeman, so it wasn't in his nature to tell lies.

'About fifty-fifty,' said John. 'I was basing it on my cousin, who does happen to be an accountant. As for your friend …'

'Boss' sister,' interrupted Tina. 'Let's get that bit straight, Jessica is by no means my friend.'

'Okay, Jessica – she could work for the intelligence service with the sort of grilling she was giving me. It's a wonder MI5 haven't signed her up by now.'

'Oooh, I like this sort of conspiracy story. We could invent a whole new life for Jessica. She could actually be part of the secret service,' said Tina, enjoying the banter between them. 'Her job as manager's secretary at the bank may just be one big cover-up. She could be working deep undercover to penetrate a money-laundering ring that she suspects certain members of staff to be involved in.'

'Now who has the overactive imagination?' John laughed and shook his head.

As her own words, flippantly spoken, sunk in, Tina's mood dropped. 'Sorry, that joke was in bad taste in light of the whole Pavel thing.'

'Hey, don't worry about it,' said John. He put his arm around her shoulders and gave a quick squeeze. 'Come on, you're supposed to be enjoying yourself.'

'Enjoying might be pushing it.' Tina looked around at the groups of guests mingling and chatting. 'Hopefully it won't be too long before they do the birthday cake and then we can go.'

'It's entirely up to you,' said John. 'You don't have to leave on my account.'

'Believe me, I'm leaving as much for my own benefit as for yours,' said Tina. 'And that's very good what you did there!'

'Sorry?'

'Leave on my account. You being the accountant.'

John groaned.

She gave him a playful tap on the arm. 'Come on, let's sneak out now. No one will notice we're not here. Not even Miss Money-Penny.'

Tina suppressed her giggles as they made their way as casually as possible around the room and in the general direction of the exit.

'I'll go first,' said John. 'You follow in a couple of minutes. I'll wait outside.'

'Copy that, Alpha One,' said Tina, pressing an imaginary hearing device into her ear and then lifting her other arm to speak into her watch.

'Now who's the MI5 agent?' said John, amusement clear in his voice. He rested his hands on her shoulders as he moved behind her, pausing to whisper in her ear. 'Rendezvous T minus ninety seconds.'

Tina brought her wine glass up to her mouth to hide her grin. Looking over its rim she watched John casually leave the room, one hand in his trouser pocket the other cupping his mobile phone to his ear, as if in deep conversation. He glanced back her way as he reached the door and winked, before disappearing out of the room.

Tina looked around the room and could see through the crowd that Jessica was heading her way. Tina avoided eye contact and, forcing herself not to break into a run, wove her way to the exit.

She bowled out of the main doors and, hooking John through the arm, didn't break stride as she took him along with her. 'Walk. Quickly.'

John didn't hesitate as he fell into step with her. 'I take it our cover is blown,' he said.

'I think the enemy had me in their sights but, if we're lucky, we can avoid engaging further with them.'

They turned the corner of the building and then, breaking into a gentle run, John took her hand and they trotted across the road towards the car park. John blipped the car open and Tina jumped into the passenger seat as John climbed into the driver's side.

'I think we made it,' said John.

Tina looked over at him and once again found herself laughing. John's own laughter was spontaneous and almost instant. The sounds reverberated around the confined space of the vehicle. It was a moment or two before Tina realised that John was silent and she was laughing alone. Still chuckling she met his gaze, his eyes held hers firm. The intensity of his look silenced her, the jovial atmosphere disappeared.

As far as Tina was concerned the world around her ceased to exist. She moved her head towards him and, in turn, John closed the gap between them. His lips met hers and she kissed him. He moved slightly away, but only for a second before returning her kiss.

Tina could barely keep her breathing under control as their kiss became deeper. It felt strange kissing someone after so long. Yet kissing John didn't give her the same sense of awkwardness as it had the last time a man had kissed her.

It felt strange and new, but it didn't fill her with fear. A hint of guilt tried to make its presence known, but she made a conscious effort to ignore it and concentrate on the here and now. Sasha was her past. A stranger in her world of the present. John, on the other hand, was very much of the now and certainly her immediate future.

John's hands cupped her face and he moved back from their embrace. He sat back in his seat. 'I'm sorry. I didn't plan that. It just sort of happened.'

'What are you apologising for?' said Tina, not moving from the edge of seat. 'I think it was me who kissed you. Perhaps it should be me apologising.'

John put his hands on the steering wheel and stared straight ahead through the windscreen and into the blackness of the night. As if deciding on something, he let out a long sigh and then turned the key in the ignition, sparking the engine into life.

Tina settled back in her seat, pulling the safety belt across her and clicking it into place. She wasn't sure what he was thinking. She knew she wasn't sorry at all. In fact, she had enjoyed kissing him and, truth be told, she would be quite happy to continue.

'We've done nothing wrong,' she said, as they pulled up outside her house. 'But if you're not comfortable with it, that's fine, you simply have to say and I won't make any more of a fool of myself than I already have.'

'You haven't made a fool of yourself at all,' said John. He opened his door and got out of the car. Tina tracked him as he walked around the front of the car and come round to her side, opening the passenger door. He held out his hand and Tina accepted the gesture. Neither let go as they walked up to the front door.

John helped Tina with her coat, laying it over the bannister along with his.

Tina stood in the hallway, facing him. What now? Where did they go from here? John didn't seem to be in a hurry to distance himself. He wasn't rushing through to the kitchen offering to make coffee to defuse the situation and wasn't making his excuses and heading for a night on the sofa either.

He was waiting for her. It was her call.

If she was going to back out, now was the time to do it. Tina rested the palm of her hand on his chest, her index finger touching the top of his shirt button. Was she ready to do this? Kissing another man since Sasha had died had been an awkward experience, but kissing John had been the opposite. He had stirred a passion deep within her that she thought she would never reach again. Her body was clearly telling her it was ready.

John placed his hand over hers and lifted it to his mouth, kissing her fingertips.

'You decide,' he said. 'No pressure from me.'

His soft voice embraced her thoughts. His tenderness caressed her senses.

She thought of her mother, telling her to allow herself to live again. She thought of Sasha and how much she had lived with him and for him. She never thought she would want anyone again, but tonight she realised she was wrong.

'I've not … since Sasha …' she stumbled over her words. Was she ready mentally to be intimate with another man? She felt her earlier bravado and eagerness waiver. What if she didn't know how to make love any more? It had been so long.

'It's okay. I understand,' said John, sliding his free hand under her hair at the nape of her neck. His thumb stroked her skin. 'We'll take our time.' He kissed her. 'Let me show you. Trust me.'

She gave one last thought to Sasha. A love of another life. A life she had lost. She had lost too much. She didn't want to lose again.

Chapter 16

John awoke first, his arm was draped over Tina's shoulder as she slept, spooned against him. He stroked her hair away from her face and dropped a tender kiss on her shoulder. If only he could suspend reality, for both of them.

In the real world, where he wasn't an accountant but a DS, sleeping with a witness or, depending whose point of view you were looking at it from, a suspect, wasn't his best move. He was only too aware of the complications this could bring. If Brogan got wind of this, John could find himself on gardening duty.

Tina stirred and rolled over. She opened her eyes and smiled at him.

'Well, hello, there,' she said. The touch of her lips on his sent his professional conscience packing.

'Morning,' he replied, returning her smile. 'You okay?'

'Is that code for do I have any regrets about last night?' She ran a finger through the hairs on his chest.

'And do you?' he asked.

'No. You?'

He shook his head. 'Not possible.'

Her fingers found their way to the scar below his collarbone. She circled the damaged tissue.

'How did you get this?' she asked.

'War wound.' He moved her hand away, kissing her, distracting her from her questions. Soldiers were bestowed medals for their bravery. John's medal, branded on his skin, bestowed for less heroic reasons.

John was in the kitchen checking his phone when Tina came downstairs later that morning. Her hair was still damp from her shower and she wore a white towelling dressing gown pulled around her, the belt holding it loosely together. Just reaching mid-thigh, it showed off her long legs.

'Hi,' she said, pushing her mane of hair back from her face. 'Ooh, cup of tea. I am being spoilt this morning.'

He stood up and, putting his arms around her waist, drew her in for a kiss. 'It's my pleasure,' he said and then sighed as his phone began to ring, vibrating on the worktop. He reached over and looked at the screen. 'Sorry. Work.'

He gave Tina another kiss and then took the call.

'All right? What we got?' he said, he ears concentrating on Martin, his eyes on Tina. She took a sip of her tea and went about making some toast. Every now and then she would glance at him and smile. She looked relaxed. She certainly didn't appear to be having any regrets about last night.

'We've found Baz Fisher,' said Martin.

'Good stuff. What's he said?'

'Nothing. Says he wants to speak to you and you alone. In person.'

John paused for a second as he smiled back at Tina. Much as he wanted to get some info from Baz Fisher, the thought of having to leave Tina tempered the result. He looked at his watch. 'Where are you? Okay. Yep. I'll be with you by midday.'

Tina rested her chin in her hands. 'It's okay, you don't have to explain,' she said. 'Will you be gone all weekend?'

'Not if I can help it. Depends how things go this afternoon.'

'What if Pavel, or whoever it was, comes back?' Although she tried to sound unperturbed at the thought, John could tell she was anxious.

'Why don't you stay at your Mum's?'

'I suppose I could. I don't really want to make a habit of it. You know, hounded out of my own house.'

'Just in case I can't make it back. It won't be forever. Once this is all over, you won't have anything to worry about.' He admired her stoicism. She certainly wasn't one to give in easily. However, he had to admit, he would prefer her not to be at home alone. 'It would put my mind at rest if you were at your mum's.'

She considered the idea for a few moments before nodding her agreement. John acknowledged the small sense of relief this brought him.

The empty feeling that had surrounded her since John's departure was persistent, if nothing else. Tina had hoped she would be able to shrug off the feeling that she felt somehow abandoned and left to fend for herself. It was unlike her. Bringing up a baby on her own had forced resilience and independence on her. She hadn't been sure how she would cope, but she knew she would have to. She had a tiny helpless baby, a new life, who was totally dependent on her and gave her a reason to carry on living herself. Flaky and unable to cope hadn't been an option.

Missing John, not simply because she enjoyed his company but also because she enjoyed the feeling of safety he brought with him, took her by surprise. She hadn't expected to feel scared being alone; it was a new sensation.

Being with her parents countered this as she and Dimitri walked along the seafront with them. They gave her the familiar sense of love and security. It was definitely what she needed right now.

As her phone sounded out a text message alert, Tina hoped it was John. She was disappointed to see Fay's name flash up on the screen. She read the message.

'Everything okay?' asked Pam.

'That was work,' she said. 'The Saturday girl has gone home sick and Fay's asked if I could come in.'

'Dimitri can stay with us today,' said her mother. 'He's as good as gold.'

'I feel a bit guilty leaving Dimitri.'

'Look at him, he's having a whale of a time with your father. It's only a few hours – he will be fine.'

'I know, but I don't like to take advantage of you either,' said Tina.

'Don't be daft. We're his grandparents; we love having him.'

'Are you sure?' said Tina. 'I know Fay will be run off her feet today. It's a Saturday and one of the busiest days. Plus, the extra money is always handy.' It would also help keep her mind occupied and give her less John-thinking time.

'Of course, I'm sure,' said Pam. 'I wouldn't have offered otherwise.'

'Thanks, Mum. I'll quickly text her back and say I'll be about an hour. It doesn't start getting busy until about eleven.' She sent a reply back to Fay. 'There, all done.'

'Is everything all right?' asked Pam. 'I don't mean with work, but with you, generally?'

'Yes, of course,' said Tina, crossing her fingers at the lie.

'You seem a bit down, that's all,' said Pam.

Tina linked her arm through her mother's. 'Just having one of those days.' She smiled at the older woman.

'Nothing to do with the date you had last night?'

Tina stopped walking and turned to her mother. She issued her best innocent look. 'Date? What do you mean?'

Pam laughed. 'Dimitri was telling us all about John.' She continued to walk along the concourse.

'He did?'

'He said you had a friend, called John, and that John played football with him.'

'Is that all he said?'

'More or less.'

Tina wasn't sure she liked the 'more or less' bit. She was certain Pam was trying to suppress a smile.

'It's nothing serious,' said Tina. They continued in silence, but the expectation of further enlightenment hung heavy between them. Tina felt compelled to expand. 'He works in London. He's a police officer.'

'And is that where he is now? In London? Working?'

'Yes, he is.'

Her mother might be getting old, but her brain was as agile as a teenager's. There was no getting away with anything.

'And that's why you're feeling fed up today,' said her mother, with a certain amount of satisfaction.

Tina didn't reply. This wasn't the conversation she wanted to be having with her mother. She couldn't tell Pam the truth about John, nor about the whole Porboski gang thing; it would only make her mother worry like mad.

'If I'm honest,' she balked at the hollowness of the expression, 'I don't know how much I'll see of him. I'm not sure it's going to be one of those sorts of relationships.'

Tina had thought about this after John had left that morning. John's work didn't lend itself to a long-term relationship and she wasn't sure if that's what she needed right now.

'Don't dismiss it so quickly,' said Pam. 'It's about time you allowed yourself to start living again.'

'Mum, please,' said Tina. She'd heard this speech before about how she shouldn't live in the past and had to move on. 'Let's not go there.'

Her mother made a humph noise. 'Okay, I'll say one thing, though.'

'Mum!' It appeared her mother's selective hearing had kicked in.

'If you can't give yourself a chance, at least give your son one.'

It was like a punch to the rib cage. Pam hadn't used that one before, a blindside comment. Tina sucked in a deep breath as she regained her composure.

'Just because Dimitri hasn't got a father, it doesn't mean he's missing out,' she said in a measured tone. 'Lots of women manage to bring their children up perfectly well single handed.'

'I wasn't saying for one moment that it wasn't possible and it definitely wasn't a criticism aimed at you.' Pam tightened her grip on Tina's hand, as it rested in the crook of her elbow. 'You're a wonderful mother.'

'Thank you.' The compliment softened the verbally bruised ribs.

'Look at Dimitri with your father. See how thrilled they are to be together?'

Tina followed her mother's gaze. Grandson and grandfather were deep in conversation, looking intently at a stone, knowing her father's interest in geology, he'd probably found a fossil of some description. Tina watched them look up and out to sea. Judging by her father's gestures and exaggerated facial expressions, Tina guessed he was telling one of his stories, which no doubt involved a dinosaur or a dragon and adventures at sea with pirates and sea- faring captains.

'Dimitri isn't missing out on anything or anyone,' she said. 'He has Dad.'

'Not forever.' Her mother's voice was so soft, the sea breeze almost carried it away.

'I know, Mum.' Tina squeezed her mother's arm. 'Nothing is forever.'

Chapter 17

John arrived in London at the safe house where Martin had taken Baz.

'Bloody hell, you look rough,' said John as he set eyes on his informant.

'So would you if you were living in a half-way home,' said Baz. He held up a holdall. 'This is all I've got right now, thanks to you.'

John exchanged a look with Martin. The latter shrugged in response.

'What's going on?' asked John sitting down opposite Baz.

'The Russians are on to you. They know you are looking for Pavel Bolotnikov. They are mighty pissed off that someone gave their fella an extra smile.' Baz rubbed at the three-day-old bristles on his chin.

'So why are you so jittery?' asked John. 'And what was it that you couldn't tell Martin you had to tell me?'

'I had a tip off that the Russians knew I had been speaking to you. Apparently, Pavel himself has been asking after me. I don't know who's talking, John, but someone knows.' He looked up at Martin.

'Hey, don't look at me,' said Martin. 'Why would I grass you up?'

'Someone must have seen you in the café with us,' said John. 'Anyway, it's academic now.'

'Too bloody right. The Porboski lot want to know where Pavel is and if one of their scouts has wound up dead, it doesn't take a genius to work out who did it. I'm not hanging around waiting for either of them to come looking for me,' said Baz.

'What are you planning on doing, hiding forever?' asked Martin.

Baz patted his jacket pocket. 'Got me passport. I'm off to visit my cousins in Ireland. I can easily get lost out there. The Paddies have got plenty of experience avoiding detection.'

'You want to have a wash first,' said Martin. 'They'll be able to sniff you out a mile off otherwise.'

'Does he have to be here?' said Baz to John. 'He's some sort of …'

'Yeah, all right, Baz. Leave it there,' interrupted John. The last thing he needed was a spat between the two men. 'What did you want to tell me?'

'Take a walk, there's a good lad,' said Baz to Martin. 'This is between me and John.'

Martin gave Baz a derogatory glare before acceding to John's nod of confirmation to be left alone.

'What's this all about, then?' said John, once Martin had closed the door behind him.

'I'm only telling you this because we go back a long way,' said Baz. He leaned towards John, beckoning him to do the same. His voice was low as he spoke.

It was a good day weather-wise and the weekend shoppers were out in force. The café was more busy than usual and Tina was glad she had come in to help out Fay.

'You're an angel for coming in,' said Fay as the swell of customers began to ebb. 'I didn't fancy the thought of Old Grumpy and his wife coming in instead.'

Tina laughed. 'No, I can imagine.'

'The afternoon tea rush is over with now, by the look of it. I can't believe it's gone four already.' Fay turned her back on the café to face Tina. 'Don't look straight away, but see those two in the corner. They keep staring over here. I wish they would hurry up and go.'

Tina made a fuss of rearranging the cake trays and took a glance at the two customers. Sure enough, as she did so, she met the gaze of the stocky, shaven-headed man. She looked away, adjusting the napkins on the counter that didn't need adjusting.

'I see what you mean,' she said. 'I'll go over and see if there's anything else they want. Maybe that will give them the hint to go.'

Picking up her order pad and pen, she pasted on her best customer-service smile and headed over to the table.

As she approached the two men, she was aware that as the first man was watching her, the second man remained looking at his phone. He had longish dark hair, which looked like it could do with a good brush.

'Shall I take these for you?' said Tina, picking up the two empty coffee cups. 'Is there anything else you would like?' The man on the phone paused with his texting. Tina could see tattoos showing from under the cuff of his jacket. Three black dots were tattooed at the 'v' between his thumb and first finger. His nails were short and his hands looked as though they had seen a lot of manual labour. His knuckles looked scarred and misshapen.

At first she wasn't sure if either of the men were going to answer, but finally the first man spoke.

'No. Thank you … err,' he looked at her name badge, '… Tina.' He gave a smile, which revealed a missing tooth at the side.

Something about the two men felt wrong. Tina couldn't put her finger on it. The man who spoke sounded English, but there was the faintest of accents. One she couldn't quite place from just the few words he spoke.

'We're closing soon,' she said. 'I'll fetch you your bill.'

She hurried off back to Fay at the counter. Old Grumpy would have a fit if he knew she was hustling customers to leave, but those two were odd. Her mind flitted to John and she wished he was here.

'You all right?' said Fay. 'What did those two weirdoes say?'

'Nothing. Have you got their bill? I told them we were closing. Hopefully that will get rid of them.'

The slam of a hand on the counter made both women jump. Tina spun round to see the first man standing there. He gave her another smile, one that wasn't at all welcoming and slid his hand across the counter. Tina looked down. There was a five pound note.

'I'll get you your change' she said.

'Not necessary, Tina,' said the man. 'See you again.' He held Tina's gaze for longer than was comfortable before turning and walking out of the café with his companion.

'Bloody hell,' said Fay. 'I wouldn't like to meet them in a dark alley.'

'Have they been in before?' asked Tina watching the men wander off, somewhat aimlessly, up the road.

'No. I don't think so.' Fay began loading the dishwasher. 'We seem to be attracting a lot of unwanted attention lately.'

'How do you mean?'

'That bloke, who's been standing across the road in the doorway. You know, the watcher.' Fay emphasised the last two words. 'Oh, Tina, the look on your face! I'm only joking. Well, half joking.'

'It's not funny,' said Tina. She flicked Fay with the tea towel and forced out a laugh. It really wasn't funny. Once again, the urge to go home and shut herself away washed over her. Then she remembered the intruder the other night. She wished John was here. Going home alone was not an appealing thought. One she couldn't ignore as she had promised Mr Cooper she would bring him some milk.

The last of the customers left and Tina locked the door behind them. She looked up and down the street and then across at the doorway on the other side of the road. Nothing and no one looked out of place.

'Right, are you okay mopping the floor?' said Fay, untying her apron before Tina could answer. 'Only, I've got to nip to the loo and make myself presentable. I have the lovely Harry picking me up from work tonight.'

Tina turned away from the doorway. 'Oooh. Harry picking you up. Where are you off to?'

'The cinema and then for a meal,' called back Fay as she headed towards the back of the café.

A loud bang on the glass of the doors sent Tina's nerves into orbit. She jumped and screamed at the same time, spinning around to look at the door. A big grinning face loomed through the glass.

This was getting ridiculous. She was jumping at the slightest thing. 'We're closed,' she mimed at the man.

'It's okay,' called Fay. 'That's Harry. Can you let him in for a minute?'

Tina returned to the door, unlocking it and letting Fay's date in. 'She won't be long.'

Harry thanked her and loitered around the doorway. Tina picked up the mop bucket and went out to the back of the cafe.

'He's hot,' she whispered to Fay, poking her head into the washroom. 'And keen. He's standing out there like a puppy dog.'

'Ah, bless him,' said Fay popping the lid on her lipstick. She took out her spray and applied a generous amount. 'Right, I'll be off. See you Monday. Have a good weekend.'

She gave Tina a hug before disappearing back into the café. Tina heard her laughing as she left. It was nice to see Fay happy, although it did make her wish John was around.

Leaving the mop and bucket in the storeroom, Tina took her coat and bag from the cupboard. She checked her phone for messages or missed calls. John hadn't called. She sighed to herself and considered for a moment if she should call him. No, he was at work. He would be in touch as soon as he could.

The sound of the traffic from outside suddenly became notice-able, followed by the unmistakable sound of the door swinging shut.

'What did you forget?' called out Tina, checking in the cupboard to see what Fay had left behind. She couldn't see anything and went out into the café.

She stopped dead in her tracks. Walking towards her was the shaven-headed man from earlier. His table-mate was leaning against the closed door, arms folded. His black, beady eyes monitoring her.

Her voice wobbled as she spoke. 'We're closed.'

A needless remark. All three of them knew that they weren't here for coffee.

Chapter 18

John listened to what Baz Fisher had to say without passing comment. On the exterior he remained calm and impassive. On the interior it was a whole different ball game.

Afterwards, he thanked Baz and arranged for a taxi to take him to the docks, where a fishing boat was waiting, its course set for the Emerald Isle.

'And?' asked Martin as they watched the black cab drive off with Baz in the back.

'Trouble,' said John already heading for the BMW. 'The Porboskis have been asking about Tina.'

'Shit,' said Martin.

'Indeed.' John turned the key in the ignition and not waiting to put his seat belt on first, accelerated away from the safe house. 'They want the money from the Moorgate robbery and think Tina may be willing to help them locate it.' He didn't need to translate that into Russian terms. They both knew what it meant. 'We need to get to her before anyone else does.'

John pulled his mobile from his pocket and, placing it on hands-free, called up Tina's number. It rang out to voice mail. He tried a second and third time. Still she didn't pick up.

'Where the hell is she?' he said to himself more than to Martin. 'Work?'

'No, she's not in today.'

'Do you completely trust her?' said Martin.

'If you mean, do I think she's playing me, no I don't think she is.' said John. He kept his eyes on the traffic as he pulled out onto the main road and headed south out of the city. 'She doesn't know anything.'

'Not even ..?'

'Not even that her dead husband isn't dead.'

Tina took a step back as the man advanced towards her. His steps were slow but with purpose.

'What do you want? Money? It's in the safe. I can get it,' she forced the words from her throat.

The man grinned again. 'Not the money.'

Tina's stomach turned one way and then the next. She took another step back and glanced at the kitchen area. She needed something to defend herself with. The man continued his advance. His steps echoed in the empty café.

Tina saw the knives. They were at the back of the work area. She would have to go behind the counter to reach them. Could she get there before he got to her? Even if she did manage to get to them, she would be trapped behind the counter that ran along the side of the café. The toilets and storeroom were at the back of the café. If she managed to get down there before he did, she might be able to make it out the back door.

'Don't waste your time thinking how to escape,' said the man. His accent was now more evident. It was one Tina was familiar with. One she had married into. Russian. As if to confirm Tina's thoughts, the man said something in his native tongue to his wingman.

The other man grunted a response and hit the light switch. He then went to the windows at the front of the café and pulled down the blinds. A shadowy greyness fell across the room.

Tina knew this was best and possibly her only chance to escape.

She had the advantage of knowing the layout of the shop. Her mind flitted to the back-door option, but this was dismissed. It was locked. There was a lock and two bolts to release. She wouldn't have enough time. Her other option was the toilets. If she could buy enough time and lock herself in the cubicle she might be able to unlock the window and climb onto the street. The small Allan key window lock was on the bunch of keys she was holding.

Tina briefly wondered if she would be able to make a 999 call. Her phone was still in her hand, along with the keys. No, she decided, by the time she had unlocked the screen and made the call, her visitors would be upon her.

The man came to a stop at the table nearest to the counter. He pulled out a chair from one of the tables. 'Don't be scared, Tina. We only want to talk to you. Tell us what we want to know and we will leave.'

Tina eyed the chair. Somehow she didn't think it would be as easy as that. Would they really let her go afterwards?

The wingman strolled over to the table and patted the chair, beckoning Tina with his other hand. 'Come. Sit.'

Tina let her shoulders drop as if compliant. 'Okay.' She let out a small sigh and made to walk towards them. The first man smiled. 'Good girl.'

As Tina spun on her heel and raced to the back of the café, she hoped to God she had given herself enough of a head start. She slammed through the swing door. It hit the rubber doorstop and bounced back. She gave it an extra push as she fled towards the toilets.

She could hear them cursing in Russian. Charging into the washroom area, Tina grabbed the chair that was in the corner and pushed it up under the handle. It would buy her an extra few seconds, if nothing else.

She slammed the toilet cubicle door shut, fumbled at the lock. 'Fuck!' she shouted as she remembered you had to align the stupid bolt up with the holder. She managed to get it in just as she heard the washroom door being shoulder-barged. Tina grappled with the keys. Her hands were damp from sweat.

The clatter of the chair skidding across the floor told her that they were in the washroom.

'Tina. Stop this! Come out. Talk to us.'

Her skin crawled at the use of her name.

A fist hammered on the door outside and words between the two men were exchanged. Tina didn't know what they were saying. She didn't know enough Russian and her brain was only focused on the keys.

Another hammering on the door made her jolt. Her phone slipped from her hands and splashed straight into the toilet. She gave it a fleeting thought – her mind going straight back to the keys.

Balancing on the toilet seat, her hands shook violently as she pushed the hexagonal metal key into the window lock. She tried turning it to the left but it wouldn't budge.

Another bash against the door. He was now trying to break into the cubicle.

She wiggled the key again. 'Come on. Turn.' Finally, there was give and the Allan key moved.

She could hear the lock on the door rattle as the screws loosened with yet another thump. Tina moved the Allan key another quarter turn. She pushed up on the handle and it lifted without resistance. She shoved the window open with the palm of her hand. The small courtyard at the back of the café was her escape route.

There was a wheelie bin against the wall. She could use that to scale the brickwork and be out in the street.

As she put one foot onto the top of toilet cistern and gripped each side of the window frame to pull herself up, the bolt on the door finally gave way.

In crashed one of the Russians. Tina didn't look behind. She let out a scream and tried to pull herself up. A hand grabbed at her flaying ankle.

'Help!' she shouted through the open window. She knew she

couldn't escape but she wasn't going to give up easily. She kicked back with her foot, catching the man in the chin.

'*Cyka!*' It was the wingman. 'Bitch!' he said in English this time.

Tina felt him release her ankle. She kicked again but this time found thin air. Once more she attempted to pull herself up through the window.

Two arms grabbed at her hips, then encircled her waist, pulling her backwards. She was yanked down, her feet clattering on the toilet lid. She kicked against it, trying to gain leverage to push her attacker away. He was too strong.

'Help! Someone!' she screamed out.

A hand clamped down on her mouth. Fingers dug into her cheek from the force of the grip. Unceremoniously she was dragged into the washroom area.

At this point, Tina became aware of another scuffle going on in the passageway outside.

Raised voices sounded. Grunts. Swearing, in Russian. There was the sound of a body being thrown against a wall. She could hear things being knocked down and then the sound of the storeroom door slamming against the wall. Somebody stumbled into the room, the clattering of brooms and mops accompanied by more dull thumps and the sound of grunting following each connection.

The door to the washroom flung open. The Russian still had his arms around her waist and as he turned towards the door, he pushed Tina forwards. Her head collided with the edge of the door. The force sent her off balance. Pain shot through her head, exploding in her skull. She staggered to the side. In the briefest of moments she caught a glimpse of the man now coming into the washroom.

She didn't have time to consider who he was. There was a flurry of fists, more grunts, more swearing. Tina cowered in the corner. Her path to the doorway and safety blocked. The mirror shattered as the Russian's head was smashed against it. As his head was then cracked against the sink, the Russian slumped into an unconscious heap on the floor.

For an eerie few seconds, silence spread through the café. Tina looked up at her rescuer. Her body began to shake violently, shock taking hold of her muscles. Her stomach went into spasm and she retched.

The walls of the washroom closed in. Her vision took on a telescopic effect – all peripheral vision deserting her. She was on the verge of passing out. She struggled to remain conscious, to fight the urge to surrender to the enclosing blackness.

She tucked her head down, leaning forwards, on hands and knees. Willing the blood to rush to her head.

She couldn't pass out. She wouldn't allow it. Not now.

She felt a hand on her back, then scooping her hair to one side, coming to rest on the side of her cheek.

She breathed deeper. The blackness began to recede.

A Russian voice, one she recognised, spoke urgently to the man in the room with her. The hand lifted from her face. She grabbed at it.

'Please …' she choked on her words as tears flowed swiftly from her eyes. 'Don't go.'

She could hear a police siren outside. Blue flashing lights bounced rhythmically off the stainless-steel kitchen appliances down the passageway.

More urgent Russian words were exchanged.

Tina raised herself into a kneeling position, any thought of standing dismissed. She knew her legs wouldn't hold her. She looked up at the two men in front of her. How could this be? She tried to speak, but her word were lost. She didn't know what to say. She could hardly believe what was happening.

She heard voices coming into the café. They were faraway and distant. She couldn't focus on them. The men in front of her turned and sprinted to the rear of the café. She heard the locks and bolts on the door, the scuffling of feet against the wheelie bin outside as they scaled the wall and were gone.

Tina slumped forwards. The wail was animal-like as she called out.

'Sasha!'

Chapter 19

In A&E John moved the curtain to the cubicle aside just enough to step into the confined area.

Her eyes were closed and for a moment he thought she was asleep. He took in the red, swollen lump on the side of her forehead, but was thankful he couldn't see any other marks. She opened her eyes.

'Sorry, I didn't meant to disturb you,' he said, moving to the side of her bed. The nurse had already brought him up to date on her condition. Bumped, bruised and shaken but otherwise unharmed. He lifted her hand and gave it a small kiss. 'I'm sorry.'

'For what?'

'Not being there. I should have stayed with you.'

'Don't be sorry.' She gave his hand a squeeze before slipping it away and placing it on the blanket across her torso. 'It's not your fault.'

'I've been briefed on what happened,' he said. 'We've got the two men in custody. They are being questioned now.'

'I don't suppose they are, how do you say, singing like a couple of canaries,' said Tina.

'What happened exactly?' said John.

'I told the police earlier,' she said not meeting his eye.

'You told them that they came in at the end of the day to rob the till.'

'That's what I assume. I didn't exactly get into a conversation with them.'

She wasn't telling him everything, that much he knew. But why that was, he didn't know.

'Who came to your rescue?'

'I don't know.' She looked down at her hands. 'I was hiding in the toilet at that point. I didn't see who it was.'

'How many?'

This time she looked directly at him. 'I don't know. I told you, I was hiding in the toilet.'

She wasn't telling him the truth, that was for certain, or at least not the whole truth. John considered his options. Now wasn't the time to press for more information. After his conversation with Baz, he knew the two men in custody, who at this point were refusing to utter a word, not even their names, were more than likely Russian. The scouting party sent over by the Porboskis. So who could her rescuers be? Who would want to protect her? Who had most to gain from her being saved? It was an easy answer. He didn't need Tina's confirmation.

Tina allowed John to take her home. He had suggested she stay at her parents, but she hadn't wanted to. She didn't want to alarm her parents any more than necessary. And she certainly wasn't ready to share the latest developments. She hadn't even told John yet, although she suspected that it wouldn't come as that much of a shock to him.

He hadn't pushed her for information at the hospital and now, as he sat her down on the sofa in her own home, he still avoided the subject. She was grateful.

If he didn't ask, she didn't have to tell any lies. She realised lies had surrounded her for far too long. The treacherous words had infecting her life like an airborne virus. She had been an unwitting carrier of the bacteria. Passing the lies on to everyone she loved and shared her life with. She felt contaminated. Plague-ridden. And, at this moment, she had no idea if there was an antidote.

Dimitri came hopping into the living room, a football under his arm.

'I've got the ball, John,' he said, eagerness in his eyes. 'You said you'd play football with me.'

'I did, indeed,' said John standing up. He looked down at Tina. 'Why don't you try and have a sleep. It will do you good.'

'Does your head still hurt, Mummy?' asked Dimitri peering closely at the bump on his mother's head.

'A little,' said Tina. She pulled Dimitri in for a quick hug. A lump rose in her throat as she thought of his innocence and how her past, her life before he was born, would now contaminate his world. His history, like hers, had been blasted away. She blinked back the tears.

'You okay?' said John. He perched on the edge of the sofa and squeezed her hand.

'I'll be fine.' She kissed Dimitri's head and ruffled his hair. 'Go on, you two. I'll have a rest.'

She listened as John went and checked the front door, offering her reassurance. She couldn't deny the feeling of unease at being in the house now. She was pleased when John had said he was staying with her for at least the next few days. He had cleared it with his boss and technically he was off-duty, although everyone knew that John was never really off-duty.

That night, after tucking Dimitri in bed, Tina sat on the sofa next to John. The TV was on, but Tina knew that neither was really watching it, just going through the motions of a cosy night in – one that might have been had she not known Sasha was alive.

Not for the first time did she question herself. Had she really seen Sasha? Had Pavel been there? She wondered if the bump on the head had confused her, made her see things she wanted to see. She didn't know what to believe.

What she really wanted was to slip back to a few weeks ago when she thought she knew her past, when she believed everything about her life, when her life was uncomplicated. Sad, yes, but it was the truth. Now, she didn't know what the truth was.

There was also the guilt factor. If her husband was alive, if Sasha really hadn't died in a car accident, then was she betraying him by sleeping with John?

Her head throbbed as she tried to make sense of the past day. Such a morass of conflicting emotions swirling around in a fog of guilt, sadness and confusion.

Chapter 20

They must have drifted off to sleep on the sofa – at some point Tina became aware of John moving restlessly in his sleep.

John's legs juddered and she felt his body jerk. Tina slipped her arm across his torso and gave a gentle hug. It didn't seem to have any effect on his sleep pattern, his arms were now beginning to move around. He flung one arm above his head, his legs moving tirelessly. Heat emitted from his body like a radiator.

'John. Wake up.'

His breathing became faster and more breathy. A bead of sweat trickled down his neck. Tina sat up, now fully awake. His face was soaked with sweat, his eyes partially open. Another convulsion and this time an indistinguishable groan.

'John. Wake up!' said Tina, this time with more insistence. She gave his shoulder a shake, but this didn't seem to make any difference. She tried again. Louder and with more force. 'John! John! Wake up.' His eyes shot open and he gave a start. It was a moment or two before he could focus on her. She stroked his hair back with her hand. 'You were dreaming. You okay?'

He rubbed his eyes, looking around him as if checking where he was.

'Yeah, thanks. I'm fine.'

He didn't look it. He rubbed his face with his hands and sat up on the edge of the seat. His shirt was damp with sweat and stuck to his back.

'Are you sure you're okay?'

'Yes.' His reply was curt. He clearly didn't want to talk about it. Male pride perhaps? He turned round to her and stretched out a hand, covering her own. This time his voice was soft. 'Sorry, but I am fine. Honest.' He stood up. 'Why don't you go up to bed? You've had a stressful day and need your sleep. I'll stay down here.'

She nodded. Relieved that the difficult decision had been taken away from her. Part of her wanted to sleep wrapped in his arms, to have the security of his body against hers. Yet, another part of her was feeling guilt at the thought.

She stood up and looked at each other. John was the first to move. He leaned in and kissed her gently on her forehead.

Tina studied him. His eyes gave him away. What was he keeping from her? What secrets did he harbour? What demons lurked behind those dark eyes?

John ran the kitchen tap for longer than necessary, watching the water gush into the sink and wind its way round and into the plughole. His nightmare unsettled him. It wasn't the first time he had suffered from them and it certainly wasn't the first time that particular nightmare had occurred. In fact, at the height of his nightmare times, it had been the one that had risen from subconscious again and again.

He thought he was rid of them, though. This was the first in two years and he couldn't deny that the timing of its return coincided with being involved with the Porboski case again and, in particular, Tina Bolotnikov.

The uneasy feeling that had begun plaguing him was growing inside like a simmering volcano. He knew it was going to erupt soon and the truth would spew out, uncontrolled, dangerous, destroying everything it touched, including Tina. He couldn't let that happen. Knowing what it would do to her didn't bear thinking about.

He made up his mind. This needed to be a controlled explosion. The truth needed to be handled with care.

He nodded at his reflection in the mirror above the mantelpiece. Mind made up. He'd tell her soon. It wasn't going to be easy, but when had he ever walked away simply because something was difficult? It wasn't in his DNA.

The thought of her smiling face and gentle laugh drifted in front of him. If he closed his eyes he could imagine the sweet soap-like smell of her perfume and the feel of her soft hair against his face. She deserved to know the whole truth about him.

The next few days passed calmly and quietly. John stayed with Tina the whole time, but had taken to sleeping on the sofa. There was an unspoken understanding between them. Something had shifted since the incident at the café. She knew John wasn't telling her everything. She was very much aware that neither of them was being totally honest with each other. John knew it too.

More lies. More half-truths.

She didn't know who or what to believe any more. She was even beginning to question herself. Had she really seen Sasha the other night?

It sounded implausible at times and as the days drifted on, she began to believe that she must have been mistaken. Sasha would not have put her through all this. He had loved her with such ferocity, with such tenderness, with such warmth; there was no way he would have intentionally hurt her. He had no reason to.

As she lay in bed, listening to the occasional car pass by in the still of the night, Tina could hear John once again prowling the ground floor of the house. She wished he would tell her what was causing his sleepless nights. She had listened to him go into the kitchen and run a glass of water. After that the living-room door opened and she assumed that was where he was now.

Tina listened for any sign of Dimitri being woken and was glad that he appeared to be fast asleep. Dimitri was becoming more and more attached to John. He badgered John to play football with him in the garden, delighted in looking at worms and spiders with his new-found friend. Unlike Tina, John didn't squeal at spiders and comment on how disgusting worms were. No, John took a great interest in examining and studying these things with the five-year-old. Tonight Dimitri had even asked John to read him a bedtime story.

Tina wasn't sure how she felt about that. How she felt about the whole John thing, really. If she could put her life into compartments, with no overlaps, she could think straight. She knew she was growing fonder of John each day. Yet it was happening very quickly. It had only been a few weeks that he had been about, but at the same time it felt as if he had been around forever. John just fitted into her and Dimitri's little world like a hand in a glove. It seemed so natural for him to be there.

A thud from the party wall to Mr Cooper's house brought Tina around from her thoughts.

'Not that bloody door again,' she muttered out loud. After the last episode of randomly banging doors, she had ended up putting a door wedge either side of the door to keep it from shutting. One of the wedges must have slipped somehow.

The noise she heard next set her senses on fire. It wasn't the gentle bang of the door against the frame, it was a regular pattern of muted footsteps. Tina strained to listen properly. A floorboard creaked and groaned as weight was placed on the top stair. A loud creak that sounded even louder in the dead of the night – then there were more footsteps. Someone was going downstairs in Mr Cooper's house and she knew, for certain, it wasn't Mr Cooper.

Tina jumped out of bed and grabbed her dressing gown. The sound travelled so easily through the party walls. With this in mind, Tina took her stairs as lightly as possible. As her feet hit the hall carpet, she felt herself bundle into someone and one arm wrap itself around her, while a hand covered her mouth, muffling the scream she let out.

'It's okay, it's only me.'

Tina relaxed immediately, recognising John's voice before her eyes adjusted to seeing his face.

'You heard it too?' she said.

'Yes, you wait here. I'm going next door to investigate.'

'Don't go on your own. If Mr Cooper wakes up and sees you, he won't know who on earth you are. I'll come too.'

'What about Dimitri?'

'He's fast asleep. Besides, I'll lock the door behind us. No one can get in.'

'But you're not dressed.'

'I have my pj's on underneath,' said Tina sticking out a leg to show the pink-checked cotton fabric. 'Just let me put my shoes on.' She shuffled her feet into her ballet pumps and, as an afterthought, exchanged her dressing gown for a hoody hanging in the hall.

'You sure you don't want to nip upstairs and do your make-up before we go? Wash your hair? Paint your nails?' He smiled, but Tina could tell he was impatient to investigate next door. 'Come on then, Tonto.'

Chapter 21

Tina grabbed a torch from the kitchen cupboard as she followed John out of the back door, locking it behind her. She passed the key to him. 'Can you put that in your pocket, please?'

He pushed it into the front pocket of his jeans and took the torch from her at the same time. 'Right, how do we get in? Through this gate?'

'Yes, it goes straight into Mr Cooper's garden. The back door will probably be unlocked. I always tell him to lock it, but he never does.'

Tina followed John through the gate and round to the kitchen door. 'When you said open, did you actually mean open, like this?'

The circular beam of light from the torch illuminated the kitchen door. It was ajar, not properly closed.

'I definitely closed it when I left,' said Tina, dropping her voice to a whisper. 'Maybe a draught has caught it.'

'You stay right behind me at all times,' said John. He took his gun from his holster and rested his hand over the other which held the torch. He swung the torch light over and around the door. He hooked the bottom of the door with his foot and pulled it open wider. 'Try not to touch anything,' he instructed. 'If someone has broken in they might have left fingerprints or some sort of evidence.'

The house was in total darkness as they entered, the shaft of light from the torch their only guide. Tina put her hand on John's back. She felt safe having actual physical contact. There was an atmosphere in the house she hadn't felt before. The kitchen she had been in countless times over the years seemed alien to her. The familiar cupboards and white goods were now just dark shadows and outlines. The stillness of the house was unnerving and she strained to listen for any sign that someone other than Mr Cooper was in the house. She wished she hadn't been so insistent on coming.

John shone the light on the closed door of what was once the dining room. 'Mr Cooper sleeps downstairs,' said Tina as quietly as she could. They paused and listened intently. The faint sound of Mr Cooper's rhythmic breathing filtered through. He gave a snuffle, mumbled something incoherent and then the steady in and out of his breathing resumed.

John gave a flick with the torch towards the living-room door, which was open. The street light cast a grungy yellow light pathway into the room. Tina smothered a startled yelp. A tall shadow in the corner of the room took her by surprise. Almost immediately she realised that it was just the standard lamp behind Mr Cooper's armchair.

'You all right?' said John.

'Yes, I'm fine.' She didn't feel remotely fine. The darkness of the house was oppressive. It felt heavy and foreboding. All Tina's senses were telling her to get out, to run back to the safety of her own home, with all lights blazing brightly.

A creak from upstairs snapped her to attention. John had heard it too. They both looked up towards the ceiling. Another creak – this one slower, more deliberate. A muffled, indistinguishable sound followed. Again it had the feel of being a controlled noise, a slow and deliberate distribution of weight.

John moved into the hall, sweeping the shadows, his torch and gun in unison, the bottom tread of the staircase becoming illuminated. John placed his foot on the stair and slowly began the ascent. Tina followed. Her heart was beating heavily. As they neared the turn in the staircase, John stopped.

The silence weighed heavy, pushing down on Tina's shoulders, squeezing her from the sides, condensing the space around her like a car being crushed at the scrapyard. Her instincts were urging her to turn and flee down the stairs. She moved ever so slightly closer to John. The movement of her feet on the tread caused a creak in the board. She stood still.

Not a sound could be heard. John moved around the half landing and up onto the first floor. Tina followed. John's light beam settled on the open door of the front bedroom. Without hesitating, he went into the room. Tina waited in the doorway.

The moon shone through the naked glass and as Tina peered into the bedroom, she watched John check everywhere, even under the bed and behind the open curtains. He turned his attention to the window and reaching up, pulled the small fanlight shut, hooking the metal catch onto the prong.

'There's nothing here,' he said, turning to face her. 'It must have been this window causing the door to bang.' He pushed his Glock into the safety of the holster.

Tina wasn't convinced. 'I didn't realise the window was open and there's not really any wind tonight.'

'I'll check the other rooms, if you like, but I'm sure this is our culprit.'

He sidestepped her as she stood in the doorway. Opening the doors to the other two rooms and the bathroom, he performed a sweep of each area, again checking under the beds and behind curtains. 'Definitely nothing here.'

'But you heard it too,' said Tina. 'It must have been sufficient for you to come and investigate.'

John looked thoughtful. 'Maybe we are both a bit jittery. If there was anything more sinister here, it's gone now.'

'I don't like it. There was definitely someone on the staircase,

I'm certain. It wasn't my imagination. Or yours.'

'As I said, nothing here now.' He steered her downstairs and towards the back door, pausing on the way to listen outside Mr Cooper's room. 'He's snoring. He hasn't been disturbed at all.'

Tina went to protest that she still wasn't happy but then remembered that Dimitri was home alone. 'Let's get back.'

Tina watched Dimitri eye John from across the top of his cereal bowl. He had that look on his face he got when he was thinking about something. Tina and John had returned from Mr Cooper's the previous night and the first thing she had done was check on her son. He was fast asleep, just as she had left him.

She had sat downstairs with John for ten minutes while they went over the events of that night, but neither of them had been able to come up with a completely plausible or reassuring explanation. In the end they had reluctantly decided to drop the subject. However, the incident was well and truly logged in Tina's mind.

'I've got to make a few calls,' said John, standing up and taking his coffee with him, he hooked up his blue Harrington jacket.

'Where's your black coat?' said Dimitri.

John looked round. 'Black coat? I don't have one.'

'Yes you do,' said Dimitri. He grinned as if John was teasing him.

'Sorry, fella, but I definitely don't have a black one.'

Dimitri dipped the spoon into the chocolate-coloured milk in his bowl. 'You had it on last night.'

'Last night?' Tina stopped buttering her toast. 'When did John have a black coat on?'

Dimitri looked from his mum to John.

'You're not in trouble,' said Tina. 'It's just neither of us can remember the coat.' She smiled reassuringly at her son, though the corners of her mouth felt tense. 'Dimitri?'

'When you came to see me in my room.' Dimitri's voice was matter of fact. He pushed the spoon into his mouth and noisily sucked the milk up.

John slowly sat back down at the table. Tina shot him a warning look. She would handle this.

'And John was wearing a black jacket?'

Dimitri gave a big sigh. 'Yes. I pretended to be asleep, but really I was peeking. You didn't know, did you?' This time his face lit up with excitement.

John shook his head and smiled.

'No, I didn't see you. That was clever of you.'

Another exchange of looks passed between Tina and John.

'You're very clever, indeed. Tell me, what was John doing when you saw him?'

Dimitri's face broke into a broad smile of satisfaction. 'You picked up Billy the Bear. Can I have him back now?'

'Billy the Bear. He's a stuffed toy.' She noted the concerned look on John's face. 'Do you have Billy the Bear?' Her voice was practically a whisper. John shook his head.

'But you took him. I want him back.' Dimitri let his spoon clang noisily into the bowl and sat back in his chair with folded arms.

'I'll find Billy the Bear later,' said Tina. 'In the meantime, we need to get you dressed for school. Come on. Let's go and brush your teeth. There's a good boy.' Tina stood up and ushered Dimitri from the table.

Once upstairs, she left Dimitri in the bathroom brushing his teeth and hurried into her son's bedroom. Billy the Bear, was a present from Sasha. He had given it to Tina when she found out she was pregnant. A gift for their unborn child. Billy the Bear usually sat on the bookshelf just inside the door. There was an empty spot the soft toy usually occupied.

Dimitri came into the room. 'I told you, Mummy, John took Billy.'

The tide of foreboding that had been brewing, rushed her like a spring tide, drenching every fibre in Tina's body with fear.

Chapter 22

Tina sat in the car beside John, with Dimitri in the back. Tina had taken the week off from work, the incident at the café being passed off as an attempted robbery for the benefit of her boss and Fay. Only Tina, John and his team knew differently.

Tina walked Dimitri into the playground while John waited in the car. From where she stood she could see both of them. Dimitri was happy running around the playground, having an early-morning game of tag. Tina tracked him this way and that, her eyes never leaving him while her peripheral vision was vigilant to any adult coming within range. Anyone she didn't recognise as a parent got a second look and a long second look until she was satisfied they were not a threat.

At last the school bell rang out, signalling the day was about to start and the children were to line up in their respective classes to wait for the teachers.

'Have a good day at school,' said Tina, bending down to plant a kiss on her son's cheek. 'Here's your book bag and lunch box. Love you.'

'Love you,' said Dimitri, already distracted by the class line that was filling up. He blindly grabbed at the two bags before running over and jumping with two feet into the line, right behind one of his class mates, leaving no opportunity for anyone to cut in between them. His feet were rooted to the spot, his toes almost touching the heels of the boy in front of him. He turned and waved at his mum.

Tina watched the line of children as they filed though the school doors, satisfied that he was safely ensconced within the confines of the building. She returned to the car, where John was patiently waiting.

'You okay?' he asked.

'Yes,' said Tina, giving another look towards the school. 'He'll be fine there, I know. Besides, if whoever it was that was in the house last night, if it was Dimitri they wanted, then they would have taken him there and then.'

John flicked the key in the ignition. 'Don't jump ahead of yourself. We still don't know for sure whether someone was there or not.'

'Save your breath trying to convince me otherwise,' said Tina. She pushed the clip of her seat belt into the holder and adjusted the tightness of the strap across her body. 'You know as well as I do, someone was in the house. We just don't know how.'

'I'll check it out when we get back,' said John. He looked in the mirrors, signalled and pulled out into a gap one of the parents made for him.

'We,' she corrected him. 'We will check it out.'

John raised his eyebrows. 'Okay, we will check it out.'

She didn't mean to sound snappy and was conscious of the edge to her voice. 'I don't mean to sound bad-tempered, but I'm seriously struggling to keep it together. This whole business is getting to me. If I let my guard down, I'm going to end up a weeping, pathetic woman.'

'Showing your feelings isn't such a bad thing, you know,' said John. 'Although, I must admit, weeping and pathetic isn't particularly helpful.'

'Exactly.'

'Right, let's get you home, then, woman of steel.' He said with his best mock-American hero voice-over.

Tina laughed despite herself. 'Now I'm picturing myself in a pair of cast-iron pants and a cape.'

'Wonder Woman-like,' said John. He looked over at Tina with a smirk. 'I kind of like that image, hot pants, knee-length boots ...'

Tina dished out a playful tap to John's arm.

The tension in the car eased and she felt herself relax back into the seat. Despite everything, she couldn't deny that she liked being with John. He had a calming effect on her, his years in the police force clearly coming into play as he took everything in his stride without so much as a stumble or falter in his step.

John stood inside the front door, Tina at his side. He closed the door firmly.

'So, let's go through this again. The front door was definitely locked, as I remember putting the chain on and checking.'

'And I had locked the back door, checked all the windows. I remember talking to Rascal,' said Tina. 'What? He understands everything I say.'

John smiled and shook his head. 'Cat woman,' he muttered.

'At least you didn't put "crazy" in front of that,' said Tina.

'We both heard a thud, a bang, call it what you like, but there was definitely a distinctive heavy noise from next door, followed by a different sort of bang.'

'More like a clatter,' said Tina.

John closed his eyes and tried hard to remember the unexpected sound. 'Yes, different to the first. Almost like two pieces of wood banging together, a door or something.'

'And then I definitely heard movement on the staircase. It really makes a noise. Admittedly the creaking noise was more indistinct, but that's what I thought immediately, that it was the staircase.'

'At which point we hot-footed it next door.'

'And found nothing.'

John wandered down the hall and back again. 'Has Mr Cooper got any pets?'

'Nope.'

'Any chance Rascal or another neighbour's pet could have got into Mr Cooper's house.'

'Nope. And let's just say a cat did. Unless it's of the wild cat-lion variety, then I doubt it would have made such a loud noise.'

John looked thoughtfully up the staircase. 'If I wanted to get from one house to the next without being detected, what would I do?'

He looked at Tina, who shrugged. He continued with his verbal thought process. 'I can't go in and out the front or back doors, they are locked and I don't have a key. How else can I get through? I'm not a ghost, I can't walk through walls.' He paused again to see if Tina had picked up on where he was going with this.

'If you know the answer, then rather than do the whole Sherlock and Watson routine, can you enlighten me?' She tagged an impatient flick of the eyebrows to the end of the sentence.

'I can't walk through walls, but I can make a hole and get from one side to the next.'

'John, please. Not a riddle.'

He took her hand and led her upstairs, coming to a halt on the landing. He looked up at the trap hatch to the loft. 'If I wanted to move from house to house …'

'Oh, shit!' The penny had clearly dropped. 'They've been coming in through the hatch.'

'Where's that torch we had yesterday?'

It was a rather precarious act, but using the small bookcase on the landing as a step and the bannister to support his other foot, John straddled the landing and pushed open the loft hatch.

'Don't you want a chair or something?'

'No. I want to see how easy, or difficult, it is for someone to do this without moving anything. If the intruder used a chair, they wouldn't be able to put it back after them.'

He pushed the torch up into the roof space, its cylindrical beam aimed into the blackness. Then he grabbed hold of the edge of the hatch on either side and heaved himself up, hooking his elbows as he did so. John was glad he kept himself in shape – he needed upper-body strength to then be able to raise himself up into the loft so that he was sitting on the edge with his legs dangling into the hallway.

'Blimey, whoever it is has got to be fit to do that.' He made a slow, steady sweep of the loft with the torch.

'If you stand up, directly above your head there's a pull cord,' said Tina looking up from the landing. 'There's a light up there.'

'Now she tells me,' said John. He found the cord and gave one swift tug, the bare light bulb in the rafters lighting up.

'I forgot. I don't go up there. Last time I was up there I was putting the Christmas tree away.'

'Did you forget about the ladder?'

'The ladder?'

'Yes, this step ladder.' John slid the aluminium steps down through the hatch. As he did so, a little shower of dust from the edge of the hatch settled on to the floor.

The soft light didn't quite reach the darkest corners of the loft. There was enough room for John to stand up straight between the trusses. He could see the loft had been boarded out, which would make navigating the space much easier without fear of putting his foot through the ceiling below. The Christmas tree, Tina had mentioned, was indeed there to the left of the hatch, within easy reach, meaning venturing into the loft fully was not necessary.

Apart from dust and cobwebs John couldn't see anything else. He turned his attention to the party wall. Ducking under one of the roof trusses, he moved closer to Mr Cooper's side.

'Have you found anything?'

John looked back to see Tina climbing up through the loft hatch.

'I thought you were going to wait down there,' he said.

'Don't go getting all alpha male on me,' she said standing up and dusting her hands off. She stepped over one of the boxes and rested her arms on the wooden A frame.

John resumed his examination of the party wall, sweeping from left to right, up and down with the torch beam. He stopped at a grey, heavy-looking blanket draped over a solid shape against the wall.

'What's that?' he asked.

'I don't remember putting it there but, to be honest, it doesn't mean it hasn't always been there. As you can see, I usually only push things up through the loft hatch.'

'My guess is that it's a recent addition.' John took a few steps closer. 'Look at the floor. The dust has been disturbed around it.'

Tina ducked under the beam and moved to John's side. 'Do you think that's how someone has been getting in?'

Her voice was less confident now, the false bravado apparent.

'Let's find out,' he said.

John held the torch firmly in his right hand, ready to use it as a weapon, if necessary. With his left hand he took hold of the edge of the coarse fabric and moved it to one side. He gave a start, flinching slightly, the knock-on effect causing Tina to let out a small scream and jump backwards.

'It's okay,' said John, immediately realising what he had actually seen behind the blanket. 'It's only our reflections. Look, it's a full-length mirror.' In truth, he felt a bit of an idiot at his reaction.

Tina gave a nervous laugh of relief. 'I didn't even know what I was screaming at. I jumped because you did.'

'Hey, it was a flinch, okay, not a jump,' said John, trying to make light of it.

'It was so not a flinch.'

'Your word against mine. I'm a police officer, remember?'

'Hmmm, exactly.' She gave him a small nudge. 'Come on then, Captain Courageous, let's see what's behind it.' Her voice grew serious. 'Do you think there might be someone on the other side?' she whispered, nodding towards the mirror.

'I shouldn't worry about whispering now,' said John. 'I think we've ruined the element of surprise. Here, hold the torch for me.'

John gripped the pine frame of the mirror. It wasn't as heavy as he anticipated and it slid easily to the left, following the track already cleared through the dust. It was obvious the mirror had been slid in the same direction recently.

A hole in the wall, about a metre high, was revealed. It was just big enough for someone to squeeze through at a crouch. A small draught filtered through the gap, refreshing the arid air in Tina's side of the loft. Several shafts of light streamed through gaps in the roof left by long-since missing tiles on Mr Cooper's side.

John took the torch back from Tina and shone the light into Mr Cooper's loft.

John could taste the mustiness in his mouth as he ran his tongue over his teeth. This was the tricky bit; going into another room that was dark and a space where you had no idea what, or who, was on the other side. Not a situation he liked to be in. If anyone was waiting on the other side for him, as soon as he poked his head through he was easy pickings.

John turned to Tina and put his finger to his lips and held his other hand up, indicating that she should stay exactly where she was. Tina nodded her understanding. He held his breath, listening hard for any tell-tale noises of someone on the other side. Anything, from a slight scuffle, weight being transferred from one foot to another, a creak in the joists or even heavy breathing. He closed his eyes. An old trick Neil had once taught him, to hone the senses, in particular the sixth sense, of being aware of the presence of someone else. Okay, it wasn't scientific or anything they taught you at police training but, nevertheless, John hadn't dismissed it, especially since it had got him out of trouble when playing cat and mouse with a particular nasty drug dealer who had waited for John behind a partition wall and with a scaffold bar. John had sensed the man on the other side of the wall and had taken him out, ankle height with his police baton. Rolling around screaming in agony over a broken ankle meant the scaffold pole was no longer a threat.

130

John rested for a few more seconds. No sixth sense, no tingling of the senses this time. He looked back at Tina, who let out the breath she must have been holding. He indicated that he was going in and she was still to remain where she was.

Still not taking any chances, John slowly extended his arm through the gap, shining the torch all around the opening. He could see the bricks that were once the wall stacked to one side and noted that this side of the loft space wasn't boarded out at all. At a crouch, he stepped through, placing his feet on the joists. He took a careful look around, until he was satisfied there was no one else up there.

'It's okay, you can come through,' he called back to Tina. 'Watch your step. Keep your feet on the joists.'

Tina climbed through, but remained just inside, choosing to watch John rather than take up the challenge of shuffling along the joists without much light.

John knelt down at the loft hatch to Mr Cooper's landing. Something shiny caught his attention and he picked it up.

'What's that?' said Tina.

'A knife,' said John. He ran his hands around the wooden plinth to the hatch, coming to stop at a rough edge, where the knife had gouged a small indent. 'I was wondering how our visitor opened the loft hatch from the inside. He digs the knife in here and flips the hatch up. As the knife is on Mr Cooper's side, we can assume that he last exited this side.'

Tina gave a small gasp. 'Do you think he's in Mr Cooper's now?'

'Maybe. Although I'm not suggesting we drop down the hatch and find out. Best we go round to Mr Cooper's the conventional way.'

'What about if he comes up here while we're down there? We could be chasing him backwards and forwards.'

'Which is exactly why I'm going to put some of those house bricks on the loft hatch. He may be able to lift it if he pushes hard enough, but we will certainly hear it.' John edged back towards her. 'Pass some bricks over.'

After a few minutes a significant stack of bricks had been placed on top of the hatch.

'What about the hole in the wall?' Tina shuffled back through to her side of the roof space.

'Shouldn't we fix that up?'

'No point if he can't get up here,' said John. 'Today I'll get a catch and padlock to put on your side of the hatch. That way, even if he does get up there, he won't be coming into yours that way.'

They made their way down the ladder and onto the landing. John put his hands on Tina's shoulders and turned her round to face him. She was doing a pretty good job of keeping it all together, but not good enough that he couldn't see the angst in her eyes. 'Don't worry, you're safe. I promise I won't let anything happen to you or Dimitri.'

He pulled her in for a reassuring hug and felt her squeeze him tightly before pulling away. 'Thank you, John. I'm not sure how I'd manage all this without you.'

'You're a very brave and strong woman. Stronger than you think. You would manage, I have no doubt. However, since I'm here, I aim to make it much easier for you.' He smiled reassuringly. 'Come on, let's pop next door and speak to Mr Cooper.'

Standing on Mr Cooper's landing, everything looked as it should.

'Whoever it was must have been quietly creeping in and out without Mr Cooper noticing,' said John.

'Well, Mr Cooper is as deaf as a post. You saw how easily we let ourselves in and came upstairs. He wouldn't hear a thing. I'm always nagging him to lock that back door.'

'Tomorrow I'll get up in the loft and rebuild that hole. I'll also have a chat to Mr Cooper about locking the door.'

'I don't want to alarm him, but I think he needs to know.'

'Don't worry, I'll handle it. I'll tell him that it's something we suspect rather than have any hard evidence.' John ushered her out of the room.

Chapter 23

Mr Cooper hadn't been overly alarmed, but he had agreed to be more vigilant with locking his back door.

'I'm an old dog,' he said. 'It's hard to teach me new tricks, but I'll do my best to remember.'

Tina knew it was the best compromise she was likely to get from him.

'So, what happens now?' asked Tina as they went back into her house.

'We're going through local CCTV to see if we can see who was hanging around the café the other night.'

'I didn't realise there was CCTV,' said Tina. She didn't meet John's look, she knew the look of guilt would speak louder than any words.

'Is there anything you want to tell me about the other night?' said John, his voice was gentle. 'Anything you may have remembered?'

Tina stared at the coffee cups she had taken from the cupboard. Her back was to John.

'Tell me a bit more about the Moorgate robbery and what happened there. Who was involved?' She needed to know for certain it was only Pavel.

'What's this, some sort of trade-off?' His tone was tetchy.

'I need to be clear who was involved and to what extent.'

133

'So you can protect people?' He was angry. 'You're not judge and jury, you don't decide who gets caught, who gets punished. If you know something and you're not telling me, then that's with-holding information. A serious offence.'

She spun round to look at him. 'If that's what you think, then arrest me.' She knew as well as he did, he couldn't prove loss of memory.

'Look, Tina. Let's cut the bullshit,' said John. 'Someone came to your rescue the other night. Who would want to protect you? Who doesn't want the local police to know they were there?' He paused and looked out of the window as if in some sort of internal fight. 'Pavel. He's over here, he wants to spoils of the Moorgate job and you, whether you like it or not, whether you know it or not, are the link.'

She thought he was going to say something else. Did he know about Sasha, if indeed it had been Sasha she had seen? She was even less convinced it was him now. Wishful thinking on her part. Hearing the Russian voices and getting the bump on her head had caused her imagination to go into overdrive. Adrenalin and fear fuelled all those subliminal connections, surging at the same time, making her see things she wanted to. Reality suspended. No, she didn't really believe it was Sasha.

Tina could see the anger and frustration in John's face, the gold flecks in his hazel eyes burned, reflecting the flames of guilt which flickered and glowed from deep within him. There was something he wasn't telling her. She needed to know one thing before she could tell him the truth.

'Was Sasha involved in the death of your partner? Was he involved in any of it? I need to know.'

He looked her straight in the eye when he answered. He didn't blink. He didn't shift his gaze for one second. 'No,' he said. 'No, he wasn't.'

'Thank you.' Relief flushed through her. Now it was her turn to level. 'Pavel was there. He came to my rescue.'

'Just Pavel?'

'No. There was someone else with him. At first I thought it was Sasha, but I didn't really see him properly.' She bowed her head, embarrassed at her behaviour. 'I think I wanted it to be him. I thought he had come back.'

'Are you certain it wasn't him?'

'Yes. I had been attacked. I'd taken a blow to the head. I was petrified.' She rubbed her temples with her fingers. 'I was mistaken.'

John exhaled. 'Mistaken is fine. We all make mistakes.'

The rattle of the letterbox and faint thud of mail hitting the floor was a welcome distraction. At the same time, John's phone began to ring. Tina left John in the kitchen answering the call and padded down the hallway to collect the post.

It didn't look like anything very exciting; a couple of bills and a bit of junk mail. The postcard amongst them, though, was rather more interesting. Who sent postcards these days?

She looked at the picture realising it was of Brighton Pier. Her heart gave a heavy beat. Brighton Pier was where Sasha had proposed to her. It had been a wet and windy, supposedly, summer's afternoon. A Sunday. The day was engrained in her memory. They had sat on the wooden bench, looking out over the English Channel, sharing a portion of fish and chips wrapped in white paper. As Tina had put her hand in to get a chip, her eyes watching the waves chase up the pebbled beach, she had felt something square and hard.

It had been a small ring box and inside was a beautiful diamond engagement ring. She had looked at Sasha, who had the most serious look on his face that she had ever seen and then, without saying a word, he had slipped to his knee and was asking her to marry him.

Brighton Pier had always been their place after that. Their special place. It didn't matter that thousands of tourists every year trod the boards of the pier, it was always hers and Sasha's place. No one else had the connection with it that they did.

She picked the postcard up and flicked it over. The message was short. She read it again, the words swimming in front of her eyes. The air in her lungs disappearing making her gasp for breath.

Dear Chris
Wish you were here.
X

Tina dropped the card and backed away, her eyes hypnotised by it. She collided with the hall table, knocking over the photo frame, which clattered to the floor.

The postcard remained on the mat within a few feet of her.

This couldn't be happening. It was impossible. She must have read it wrong.

She waited a few moments while her breathing settled back to a more normal level. Taking slow steps as if the postcard was going to out-manoeuvre her somehow, Tina stalked it like a lion creeping up on its prey.

She stopped in front of it. The tips of her black court shoes were now a centimetre away. Steeling herself, Tina crouched down and tentatively reached out, her fingertips picking at the corner of the card. Securing it between her finger and thumb she slowly stood up and looked at the message again.

This time the words were clear. The message was clear, the impossibility of its meaning still knocking the wind from her. The tears took her by surprise and she swiped at them with the back of her hand as the anger ignited from deep within her.

How dare he do this to her? She hadn't been mistaken. Sasha had been there the other day. These past five years she had cried an ocean of tears for her dead husband. And now … now, he clearly wasn't dead.

Tina looked back down the hall. She could hear John ending his call. He called out to her to see if she wanted a cup of tea. Somehow she managed to answer.

'Yes please.'

Her thoughts were running riot, rattling around inside her head like a Roman chariot race, thundering so fast she couldn't focus on a single one of them, they came and went so furiously.

Tina gathered up the letters. She folded the postcard in half and slipped it into the back pocket of her jeans. The sounds of John moving around in the kitchen were magnified in the silence of the house.

The kettle rumbling to the boil. The chinking of cups. The opening of the fridge as the suction released the door from its hold. The milk trickling into the cups and the clank of the teaspoon as he swirled the tea bag in the hot liquid. She imagined the dark streaks of the tealeaves, colouring the milky water, staining it to a shade of Mediterranean tan.

'You okay?' John called down the hall to her.

She coaxed a cheerful expression to her face and turned. 'Yes, fine.'

Another lie.

'Anything exciting?' asked John, nodding to the letters in her hand.

'No. Bills, junk mail. That's all.'

Liar! The word echoed around in her head.

'I've got a meeting with Martin this morning,' said John. 'Will you be all right on your own for an hour or so?'

'Of course.' She hoped she sounded convincing. 'I've got my new phone now, so I can easily get hold of you if needs be.'

'I won't be far away.' He dropped a kiss on her head and held her for a moment in his arms.

It felt good. It was comforting. It fed her need to feel safe. The world around her was collapsing. It wasn't a new thing. It had collapsed once before, when Sasha had … had died. Yes, he had died then. The Sasha she loved, and was married to, had died five years ago. The Sasha who was alive now had been reborn into a world she wasn't part of. And now he was back destroying her new life. Anger licked at her heart, curling the edges of once-cherished memories – ashes to ashes, dust to dust. Her belief in her past, her history, flaky and charred.

Chapter 24

Tina checked both the front and back doors after John left, ensuring they were locked. She hated this new routine that she had been forced to adopt, but until all this mess was sorted out she needed to take extra care.

She looked at the side of her head in the mirror. The swelling had gone down and a yellow and purple bruise was blooming in its place. She acknowledged that it could have been a whole lot worse had Sasha and Pavel not turned up.

Taking the postcard from her pocket, Tina went about making herself comfortable in the living room. She had intended to lie down on her bed, but from the sofa she could watch TV. Not normally one for daytime TV, Tina hoped it would be a welcomed distraction.

It was chilly in the north-facing living room – autumn was definitely upon them. Tina gave a small shudder. She'd borrow John's sleeping bag to keep her warm. It was folded on the floor at the end of the sofa, near the window. Tina pulled it out. The faint smell of John's deodorant lingered on the fabric and she lifted it to her nose, breathing in the familiar and comforting scent.

As she gave the sleeping bag a final tug from down the side of the sofa, it pulled John's briefcase out too. She hadn't seen it tucked down there. As she went to pick it up, Tina noticed that one of the locks was open. She went to flick it shut, but paused, her thumb hovering over the latch.

Tina placed the briefcase on the coffee table and sat down on the sofa. The leather around the edges of the case was worn and the shine had long gone from the handle.

There might be papers relating to the investigation of Pavel inside. Should she look? No, she had no right to go rummaging through his briefcase. But, if she did, she might find answers to questions John wouldn't answer. She might find out if he knew about Sasha or not.

She was torn between the two men. Loyalty and trust, where did hers lie?

It didn't matter. She needed to know the truth. Tina flipped the left-hand catch and it sprang open. With trepidation about what she might actually find, Tina lifted the lid. There were two manila files and a brown envelope, plus an assortment of pens, sheets of paper, a small notebook and a mobile-phone charger.

She lifted the first file out. The name-tag caught her attention first. It was dog-eared and partially missing, but unmistakably the end part of her surname was still intact. It was quite bulky and the folder itself showed signs of being manhandled many a time. A coffee-cup stain marked the bottom corner.

Tina's hands shook as she held the file. The word 'confidential' was stamped across the front in red ink. A label with a case number and title 'Porboski Investigation' was stuck on the front.

Tina opened the cover. A passport-sized photograph of Pavel was paper-clipped to several sheets of paper. Another pile lay underneath, this time about Sasha. Tina scanned the documents. The front cover was like a summary: date of birth, physical description, where he was born, where he went to school, his address. Then Tina gulped. It was the address of their flat above the deli.

Tina looked at the second page. An account of what Sasha had been doing at what time and on what dates – a log of his daily routine. She riffled through more pages. Some events were highlighted in yellow. There were scribbled notes in the margins. Each page relayed everything Sasha did, every place he went, every person he came into contact with, her own name cropping up time and time again.

The folder slipped on her lap and out slid several black and white photographs. Her heart thundered in her chest. Her stomach churned and she felt the pulse in her neck throb. She reached down and picked up the photographs.

Herself and Sasha walking arm and arm down the street. Taken from a distance through a long lens. They were looking at each other, laughing at a shared joke. They were young, happy and clearly in love.

Another photograph was taken through the deli window. Sasha at the counter serving a customer. Another was of them both locking up the shop for the night. Another of her and Sasha talking to a man in a suit in the doorway of the deli. She didn't recall the conversation but it had obviously taken place.

And so the photographs went on. There were about twenty of them, taken over a period of time. The last one choked her. She cried. Silently. She rocked back and forth. Memories and pain hurtled towards her, coming back to torment her as they had done five years ago. The picture was of her alone in their flat, curled up on the sofa, surrounded by opened photo albums. She knew exactly when that had been taken: two days after she had heard about Sasha's death. She had spent three days huddled there – not answering the phone or the door to anyone, alone and in the deepest pit of grief. In the end her dad had forced the lock and her parents had scooped her up and taken her home with them. She hadn't wanted to go. All she wanted was to be with Sasha. She didn't know if she would be able to make it alone.

Tears spilled as she thought back to those dark days. If it hadn't been for her parents and the knowledge she was carrying Sasha's baby, she wasn't sure she would be here today.

Chapter 25

Martin had been waiting outside in the car for John. The two men were now heading for an address a few miles away. As they joined the A259, a black 4x4 slipped into the traffic behind them.

John looked in the wing mirror.

'They're letting Adam drive?' he said.

'Yeah, he's been nagging them so much to let him drive the Range Rover, I think he wore them down in the end.'

John looked at the road ahead of them. 'How certain are we that this is the address for the Bolotnikov brothers?'

'About as certain as we can be with anything in this game,' said Martin. 'It's an old farm cottage on a back road which has been empty for a couple of years, apparently the owner went into a nursing home. A few weeks ago, the farmer who lives at the end of lane noticed lights on one night. He thought it was squatters or something and phoned it in.'

'Did the local police go and have a look?'

'Yep. All checked out, apparently. It was the nephew. Just visiting, making sure everything was okay with the house. '

'So, this is where you tell me how our Russian brothers are connected,' said John.

'The house is owned by one Alice Smith, or as she was formerly known, Natalia Muratov.'

John mulled the name over. He knew it, but was having trouble placing it. He saw the grin on Martin's face. He was enjoying having one up on his partner. John thought hard.

'Muratov. I've got it. Ivan Muratov, cousin to the Bolotnikovs' grandfather.'

'Yep. Now you can see where we're coming from.'

'Makes sense. Those boys have got to be holed up somewhere,' said John.

'How's Tina?' asked Martin as they powered east along the dual carriageway.

'Bearing up,' said John. 'She's a strong woman.'

'Has she said any more about the attack?'

'Only confirmed what we thought. It was Pavel who came and sorted out our two Russian guests.'

'On his own?'

'No. He had someone with him. Sounds like it was Sasha,' said John, checking his mobile phone. 'She said she thought it was Sasha at first, but that she was mistaken.'

'And you believe her?'

'You seem to ask me that question on a regular basis,' said John.

Martin shrugged. 'You've neatly side-stepped giving me an answer, though.'

John tapped the screen absent-mindedly with his forefinger. 'There's something. I don't know what it is yet. Whether she's waiting to tell me something or ask me something, I'm not sure.'

Martin left the dual carriageway at the next roundabout, turning left and heading north.

'ETA two minutes,' he said.

Both men lapsed into silence as they considered their arrival at the cottage.

They cruised to a stop a few metres short of the entrance to the dwelling.

'I can't see any cars in the driveway,' said John. 'I suppose they could be parked up in that barn at the back.' He took out his binoculars and scanned the area, then the house itself. 'No sign of life anywhere. Come on, let's move in. Nice and easy, we don't know if they are armed.'

It was a frustrating raid. The cottage was empty. There were signs that it had been occupied very recently; the bins contained discarded food and empty takeaway cartons.

John swore as they regrouped at the vehicles. 'Looks like we were too late. They must have had the jump on us.'

'No one outside this circle knew we were coming,' said Martin. He kicked the tyre of his car in frustration.

'But the Bolotnikovs did. How the hell did they know?' said Adam. 'What about the wife?' His voice faded.

John's glare was enough to stop him mid-flow.

'Don't even go there,' warned John. Then, to reassure his team, he added, 'She didn't know about this. She couldn't have given them the heads-up, even if she wanted to.' He made a point of making eye contact with each man, daring them to even think Tina might have been a mole.

'There is one way they could have known,' said Martin. 'If they were in Belfour Avenue watching the house.'

'So, if we're here and they're there …' said Adam.

'Shit,' said John. 'Let's go.'

The knock at the front door startled Tina. She hadn't been expecting John back so quickly. She stopped as she saw the silhouette through the door's glass panel. That wasn't John. It was too short, too stocky.

She knew who it was, though. Oddly, she was neither surprised nor frightened. She had been half expecting this. Maybe not quite so soon, but she knew it would happen at some point.

Tina opened the door.

'Hello, Pavel,' she said, her voice measured. She couldn't claim to be pleased to see him. This was no happy family reunion.

'Hello, Tina.' He gave a small nod. 'Get your coat. We do not have much time.'

Tina did as she was told, picking up her handbag at the same time.

Sitting in the car as it sped along the A27, Tina took out her phone and arranged for her mum to collect Dimitri from school.

'I'm meeting an old friend. It's all a bit spur of the moment,' she said. A lie. 'Thanks ever so much, Mum. I really appreciate it.' A truth.

Chapter 26

John was out of the car, almost before it had stopped. He sprinted up the path and, using the spare key Tina had given him, he pulled himself up and walked calmly into the house.

He called out her name, but he could tell she wasn't there. The house had that empty feel; one when you knew you were alone. The kitchen door was closed. He took it as a good sign. She must have left of her own accord, allowing time to shut Rascal in the kitchen. Maybe she had gone for a walk or to the shop.

When he looked in the living room, however, his relief turned sour. He took in the open briefcase, the confidential file and the photographs scattered across the coffee table and sofa.

'Fuck. Fuck. Fuck.' He pulled his hand through his hair and thumped the door with his palm.

'John?' Martin came up behind him and looked into the room, taking in the debris of papers. 'Yep, it's definitely a fuck moment.'

John began gathering the photos up and replacing them in the briefcase. He stopped at the postcard on the floor. Picking it up, he looked at the front and then at the back. He stood up.

'I think I know where she's gone.' He handed the card over to Martin.

'Brighton?' said Martin. 'But it's for "Chris" – whoever that is.'

'Chris. Short for Christina.' John picked up the file from the floor and threw it into his case. 'Tina. Also short for Christina. It's what he called her. A pet name for his wife.'

Tina stepped onto the boardwalk of the pier and for a moment she wasn't sure if her legs would take her forwards.

The off-shore breeze licked at her arms. Step by step, Tina walked further along the pier. The fourth bench on the right, facing east, her destination.

And then he was there. He must have seen her at the same time. The world around her stopped spinning. Life was put on pause as he looked back at her. For that moment, there was no one else on the planet.

He'd aged a lot in five years. More than she was expecting. He had deeper frown lines on his forehead than she remembered and his dark hair had a few flecks of grey above his ears. His eyes were the same dark pools of ebony, but now there was an intensity, a haunting that hadn't been there before.

His skin looked more weathered and he had lost some weight. He had the look of a troubled man. But, despite all this, he was still Sasha Bolotnikov. He was still the man she had married and had loved so completely.

Then he was walking towards her, his pace increased with every stride. Tina realised her legs were already carrying her forward. The metres between them rapidly diminished. The last few steps found her running and in seconds she collapsed into his arms. She held onto his neck as if clinging to the last strand of grass on the edge of a cliff. As if her life depended on it. In actual fact, she was clinging onto her past.

'Tina, Christina, my Chris,' he muttered over and over again into her hair. 'I knew you would come.'

She pulled back from the embrace. This was where she wanted to slap him as hard as she could.

'You sent me to hell and back,' she said, her voice wavered slightly. His eyes dropped away and when he looked back at her she could see tears fighting to escape as he struggled to compose himself. 'How are you?' she asked him like she had just met up with an old friend but she needed to hold onto a bit of normality.

'I'm okay,' he said. His accent was stronger than before. A sign he had not been living in the UK. 'You?'

Tina nodded. 'I was,' she managed to say. She wondered when she was really last okay. Before Sasha died she was okay. She was very okay. But since then, she wasn't sure. Maybe since John had been about she had become okay again.

'I'm sorry,' said Sasha, his hands held the tops of her arms and he looked directly into her eyes.

'Since I got your postcard, I have been going through all the possible things you would say to me,' she said. 'Sorry was top of the list, but it doesn't even begin to cover what I've been through.'

'I know …'

She cut him off. 'Don't you dare tell me you know. You have absolutely no idea.' The anger was simmering inside her. 'I thought you were dead. My heart broke. I was broken. I have never known pain like it. I didn't think I could come back from it. I was free-falling into an abyss of pain and desolation that knew no end. Do you understand what you did to me? Do you?'

Tina was aware her voice had risen an octave as the anger turned into a rolling boil. She shrugged his hands from her and thumped his shoulder. She didn't care. She punched his chest with her other hand. Then both together. She pummelled him.

For a while he stood still and allowed the blows to batter him. Then he held her wrists, saying her name over and over again. He pulled her into a bear hug.

'I hate you,' she sobbed. At that moment she really meant it. She hated him and yet she loved him. She cried for a long time, vaguely aware that Sasha had led her over to their bench. Eventually she calmed down and began to regain her composure, whilst reassuring a concerned passer-by that she was okay.

Tina disentangled herself from Sasha. She needed a physical

distance. She looked out across the English Channel, desperately suppressing the thoughts and memories of that time long ago when they had sat there. When they had been so happy.

'You do not hate me,' said Sasha. 'You just hate what I have done.'

'Isn't that the same thing?'

'It is not the same.' His voice was soft but firm.

'Convince me.' Tina threw the challenge down to him.

Sasha looked around. Tina watched his eyes scan the faces in the crowd. He shuffled uncomfortably on the bench, turning slightly to face her.

'It is not what you think,' he said.

Tina gave a derisory laugh. 'I was told, by your own brother, that you were dead. That you had been killed in a car accident. I believed him.' Her voice was ragged as the feeling of utter misery came storming right back to her, like it was only yesterday. The taste of the salty air settled in the back of her throat. 'I thought you were dead. My soul partner, the father of my unborn child, the love of my life, the man who I loved more than anyone else in the world, had been taken from me. Never had I known pain like that. Before or since.'

'I want to explain,' he said.

'You have exactly ten minutes to explain, otherwise I'm walking away and going back to my life as a widow.'

Chapter 27

'It is very complicated,' said Sasha.

'I'm hoping so,' said Tina, not able to keep the sarcasm from her voice. 'I wouldn't want it to be a straightforward, easy reason, like you didn't love me. No, I definitely want it to be a long, complicated reason.'

He didn't say anything for a moment, waiting for the spike of anger to dull. He wet his lips before speaking.

'When we lived in London and had the deli, I always told you that the money to set it up had been a bank loan,' he began. 'Well, that was not the truth.'

'So, you lied to me from the very start?' Her heart began to sink. The betrayal had begun from the moment they met.

'It was from my grandfather,' said Sasha, choosing not to answer her question. 'He made me promise not to say where it had come from. The money was not supposed to come out of Russia.'

'Why?'

'Please, Tina. My grandfather, he had a hard life, he had to make his own way in the world. He came from a very deprived background. His family were very poor and they had to do many things that would not be accepted in the Western world – just to put food on the table.'

'Are you trying to tell me that he got the money through

criminal activity?'

'Yes.' He held her gaze, his own was challenging. 'He became a very successful businessman, but he could not keep all the money in Russia. He expanded into Europe.'

Tina couldn't help the laugh that freed itself. 'Oh, my God, Sasha, you make it sound like something from a gangster movie. Your grandfather was involved with organised crime in Russia and he smuggled money into the UK.' Sasha wasn't laughing. He sat silently, his eyes answering her questions. Then she realised what Sasha was telling her. The laugh died. 'Money-laundering,' she said. 'Your grandfather was money-laundering through the deli business.'

Sasha shrugged. His indifference firing the outrage within her. 'You knew and you didn't say anything. You let me become involved. You let me become party to a big international criminal ring.' It was beyond belief and, yet, it was totally believable given what else she had learned in the last few weeks. 'You bastard.' She hissed the words at him. She gripped her hands so tightly together that her nails dug into her palms. When she opened them, she had drawn blood. It didn't hurt. The pain of what Sasha had done was far too great. It swamped every other feeling in her body and soul.

'I could not tell you. If I did, then you could be implicated if it all went wrong,' said Sasha. 'I was protecting you. The less you knew, the better it would be.'

Tina didn't know if that was true or not. Would that argument stand up in a court of law? She had no idea. She didn't say anything, but waited for him to continue.

'Everything went well with the deli. You know that. We were busy. We had lots of customers. All that was real, that was true. We had a good life together, didn't we?'

His arm rested on the back of the bench and his fingers stroked her shoulder. Tina wanted to pull away but she couldn't. They were so happy together in London. They laughed. They loved. They enjoyed life. They were in their own cocoon. They hadn't

151

needed anyone else. Sasha and Tina, an independent unit; they functioned as one. Well, that's what she believed. But in the end it had been a lie.

Tina felt the tears sting her eyes. Sasha's touch stirred up such conflicting emotions. She buried her face in his arm and allowed him to draw her towards him. She had grieved for him and now she was grieving for their past. The past that had only been a half-truth.

'What went wrong?' she said, lifting her eyes now the latest round of tears had abated. She felt exhausted. She needed to know. She couldn't walk away and not know the truth.

Sasha held her hands. His palms were rougher than she remembered, his nails shorter, the skin around the tips of his fingers jagged and torn.

'I have much more manual work to do these days,' he said, answering her unspoken question. Tina thought how they used to do that a lot. Be able to anticipate each other's words. Finish the other one's sentences. A single look between them could share the amusement of something they had seen, no words needed. They had been good together.

She caressed his hands with her fingers. She wanted to kiss them better. To kiss away the present and the nightmare she was an unwillingly part of. She looked long and hard into his eyes and, with unspoken words, urged him again to continue.

'What went wrong?' he repeated. 'Pavel went wrong.'

Tina knew how much it was hurting Sasha. He adored his older brother. Sasha looked up to Pavel with a reverence reserved for the best of church-goers.

'He got greedy. Got himself involved in some bigger fish.'

'The Porboski gang.'

'I did not know at first, I swear to you,' said Sasha. 'But I found out. I told him it was dangerous, that we were out of our depth. But, you know Pavel, he would not listen. He had a taste of life in the fast lane and he was not slowing down. He became involved with armed robbery.'

Tina sucked in a deep, salty breath of air. 'And you?'

Sasha shook his head vehemently. 'No. Well, not at first. I did not want to become involved in anything like this. I had you to think about. How could I put you in that position? Put you at risk? You were the most precious and pure thing in my life and I would not risk it for something as dangerous as that.'

'But not precious and pure enough to stop you money-laundering,' said Tina.

'I kept you out of that. Why do you think I never let you become involved with the finances of the deli? I did not even like you handling any of the cash. I did not want you even touching what was not true.'

He was right. He had always done the cash-handling himself. She hadn't questioned it at the time. It was his business and seemed only natural that he would want to deal with the banking.

'It still doesn't make it okay,' she said.

'I know.' He dropped his head for a moment and pinched the bridge of his nose between his finger and thumb, a gesture he always made when under pressure. Tina quelled the ripple of sympathy this evoked within her, countering it with thoughts of his ultimate betrayal.

'You have a son,' she said at last, her voice so quiet, she could barely hear it herself. 'He's called Dimitri.'

'Dimitri. It is a good name,' said Sasha.

She looked down at her hands, blinking back the tears gathering in her eyes. This was so hard. They were talking about their son and, yet, only one of them knew him. It just shouldn't be like this.

'He's a good boy,' she said.

'Like his mother.'

'He looks like his father.'

'I know. I have seen him.'

'So it has been you following me. You've been in the house when I wasn't there. Was it you … that night … on the stairs?'

153

'No. That was not me,' said Sasha. 'I am sorry. It was Pavel. He was impatient. I did not want him to go. He thought he was helping me.'

'But it was you the other times?'

'Yes.'

'Part of me wishes I never found all this out. But now I know, I can't undo it,' said Tina. 'I don't understand why you were creeping around. What were you looking for? What else has Pavel done?'

Sasha shifted position. His jaw tightened and a pulse thumped in his neck. He shook his head. 'He has done what needed to be done.'

'The Russian at the dock.' It was a statement, not a question. Sasha didn't need to answer. His silence told her everything.

They sat side by side for a few minutes, looking out to sea, as if admiring the view. Tina watched the waves roll back and forth, scrambling over the pebbles. A couple walked along the water's edge, hand in hand, laughing together, sharing a moment. On the outside the world was a sunny and bright place, on the inside, Tina knew life was much darker.

'You didn't answer me. Why you were in the house. Why you faked your own death,' she said, hoping her voice would hold and not break with emotion.

'Can we walk?' Sasha asked. 'I do not want to sit here for too long.' His eyes swept the pier, checking the faces that came their way.

'Who are you hiding from?' she said, suddenly feeling unsettled. Memories of the attack back in the café resurfacing.

'No one. I just do not like sitting in one place for too long.'

'The truth, Sasha! Tell me the whole truth,' said Tina. She wasn't going to be lied to any more, no matter how big or small the untruth.

He took her upper arm in his hand and hoisted her to her feet.

'Tina, please?'

She considered refusing but didn't know what that would achieve, apart from drawing attention to them. Despite everything,

154

her natural instinct to protect Sasha kicked in. She fell into step as they made their way off the pier. Tina and her un-dead husband.

Chapter 28

The sun's rays danced and bounced off the sea. It looked so blue today, so still. The beach itself was busy with visitors and locals alike, enjoying the warmth of the late-September weather. Tina walked along the promenade, Sasha at her side. They milled in and out families with pushchairs, roller-bladers, dogs and cyclists. Tina thought they probably looked like any other couple that day, taking a stroll along the seafront.

Even though Sasha had put his sunglasses on, she could see from her side-on view that his eyes were alert. This was not a leisurely stroll for him, where he absently took in the views around him. No, his eyes were darting back and forth, checking for what, she wasn't sure, but she knew there was an anxiety there. As they walked further along the seafront, the crowds began to thin out and Tina sensed Sasha begin to relax.

They found an empty bench and sat down. Sasha fiddled with his black leather watchstrap. Another one of his tell-tale stress habits.

'Pavel got more heavily involved with armed robberies. The last job they did went wrong. Badly wrong. A policeman was shot and killed. Another was injured. It was all over the newspapers and TV.'

'Yes, I know,' said Tina.

'Pavel was there. They had robbed a small private bank.'

'They never caught who did it,' said Tina. She knew all this from John, of course.

'This time, though, I *was* involved,' said Sasha. 'Their lookout was sick and Pavel asked me to step in at the last minute. He said I did not have to do anything, only watch the street.'

Tina felt sick. Her stomach churned. John had lied to her. She looked at her husband. He had lied. Two betrayals. 'You and Pavel, you went home to Russia afterwards.'

'Yes. He had some money he had saved over the time. I had a little of mine…'

'What? Wait a minute.' Her voice was louder than she had intended and gained her a curious look from a passing couple. Tina modified her volume. 'You took money? You had a cut? How did that work?'

'Call it commission, but I got paid to launder the money.' His reply was matter-of-fact.

'What did you do with the money?' She knew they were comfortably off at the time but they certainly hadn't been living a life of luxury. The feeling of sickness returned – they might have been out enjoying ourselves on what she believed to be their hard-earned cash, when, in fact, it was the proceeds from criminal activity.

'I saved the money. We never spent it.'

'That's something, I suppose,' she said. 'I still don't understand why you faked your own death. You still haven't told me.'

'The heat was on all around. The police were getting closer and closer. They had already taken an interest in the deli. They had been watching my every move.'

Tina knew that now. She hadn't at the time, but Sasha had. 'And you still never told me.'

'I was protecting you.'

'You were keeping me in the dark and treating me with zero respect.'

Sasha leaned forward, his forearms resting on his knees, his hands together as if in prayer. 'I did not see it like that. I still do not.'

Tina knew this was difficult for him, but not as difficult as it was for her. He was wrestling with his conscience, trying to justify his actions to her. Something he knew he could never really do.

'Pavel had more than his fair share. He took some diamonds from one of the jobs and he sold them on, getting a large sum of money. The remaining members of the Porboski gang did not take too kindly to this information once they found out. They wanted what they considered to be their cut. We were both coming under threat from them, Pavel and me.' He was struggling for words now. The effort of speaking in English taking its toll – he had spent five long years away, speaking in his mother tongue. 'I needed to hide. The word was out that I was on their hit list too. I knew as long as I was alive they would keep coming for me. They had gone after Mario and you know what happened to him.'

Tina certainly did know what happened to one of Pavel's friends. He was found tied to a chair in a garage in Dalston, beaten and tortured to death. She couldn't believe that she never made the connection then. She truly believed that she and Sasha had no more of a connection with what was going on other than that Sasha hailed from the same country. How could she have been so naive?

'There's something else,' he said.

'Oh, God, what?' She wasn't sure she could take any more.

'I had been forced to speak to the police.'

Tina frowned. 'Speak to the police? I don't understand.'

'An informer. The police were blackmailing me.' He sat back against the bench. 'They had evidence on me for the money-laundering. They said I could be kept out of prison if I gave them information.'

'You grassed on the Porboski gang? Your own brother?' Tina let this new information sink in. John had never told her that bit. He must have known, surely?

Yet another lie.

'I had no choice. I was stuck in the middle.' Sasha let out a long sigh. 'The only way I could stop both the police and the Russians

158

coming for me was if they thought I was dead. The Porboskis wanted their share of the money and they wanted revenge. They wanted my blood.'

'If you had told me, we could have disappeared together,' said Tina. There was a bleakness in her voice as she began to understand what her husband had been involved in. How she thought she had known him but really she hadn't. It hurt. Badly.

'I could not take you with me.' Sasha held Tina's hand as he had done so earlier. The roughness of his skin still felt alien to her. He felt alien. He wasn't the Sasha she had been married to. The Sasha she married had never really existed. He was a front, a disguise for the real one. She kept her hands within his. She wanted him to tell her more. She needed to know exactly what happened. 'If I had taken you with me, you would have given the game away. An English woman in Russia, who could not speak a word of the language, it would have been easy to find me and you would have been in grave danger too. You and our unborn son. I could not put you in that position. I couldn't let there be any chance that they would come for you. The only way I could escape and keep you safe was if I died. I could not tell you. If you knew the truth you would not have let me go, I know you too well. You would have tried to do something crazy to put it right.'

Tina nodded. Yes, she probably would have. She would have done anything to keep the love of her then-life.

'So you faked your death. You and your brother and your family were all in on it,' she said, as realisation about the extent of the lie hit her. 'They all knew. No wonder Pavel didn't want me to come over for the funeral. There wasn't one.'

Sasha bowed his head. Shame settled over him like a shroud. At least he had the decency to be ashamed of what he had done. She remembered the pain of the grief. It was still raw, but it was all needless. How tragic.

'You deceived me. You betrayed me. You have come back and rewritten my history. I can't just say, "Oh, that's okay Sasha, don't worry about it. It's all okay now".'

The sound of a car horn, tooting several times, made Sasha look round. He stood up, anxiety etched across his face. 'I have to go,' he said.

'Go? But … why?' She couldn't let him go without some sort of resolution.

She followed his gaze. Pavel was sitting in a car, the engine running, beckoning to Sasha.

'Meet me again,' said Sasha urgently. He kissed her on the forehead. 'I will contact you.'

Tina stood and watched as he ran across the grass strip, hop over the wall and jump into the waiting car.

As the car disappeared out of view, swallowed up by the traffic, Tina turned and looked out to sea.

She felt numb. Shell-shocked. Confused. Broken. Betrayed.

She had no concept of time. No idea how long she stood there for. She was vaguely aware of the tide drawing in and the coastal breeze picking up as high tide peaked.

A touch on her arm brought her back from her thoughts. 'Tina.'

She didn't move. She didn't turn. She knew who it was.

Chapter 29

'Tina,' he said her name again, this time louder. She remained impassive, almost in a trance, looking out at the horizon.

John and the team had driven straight over to Brighton. It was more than a hunch. John knew she had come to meet Sasha. The atmosphere in the car had been tense. Neither John nor Martin spoke as they travelled to the destination, the 4x4 in its familiar position in their rear-view mirror.

Sweeping up and down Brighton seafront in their vehicles, on the prowl for their prey, they had missed him. As John and Martin had cruised along, scanning the faces of the crowd, the people had thinned out and that's when he had spotted her.

A lone figure, standing still as the people trickled past her. The wind had picked up and was lifting the ends of her hair, cocoa-bean-coloured strands of hair floating up and down, caressing her face and shoulders.

'You lied to me,' she said, still not turning.

'I wanted to tell you, but I couldn't,' he said. 'It could have compromised the operation.'

'Is that all you care about?' she turned to look at him. 'The operation. I thought you cared about me. Obviously, not as much as I thought.'

'I do care about you,' said John, 'but I also care about the death of Neil Edwards.'

'What about the death of my husband? You know, the death that never happened. I suppose you knew about that too.'

'That came as a surprise to me too,' said John, the guilt for both his deception to Tina and his loyalty to Neil fighting for pole position. 'And that's the truth.'

'The truth. Dear God! Don't speak to me about the truth,' she shrugged off his hand. 'Your life, your job, brings you into so much contact with lies and deceit that I think you don't know where one ends and the other begins. You're surrounded by it all day and at some point it seeped into your soul. You tell lies like some people breathe.'

She brushed past him and began walking back towards the pier.

'Tina, wait.' He ran after her.

She didn't break stride, her eyes once again fixed firmly in front of her. 'The bottom line is, John,' she said. 'You lied to me.'

'And you've been totally honest with me?' he said, his own indignation surfacing. She stopped and looked at him as he continued. 'We all tell lies. We all keep things to ourselves for our own personal reasons. I'm not the only guilty one here. Think about it.'

'Some lies are bigger than others,' she said.

'They are still lies. Whatever the size.' He was being pedantic, he knew, but morally he was right. She couldn't argue with what he was saying.

He watched her shoulders sag. She looked down at her feet and when she looked back at him there were tears shining in her eyes.

'All these years I've grieved for Sasha, the pain of losing the love of my life, the father of my son, has at times been almost too much to bear. I thought I had lost someone who loved me as much as I loved them. I thought I had experienced the most painful thing possible.' Her voice caught in her throat. 'I was wrong. This is worse.'

She swayed. John drew her to him. He felt her knees give. He held her tight.

Eventually, she pulled away from his hold, the strength returning to her body and her mind.

'I need to pick Dimitri up from my parents.' Rummaging in her bag and pulling out a tissue, she wiped at her eyes.

Referring to herself only wasn't wasted on John. She was distancing herself from him. He couldn't blame her. This understanding didn't mask the stab of the rejection which sliced through him.

'Come on, I'll take you home,' he said. There were more truths he needed to tell her. She had more pain to come. He had more confessions to make.

John listened to the soft tones of Tina reading Dimitri a bedtime story. Her voice drifted down the stairs and into the living room like a clement breeze, the pain of what happened earlier, hidden from her son.

A few minutes later she came into the room.

'He's asleep now. I think Dad must have worn him out. They've been gardening, so Dimitri tells me.'

John smiled. He loved the way she looked so relaxed when she spoke about her father and Dimitri. For a while it was as if she had no troubles whatsoever. He wished he could keep it that way.

He passed her a glass of wine.

'How are you feeling?'

Tina took the glass and sat in the chair by the side of the fireplace. 'Confused. Happy. Sad. Ecstatic. Heartbroken. And everything in between. I've been duped.' She took a large gulp of wine. 'By both of you.'

John crouched in front of her. 'I couldn't tell you before. I wanted to. But I couldn't compromise the operation.' He took the wine glass from her, placing it on the table, then held both her hands in his. 'I'm sorry. I truly am.'

She didn't reply for a while as she looked at him, studying his face.

163

'I suppose I understand,' she said. 'It's not a nice thought, but I do get it.'

'It goes with the job, unfortunately.'

'There's something else, though,' she said, leaving her hands within his. 'I can tell there's something you're not telling me. And don't say it's confidential or you can't disclose that information. I'm not buying it. I want the truth.'

He looked at her. There was no easy way to do this, he'd simply have to tell her. Could he tell her everything, though?

'Sasha was my informant. He passed information onto me about the Porboski gang which meant he passed information onto me about his brother too.'

Her eyes widened. 'It was *you* who was blackmailing him.' He could hear the shock in her voice.

'He was there when Neil Edwards was shot. No, it's okay, *he* didn't shoot Neil.' John fought his customary mental battle, dispelling the images, regaining control. 'But he was involved with hiding the money from the job. All I want is to arrest Pavel and get the money back.'

'What about Sasha?'

'If he agrees to talk to me again, I can arrange immunity for him. I can get him on the Witness Protection Scheme. He can walk away from all this. From the Porboski gang too.'

'And from me, again,' said Tina, her voice was bleak.

He chose his next words carefully.

'I don't know if he was coming back for you in the first place.' He felt a complete bastard saying it, but he was certain Sasha hadn't come back for her. Not with Pavel in tow. No, there was a completely different agenda.

She nodded. 'In my heart of hearts, I know you're right.'

'Did he say why he was back?' John asked.

'No. It was him and Pavel who were in the house though.'

'What did he say they were looking for?'

'He didn't. We never got that far. He suddenly said he had to go and that he would contact me again. I don't know how or when.'

He stroked the top of her hands with this thumbs. 'I think he's back for the money. There's no other logical reason. That's why Pavel is with him and that's why the Russians are after him. And after you.'

'What? I don't understand.'

'You are the link to the missing money, whether you know it or not. And all the time it remains hidden, you are in danger.' He wasn't sure he was getting through to her. 'Tina, the Russians think you know exactly where the money is and they want you to share this information with them. They will use every method to persuade you to co-operate. People close to you.'

He watched as realisation dawned on her. 'Dimitri?' she whispered. 'Oh, God, this is a nightmare. I don't know where the money is. What if they don't believe me? What if they do something to Dimitri?'

'Hey, hey, calm down, it's okay,' said John. 'We can sort this. I've got it worked out.'

Monday morning finally limped its way round. They had spent Sunday playing happy families for Dimitri's sake: football in the garden, a walk along the seafront, helping John wash the car and all the time Tina acutely aware that the wrong father figure was there.

Tina waved Dimitri off at the school gates and drove back home with John.

'Are you going to tell Dimitri about Sasha?' asked John.

'Tell him what, exactly?' Tina fiddled with the wedding ring on her right hand. 'That his father walked away from him and made a new life. No, what would the point be? It wouldn't achieve anything.'

'So you're going to continue the lie?'

Tina removed the wedding band from her finger. 'I was brought up to believe there were only truths and lies, nothing in the middle, no grey areas. It's something my parents instilled in me from a very early age.'

'And now?'

'I'm beginning to realise that some lies are good lies. Sometimes it is best to lie than to tell the truth.' Tina slipped the ring into the interior pocket of her handbag. She looked down at her now-naked hand. 'Not telling Dimitri the truth will be my good lie.'

Chapter 30

He was already waiting for her when she approached the coast-guard tower. He looked on edge. The wariness was still in his eyes and he glanced around repeatedly. The sea breeze was playing with wisps of his hair and Tina was glad she had tied hers back into a ponytail. She took her cardigan, which had been resting in the crook of her arm, and put it on to tame the goose bumps that had appeared on her arm, taking care not to knock the pin from the collar of her blouse.

She knew what she had to do

As she walked towards Sasha, Tina tried to work out what she was feeling. Trepidation, certainly, was the most overriding emotion. She was getting over the shock of him being alive and now she was pretty certain of his agenda – one which wasn't for the love of her or their son.

'Hi,' she said as she came to a stop in front of him, making sure it was just out of kissing distance. He seemed to read the body language and checked himself from embracing her.

He greeted her in Russian. 'Kak pozhivaesh?'

For a moment she was taken back to their married days. He always said hi and asked her how she was in his native tongue. It had been an endearing gesture, one that had always made her smile.

She nodded, keeping her emotions in check, refocused on the

here and now. She mustn't let him get to her like this. 'I'm fine, thanks,' she said, aware that they both knew it was a lie.

'Do you want to get a coffee?' he asked.

Tina shook her head. 'No, let's sit on this bench,' she said, remembering John had told her to keep within range of the car so the listening equipment could still pick up the bug in her collar.

'Why are you back?' she asked, not looking at him but keeping her gaze fixed straight ahead. The tide was out, the sun shone down on the wet sand, reflecting back in the rivulets of water which filtered their way out to sea.

She heard him sigh. 'As I said the other day, it is complicated.' He sat down beside her. Sasha turned her towards him and rested his hand on the side of her face. 'My darling, Tina, I have loved you from the first day I saw you and I have never stopped loving you. But ... things have happened.'

'Tell me,' she said, placing her hand on his. She knew John would be listening to their every word, but she didn't care. This would be her only chance to find out what had made Sasha leave her.

'When I went back to Russia I had to build a new life for myself. I knew I could not have you or our child, I could not put either of you in danger. You do understand that?'

Tina gave a slight nod of the head. 'Sort of.' She didn't want to stop him talking, not now. She felt she was close to finding out what had brought him back.

'I met someone, a woman. We married.' He paused, allowing her time to take this in.

'What's her name?' She didn't know why this was important, but she needed to construct the new Mrs Bolotnikov in her mind. 'What does she look like?'

'Please, Tina, it is not necessary.'

'It is. For me, it is very necessary.'

'Her name is Rozalina. She has dark hair. Brown eyes. About your height.'

'Do you have a photo?'

He hesitated, his hand resting on the back pocket of his jeans. 'There's something else.'

'You have a child.' It was a statement, not a question. Why else would he hesitate to show her a photo?' Pain surged through her veins straight to her heart.

Slowly he removed the wallet and opening the soft, brown leather, he showed her the photo. Tina had been right. A young woman smiled back at her and beside her was a boy of about two years old. Dark hair, like his parents. He was smiling at the camera. The little dimple in his cheek made Tina catch her breath. It was like looking at Dimitri a few years ago. The dimple that both boys had inherited from their father. Her eyes blurred and she realised it was tears. She blinked hard, not wanting to allow them to escape. 'What's his name?'

'Nikolay.'

'He has your smile.' A thought struck her. 'He's like his brother.' The tears came now. Dimitri not only now had a father who was alive, he also had a brother, albeit a half-brother. She looked up at Sasha and a tear rolled down his cheek. She wiped it away with her thumb. 'Oh, Sasha, what a mess.'

They clung to each other and both cried. It truly was a complete mess. How had it come to this and what was the purpose of it all?

'He is not well,' said Sasha eventually, as he pulled away. 'He is a very ill boy. He needs treatment, which I cannot afford. I need money for the operation.'

'I'm so sorry,' said Tina, with genuine emotion.

'I need your help.'

'Me? What can I do? I haven't got any money, Sasha.' She dropped her hands away.

'You have something that I need. Something I gave you.'

'What are you talking about?'

'Okay, listen very carefully.' He ran his hands down his face and then holding her at the tops of her arms, looked intently at her. 'Do you remember your last birthday we had together. We went to Covent Garden for a meal?'

'Of course. You ordered a huge bottle of champagne.'

Sasha nodded. 'That is right. And do you remember what I gave you?'

'A necklace.' The memory washed over her. It has been a lovely evening, one she had treasured in her memory as the last time they had been out together. A bittersweet thought.

'What else did I give you?'

'A key,' she stumbled over the words as her emotions fought to take control and send her into another ocean of tears. 'You said it was the key to your heart. That it locked the happiness in for a lifetime.' Oh no, now she realised he had been laying the ground-work in case something went wrong with the robbery. Her once-beautiful memory of their evening out for her birthday had, in fact, been the last supper, except she hadn't known it then. Hadn't known that a week later he would be gone, seemingly forever.

She realised the sob was her own.

'Tina, stop, please. You must listen.'

He sounded desperate. Who the hell was he to tell her to stop crying, to stop feeling? 'You have no idea how much pain you have caused.'

'I'm sorry. More sorry than you can ever understand, but please listen. I have not got much time.' He glanced around, up and down the seafront. 'Do you still have the key?'

Tina wiped her eyes, quashing the grief that was churning in her throat. 'I do. It's at home.'

'It's for a safe deposit box in Brighton.' He handed her a piece of paper. 'These are the details. You must get me the money so I can pay for Nikolay to have the operation he needs. Without it, he will die.'

In that instant she knew she had made a mistake. She stood up, pulling Sasha to his feet. She had only seconds to act.

Tina threw her arms around him. She kissed his cheek long and hard.

'I'm so sorry,' she whispered.

'What for?'

'You must forgive me.' She felt his arms tighten around her. 'Trust me. I will do it.'

He pulled back to look at her.

'Thank you.'

She leaned in and whispered in his ear.

Chapter 31

'No!' John shouted, pulling the headphones from his ears.

'What did she say?' said Martin, doing the same to his headset. John was already throwing the driver's door open.

'Run,' shouted John as he slammed the door shut. 'She's telling him to run.'

The two men raced towards the seafront, it was over fifty meters away and Sasha now had a head start. Their feet pounded the tarmac, covering the distance at speed.

They rounded the corner of an ice-cream stall. The bench was just along from it.

There sitting, her hands on her lap, waiting for them, was Tina.

'Where is he?' demanded John coming to a halt in front of her.

She shook her head. 'I'm sorry. I couldn't do it.'

'For fuck's sake, Tina!' He was aware he had shouted. John scoured the promenade. Apart from a couple of joggers and someone walking their dog, it was empty. John spun round, his eyes scanning every direction.

'There! In between the cars,' said Martin. 'I'll go. You stay with her.'

Tina stood up and watched Martin thunder across the crazy golf course, hopping over the small stone wall in pursuit of Sasha.

'What the hell were you playing at?' demanded John, fighting to keep his temper in check.

'You heard what he said. His son is sick. He needs the money to pay for life-saving treatment,' she said. 'I couldn't let my son's brother die.'

After everything Sasha had done to her, she could still find compassion. John felt humbled and shamed.

A crackle of a radio splintered the quietness between them and a rasping, out-of-breath voice sounded out.

'Lost him … Can't see him anywhere.' John saw the relief on Tina's face. Martin's voice came again. 'John? You there, mate? Did you hear me? He got away.'

John lifted the radio to his mouth. 'Yep, I heard.' A twiddle of a button and the radio fell silent.

John and Martin walked into Brogan's office and stood in front on their boss's desk.

'Sir.'

'Sit down, you two,' said Brogan. 'Do you want to tell me what exactly happened today?'

'Sasha Bolotnikov gave us the slip,' said Martin.

'And how exactly did that happen?'

'Took off. Caught us off guard,' said John.

'And the listening bug you put on Tina Bolotnikov didn't work?' said Brogan, tapping the edge of his desk with his pen.

'No, Sir,' said John.

Brogan leaned forwards. 'So that's the official line. The one going in the report. Shall we have the truth now?'

'That is the truth, Sir,' said Martin.

'I don't know what went on there today, you two, but I wasn't born yesterday and I can make a good guess. Covering for a suspect is not something I approve of.'

'She's not a suspect,' countered John.

'You don't know that for sure. She could be playing you at your own game,' said Brogan. 'You're getting too close to all this, John.

173

Boundaries are blurring. You need to watch your step because I'm going to be looking very closely at this now. Do you understand?'

'Yes, Sir,' said John. 'Is there anything else?' He was keen to file his report and get back down to Sussex. Brogan had insisted both he and Martin come back to HQ for a personal face-to-face debriefing of that day's events. In other words, a sophisticated bollocking.

'That's it now, you can go.' Brogan dropped his pen onto the desk. 'Oh, actually, John, you wait behind, I want a word with you.'

Martin closed the door as he left.

'My wife bumped into Hannah Edwards the other day,' said Brogan, his voice too casual for John's liking. 'Hannah mentioned that you had been round to see her.'

'That's right.'

'Lovely daughter, she's got. My missus said they both seemed happy. They're moving on with their lives.' John wasn't sure where this conversation was going, so he said nothing and let Brogan continue. 'It's a good thing, John. You need to move on as well.' Brogan paused but John remained silent, he had no desire to get involved in a conversation about moving on with his DI. Brogan sighed as he realised he was getting nothing from John. 'Right, get out of here before I change my mind about leaving you on the Porboski case.'

John knew the last time he saw Hannah they hadn't parted on the best of terms. His realisation that he was, in fact, damning Hannah for doing exactly what he wanted Tina to do, move on from her dead husband, had plagued him tirelessly. The hypocrisy wasn't wasted on him.

He pulled up outside Hannah's house. He hoped he had timed it well. By his reckoning, Hannah should be back from the school run within the next few minutes. With a bit of luck, the boyfriend wasn't about.

The blue Ford C-Max swung onto the drive. John could see

Ella in the back seat.

John got out of his car and stood at the end of the driveway. Hannah was now at the front door with Ella.

'Hannah,' said John, standing at the apron of the driveway.

She turned. He saw her face register him. A frown followed. She turned back to the door, unlocked it and ushered her daughter inside.

'Go in, darling,' she said. 'Mummy will get the shopping out of the car.' She walked to the boot of her car. 'I wasn't expecting to see you,' she said opening the hatchback.

'I wondered if we could have a chat.'

'A chat? Honestly, John, I don't think we need to chat about anything.' She heaved two bags of shopping from the car.

'Here, let me,' said John.

'No, I've got it. I can manage.' She put the bags on the ground and faced John. 'It's not a chat you want. You want forgiveness.' John took a step back on to the path, the words unexpected. Hannah continued. 'So listen to me. I. Forgive. You.' She slammed the boot down hard and grabbed the shopping bags. 'Now you can get on with your life and let me get on with mine.'

Hannah strode up the path and in through the front door without looking back once.

John's feet may as well have been welded to the spot and his throat fused closed. He couldn't form a reply. This was not how he had envisaged this encounter. It appeared he had just angered Hannah even more.

Finally, his feet responded to the message from his brain and he walked back to his car feeling no better than he had before. If anything, he felt worse.

Chapter 32

Tina was at her parents with Dimitri. John had taken her straight there after leaving the beach that morning and before heading back up to London for his meeting with Brogan. Tina was glad to be able to sit with her parents and talk of normal mundane things. She wanted to put all thoughts of Sasha and what he was involved in right from her mind.

'Stay for some tea,' said Tina's mum. 'I've made plenty.'

'Yes, stay, love,' said her father. 'Your mother is happiest when you are all eating.'

So Tina stayed and although she thought she had no appetite, once her mum had put a plate of shepherd's pie in front of her, Tina realised she was actually very hungry. She was heartened to see Dimitri tucking into a second plateful. He always said it was one of his favourite dinners his nana made.

'Are you all right?' said her mother as Tina helped clear away the empty plates later on. 'You don't look yourself.'

'Oh, I'm fine, mum,' said Tina. 'Don't worry about me. Just a bit tired.'

'No, you don't look tired.' Her mother began to rinse the plates. 'You look like you have the weight of the world on your shoulders. I can always tell when there's something wrong.'

Tina went to protest but changed her mind. There was little

point. Her mother was right. Pam had always been able to tell when something was bothering Tina, right from when she was a young child, coming out of class, upset because she had been told off for talking too much, as a teenager when she had first falling out with a boy and through to adulthood. The strain of the past few weeks was clearly evident to her mother.

'I've got a few things I'm trying to sort out at the moment,' said Tina. Might as well tell her mother the truth, or as near to the truth as she dared.

'Anything I can help you with?'

Tina took the rinsed plates from the drainer and began loading the dishwasher. 'Not really. Not yet, anyway. But thank you.'

Pam turned off the tap. 'You know where I am if you need me. Or your father, for that matter.' As if on cue, a screech of laughter came from the living room.

Tina raised a questioning eye to her mum. 'What are those two up to?'

'You know what your dad's like – he's as big a kid as Dimitri. They were like this the other night when Dimitri stayed – laughing their heads off at cartoons.'

Tina looked fondly back towards the living room. 'I hate to be the one to break up the party, but I really should be getting back home. Dimitri has school tomorrow and I've got work, plus I'd like to look in on Mr Cooper.'

'Why don't you leave Dimitri here? He can stay the night. In fact, why don't you stay as well?'

Tina looked at the concern etched on her mother's face. A simple yes would take away the worry lines of the older woman. 'But I haven't got any of our things and I need to feed Rascal.'

'Why don't you nip home, do what you have to and then come back?'

It was a tempting offer, but Tina knew if she said yes now, it would be too easy to continue saying yes. One night would turn into two, then three, then four, then … well, she'd be moved in before any of them knew it. She was aware her parents would be most pleased at this – they regularly asked her if she wanted to move in with them. And, yes, it would make life a lot easier, more convenient and, at times, a lot less lonely, but Tina had thus far refused. She needed her own space and she didn't want to become a burden to her parents. She had always envisaged that one day she might meet someone again. She hadn't envisaged, however, that it would be the investigating officer of the secret criminal past of her husband who had faked his own death.

It occurred to her that Sasha might be waiting for her. She was his only hope of getting the money he needed for his other son. She gulped at the thought. Another son. Dimitri's half-brother. She had to be there for Sasha, no matter what she felt about his deceit, his lies, their life built on lies. The truth was, there was a child's life on the line.

'Look, I'll go home,' said Tina. 'If Dimitri could stay, that would be great.' The concern in her mother's eyes took on a fiercer glow. 'It's okay, Mum, honest. There's nothing to worry about. I just need a bit of time to sort a few things out.'

'Anything I can help you with?' said Pam.

Tina hesitated. Could she bring herself to tell a lie to her mum? In the end she settled for a white lie, or rather, an adaptation of the truth. 'It's John. I'm quite fond of him, but I've been thinking about Sasha a lot these last few weeks and it's all getting to me.'

'You shouldn't be so hard on yourself. You can't drag the past around; you have nothing to feel guilty about.'

Tina nodded. 'I know.'

'Why don't you go home and have a long, hot bath, pamper yourself and have an early night.'

'Thanks Mum, I really appreciate it. And please don't worry. I'll be fine.'

Tina gave her mother a hug. She hated telling lies to her, but she couldn't exactly tell her the truth.

As soon as Tina walked through the front door of Belfour Avenue, she knew something was wrong. Rascal mewed a greeting as he trotted through the open kitchen door. The first giveaway. She knew she had most definitely shut the door to the hallway before leaving.

Her heart gave a sprint. Someone had been in the house. Or worse, someone was in the house. She knew they wouldn't be able to get in through the loft hatch any more, not since John had fitted it with a padlock, so this meant they must have got in by some other means, via the kitchen, judging by the open door.

She wondered if it was Sasha and called out his name. If there was someone else in the house, now would be their time to escape out the back, the way they had come. She waited by the front door, her hand on the lock, ready to make her escape if it wasn't Sasha.

Rascal rubbed his arched back against her leg and mewed some more. Tina bent down and lifted the cat into her arms.

'Hello, boy,' she whispered, holding him close to her racing heart. Rascal twisted his body, a protest at being held too close. Maybe he sensed her unease. Tina let him jump to the ground.

Flicking the latch to stop the door from locking, Tina eased the front door fully open and picking up a shoe, wedge it under the weatherboard. She wanted a clear escape route.

She edged over to the bottom of the staircase and craned her neck to look down the hallway and through into the kitchen. A small pane of glass in the back door was broken; the intruder's way in.

Tina took her phone from her handbag and tapped in 999, but didn't press the call button. If it was Sasha, if he was in the house, she certainly didn't want the police here. If, however, it turned out to be someone else, then that was a whole different matter.

'Sasha? Are you there?' she called down the hallway. 'I'm on my own. It's okay. I promise.'

Tina glanced back towards the open front door and the safety of the empty street. It was tempting, but what would she do then? Call the police? Call John? She mulled the latter option over in her mind. No, she didn't want John here. Not tonight. Possibly not ever.

Tina took a deep breath in an attempt to settle her pulse rate. She needed to keep calm and clear-headed. Thinking of John was not conducive to the current situation.

Just as she knew straight away something wasn't right when she first came home, instinctively she felt sure there was no one else in the house, despite her caution. She forced one foot in front of the other, stopping at the living room and looked through the crack between the door and the doorframe. The room appeared empty. She stepped in, scanning the room, noting its slightly dishevelled look. Things had been moved and replaced, but not to their exact position. The books on the shelf in the alcove weren't lined up as neatly as usual, one or two were poking out, the photo frame on the mantelpiece wasn't at its usual angle and the sun-catcher hanging from the sash window had been turned, the sailing boat no longer facing left but right. Someone had been in, clearly looking for something, but had done it with care. Not a callous burglar, to whom the crime was victimless, no this burglar, if indeed, she could call them that, had shown respect.

Tina ventured tentatively into the kitchen, pushing the door wide open and looking in, satisfying herself that her intuition was on point.

One of the kitchen drawers, the one found in most houses – reserved for all the odd bits and pieces that didn't have a particular home – wasn't shut property. The end of a screwdriver was sticking up, preventing its closure; a sure sign the contents had been riffled through.

Tina moved further into the kitchen and, looking over the breakfast bar to the back door, could see jagged pieces of broken glass had been scuffed to one side, as if the person responsible for the damage had a conscience and was keeping the fragments from being accidently trodden on.

The tension in Tina's shoulders fled her taut muscles. No burglar would bother doing that. It would have been Sasha – that she was convinced of. He wouldn't want her or Dimitri walking on the glass, or even the cat, for that matter.

She leant back against the worktop.

'Tina?' The deep but soft voice from the hallway made her jump. She spun round and managed to suppress the scream that attempted to erupt from her throat.

Chapter 33

He hadn't meant to creep up and frighten her like that, but seeing the front door wide open was unusual enough, given the recent events, to send John's senses straight to red alert. Despite his intentions to stay out of sight, these were thrown to one side without a second thought.

'You okay?' he glanced around the kitchen, his hand twitched at his hand gun lodged in his shoulder holster.

'Yes. Everything's fine,' she said, her eyes shifted to his hand.

'Sure?'

'Positive.'

John relaxed and let his jacket fall from his grasp. Yet, years of experience and habit didn't stop him carrying out a quick check of the house before closing the front door. As he did so, he signalled across the road to Martin that everything was okay and then returned to the kitchen. Tina was crouched down on the floor with a dustpan and brush, sweeping up broken glass. He clocked the missing pane in the back door.

'You've had a visitor?'

'Mmm. They let themselves in.'

Tina stood up and, pressing the pedal on the bin with her foot, slid the glass off the dustpan. The lid closed with a clap that reverberated around the kitchen.

'Is anything missing?'

'Not as far as I can tell.'

John watched her replace the dustpan and brush in the under-sink cupboard. She turned and faced him. The strain of today was evident. Her eyes looked heavy and her whole body language looked weary and defeated. He wanted to go to her, to hold her in his arms and tell her he was sorry. He wanted her to say it was okay and she understood.

'Where's Dimitri?' he asked, suddenly realising the little lad wasn't in the house.

'At my parents,' she said. 'What are you doing here anyway? I thought I made it clear that I wanted some time alone.'

'All the time Pavel is still roaming around, not to mention Sasha and the Russians, I still need to keep you safe.'

'Well, you've done your duty. I'm all safe and there's no burglar.'

'You need to get the back door secured for the night. I don't suppose you've got any hardboard and hand tools?'

'No, but I'm sure Mr Cooper has in his shed. I'll go and look.'

'No, I'll go and look, you wait here.'

'Ever the hero.'

John wasn't sure how to take that last comment, but whether she was being sarcastic or not, she was letting him help her and that had to be a good sign, right? He rummaged around in Mr Cooper's shed, finally locating an old tin toolbox in the corner.

He returned with the necessary tools and a piece of hardboard. 'I'll tack it in place for now, from the inside and outside, to keep the door secure for the night. I can put a pane of glass in it for you tomorrow.'

She didn't contradict him and John carried out the impromptu DIY tasks in silence as Tina made them both a coffee.

It didn't take John too long and when he was confident the hardboard was secure, he drank the coffee she had made.

'So, are you the male version of the honey-trap? That's what they call it, isn't it?' said Tina as he sipped his coffee. 'You were

183

tasked with getting into bed with me, in the hope I'd reveal secrets and information across the pillow.'

'No,' said John exasperation creeping in. It seemed to be the day for dealing with stressful women. 'It wasn't that at all.'

'What the hell was it, then?' Her eyes blazed with anger and hurt, but there was hope there too. John had seen it before in victims he had interviewed. They were in a nightmare that they didn't want to be in and there was a slither of hope that he could pull them out of it, wake them from their terror.

He sat down at the table, his voice controlled. Soft. Reassuring. Honest. 'I was never meant to get involved with you. I promise. In fact, my boss has threatened to take me off the case because he thought I was too involved and my feelings for you were impairing my judgement.'

'Feelings?' The hope burned a fraction brighter.

'Yes. I knew I was getting more involved with you than I ever intended but I also knew that I couldn't stop it. Believe me, Tina, I've struggled and wrestled with this over and over again.' He waited while she took in his words.

'There's another but, I can tell.'

God, she was perceptive. 'Bringing Neil's killer to justice comes before anything else. I need to do this.'

A small tear wound its way from the corner of her eye. 'Sasha is not a killer.'

'I believe that. In fact, I know that, but he is our only lead to Pavel and to the money. Ultimately, it's the way to your safety.'

'Are you telling me the truth?' More tears followed the first.

'Yes. I promise,' said John. 'About everything.'

'I can't deal with the "us" bit at the moment,' said Tina, she palmed away dampness on her face. 'I'm totally drained, I literally can't think straight.'

'What's his next move, Tina? What's Sasha going to do now?' asked John.

Tina looked at John and then past his shoulder. She sucked in a deep breath. Her eyes widened.

'Sasha.' Her voice was filled with fear.

John swung round, his hand automatically pulling the Glock 26 from inside his jacket. A gun barrel greeted him, shaking ever so slightly in Sasha's hand. *Fuck.*

'Hello, John,' said Sasha. He smiled at the detective, but a band of sweat across his forehead, belied his casual tone. 'Now, let's not all get jumpy and start pointing guns at each other, they have a tendency to go off unexpectedly.'

'I agree,' said John, not wavering. 'We seem to have got ourselves in a bit of a stalemate position.'

'Put the gun down,' said Sasha. He swallowed hard and used his left hand to steady the gun in his right.

'I can't do that,' said John. 'Goes against company policy.'

'Do not fuck with me,' said Sasha.

'Listen to me.' John held his arm still, applying gentle pressure with his finger over the trigger. 'You're no killer. I know you. However, I, on the other hand, am. I've been trained to kill.'

'Stop, both of you.' It was Tina. She placed herself between the two guns, looking from one man to the other.

'Tina, move away,' said John, his eyes never leaving Sasha.

'You will not shoot now,' said Sasha, his tongue moistened his dry lips. 'You might hit Tina.'

'Remember, Sasha, I'm a trained marksman. I can take you out with one shot to the head any time I like. Tina is not in my way.' This wasn't strictly true and it certainly wasn't in his training manual. 'Your call.'

The sweat patch had now become a river, flowing freely down Sasha's face. He rubbed his mouth and nose over the shoulder of his shirt.

'Tina, take the gun from John.'

'Wait. Let's talk about this,' said John. 'I know you're not a killer. I'm not interested in framing you up or anything like that. I just want to know where Pavel is. Where the money is. We can deal.'

'I cannot deal,' said Sasha, shifting his weight from one foot to another. 'I have to go back.'

'Tell me where the money is. Where your brother is. I can help you and your family. Your son needs treatment. It can be sorted.' John willed Sasha to take the bait. He couldn't promise him everything, but he was throwing as much at him as he possibly could. 'Work with us and we can help you. We can offer you protection.'

'No. It is not that simple.'

'Sasha needs immunity. He needs a new passport. He needs to be able to go back to Russia,' said Tina. She turned to Sasha. 'Trust me, I can help you. Give John what he wants. I'll find the money you need.'

'Tina,' said Sasha, the quake in his voice audible. 'Take the gun from him.'

Tina looked at Sasha for a moment, he nodded encouragement and slowly she turned to face John. 'I'm sorry,' she said. Then she stepped towards the Glock, its muzzle pointing directly at her head.

'Move out the way, Tina,' said John, his voice calm but firm. She shook her head, the tears trickled down each side of her face.

He had no choice.

Chapter 34

John let the pistol swing round on his finger like a pendulum, coming to rest upside down pointing towards him. Tina stretched out her hand, which was shaking with nerves and adrenalin.

'Nice and easy, does it,' said John. 'Just take the gun by the grip. Don't touch the trigger, it doesn't have a safety lock. That's it. Keep it pointing to the ground. Don't be frightened. If you don't touch the trigger, you can't fire it.'

John watched her shaking hand take the Glock from him. She backed away and, with an outstretched arm, held it in Sasha's direction.

John didn't take his eyes from Sasha for a second. If he was going to disarm the Russian, he had to get the timing absolutely right. Even the slightest of unexpected movements could induce a flinch response from Sasha and in the hyped, adrenalin state he was clearly in, this could easily cause a trigger-finger reaction.

John needed to wait for what was known as a break state; a break in Sasha's state of mind. He needed Sasha's focus to be taken away from the trigger, to wait for an interruption in the flow of thought from brain to finger. He had been trained for this and on more than one occasion had put this into practice.

As the Russian stepped forward, still holding the gun in John's general direction, he made to take the pistol from Tina. Neither

Tina nor Sasha were looking at the gun, the baton handover was fumbled. Tina let go before Sasha had hold of it properly. The Glock clattered to the ground. Tina screamed and jumped back. John knew this was his chance, probably the only chance he would get. It wasn't the ideal time

John leaped towards the Russian, grabbing his arm and pushing it as hard and fast as he could into the air. Sasha was stronger than John expected and once Sasha realised what was happening tried to twist away from John's grasp.

John used his body weight to knock Sasha off balance and the two men bundled into the doorframe. John smashed Sasha's hand against the wall, shattering the glass of a picture hanging behind them. Streams of blood flowed down Sasha's hand from his knuckles. Again John thumbed the hand back against the glass, turning his head away from Sasha free hand, as the Russian's fingers tried to gouge at John's eyes.

John brought his knee up and hammered it into Sasha's crotch and once more rammed his opponent's hand against the wall.

Sasha let out a cry of pain, he hunched over, gasping for air but still kept his grip on the gun. John looked at the weapon as Sasha turned his wrist, attempting to point the muzzle at John. In one last attempt to overpower Sasha, John brought his left elbow up, catching Sasha under the chin. The pain inflicted was enough for Sasha to momentarily ease his grip on the gun. John yanked the pistol free.

A shot rang out, followed by a scream from Tina. Bits of plaster from the ceiling fell down onto John.

'Stop it!' shouted Tina.

Both men froze at the sight of Tina standing in the middle of the kitchen with the police-issue Glock in her hand. Her whole body was shaking as she stood holding the gun out in front of her, two hands clasped round the weapon; it wavered in the air as if fighting against an unseen magnetic force.

'Give me the gun,' said Sasha to Tina.

'Don't even think about it,' said John, now turning Sasha's own weapon on him.

Sasha let out a laugh. 'Take another look at what you have in your hand.'

John should have realised as soon as he had taken it from Sasha. The weight was all wrong for a start, and now the texture, the finish, the whole look of it was off kilter. It was a replica. Not a bad replica – good enough to fool someone from just a few feet away, but once in possession, John should have spotted it immediately.

All the same, he checked the breach and magazine holder. Empty. Not even a blank. Sadly, not the same could be said of what Tina was holding.

John slowly lowered the imitation firearm to the floor, kicking it down the laminated hallway.

'Tina, look at me,' said John. 'At me, Tina. Look at me.'

'Ignore him, Tina,' said Sasha. 'Don't betray me. Remember what I said.'

'Betray you? After what you've done to me?' She looked at John and then back to Sasha.

'You know why it had to happen. I was protecting you.'

'Protecting me? What you did was so cruel. One of the cruellest things a person could do to someone they supposedly loved. You never gave me a choice. And you know what? If you had asked me what I wanted to do, I would have taken my chances and not become a widow.'

'I am sorry.'

'Maybe you are, but you've come back and caused me so much pain, all over again.'

John watched and listened to them. He knew at that very moment, neither were aware of him. They were having a deeply private and emotional exchange, totally unaware of the world around them. It hurt him to see Tina in so much pain. He wished he could just take her in his arms, right there and then. Comfort her, protect her and love her. Show her that *he* wouldn't let her down.

'I know how much this has hurt you. I wish there was another way. I have come back to try and explain everything.' Sasha ran his blooded hand through his dark hair.

'No, Sasha, that's not why you're back. You've come back for your son. Explaining what you did is out of necessity, not choice. You came back for your son, Nikolay.'

'I stayed away for you. I stayed away so you could have a new life, safe, without me.' There were tears in Sasha's eyes. 'I dreamed so many times of a life with you and our child. Instead I had to build a new life to block out thoughts of what could not be mine. In that new life, I was given Rozalina and Nikolay. It was as close to my dreams of you as I could get.'

John's eyes darted to Tina, her face a bed to a river of tears. This conversation was going off in totally the wrong direction. Getting involved with feelings and emotions meant things could get messy. Emotions caused people to be unpredictable. Unpredictable was no friend of his right now. He needed to get them back on track.

'Look, this is no time for a Relate session and right now I need that gun, Tina. Then we can all sit down and talk this through.' He took a couple of steps towards her, his hand held out.

'Do not give it to him, he will arrest me,' said Sasha.

John looked back at Sasha. 'You can't escape and the money you want, well, you won't get that either if you run now. Stay, work with me, the police, we can help you. We'll get you a safe house. We can protect you. Whatever you need, we have the power to make it happen. I'm not interested in you, I just want Pavel and the money.'

'John's right. You must let him help you. It's the only way you can help Nikolay,' said Tina, her voice choking. 'Whatever I do now, isn't for you, it's for your son.' She lowered the gun, her hands dropping to her sides.

Immediately John was there, taking the firearm from her hand. He spun round, pointing it in Sasha's direction, half-expecting to see him already fleeing down the hallway. John really didn't want to have to chase him or, worse, shoot him. He was relieved to see Sasha flop back against the wall, his eyes closed.

Tina brushed past John and went to comfort Sasha.

'I'm sorry, Sasha. I'm sorry,' she repeated as she held her hand to his grazed cheek, a result of his and John's tussle. Sasha looked down at her, nodded and pulled her into his arms. John watched, as husband and wife clung onto each other, both crying. John turned away, driving down the unexpected bitter taste of jealousy that caught in the back of his throat. She still loved Sasha the man, not Sasha the memory.

John took out his phone, swiped at the screen for Martin's number.

'Yep?' Martin answered on the first ring.

'Looks like we're taking a ride to the safe house.'

Chapter 35

Tina sat at the kitchen table, her hands cupped around an untouched mug of tea. John had made it for her before he had left with Sasha and Martin. She didn't want it. The thought was turning her stomach; a place where her heart had dropped to and now lay heavily. John had wanted to call a female police officer over to sit with her, but Tina had refused. She didn't want anyone with her, she didn't need baby-sitting. She just needed to be alone. So much had happened in one day, she needed time to sift through the events and try and make sense of everything.

Sasha was gone and in his wake had left a torrent of emotions, all jumbled up by a raging storm. And now, it was calm, but was this the eye of the storm? Would she have to face another hurricane before emerging the other side into calmer waters or was she already there? Her emotional compass was broken, her sails of resilience tattered; she felt adrift and alone.

She had both Sasha and John and yet she had neither. Sasha was no longer her husband, even though he was still alive. Sasha, her husband, really did die five years ago. The Sasha who was left was someone else's husband, a father to someone else's son. He didn't belong in her world – that much she realised. The irony was not wasted on her. How many times had she wished it was all only a dream and that Sasha would walk through the door and everything could go back to normal? And now that wish had come true, but in the cruellest of ways. Sasha might still be alive as she had wished so many times, but having him back again would always be a dream.

Tina knew she should console herself with the fact that John had come into her life. Again, the irony of his appearance was not wasted on her. Death had taken Sasha and given her John. Yet John, too, was far from straightforward. He was with her, but his affection had come in disguise and she wasn't really sure who she had begun to have feelings for or how much he felt for her. Did he care about her for herself or for who she had been married to and what information she could give him? Did he care about her for Neil? Once he had brought justice to Neil, would John no longer need her? Was she enough for him without the Bolotnikov connection?

Her head was spinning and thoughts were chasing each around her mind – a never-ending carousel of questions.

19 De Beauvoir Square was an unassuming Edwardian terrace house, situated in north London, innocuous and typical of the area. It didn't stand out in any way from the other houses clustered around the central gardens of the square. And that was how John liked it.

Contrary to Hollywood films there were no security cameras, intricate door-entry systems, banks of computers and monitors, an arsenal of weapons, a hidden maze of tunnels, complete with panic room or a self-destructing safety mechanism should the premises be breached.

A colleague was there to let them in, having stocked up with food supplies. The two- bedroom house was sparsely furnished, the Met not known for its generous interior-design budget, although a TV had been acquired to help pass the hours.

The *housekeeper* left John and Martin with their guest.

'Welcome to Chez Met,' said John as Sasha stood in the living room. 'We're not quite up to the Savoy standards, but I hope you have a pleasant stay.' He indicated the sofa. 'You might as well sit down and make yourself comfortable, we're not going anywhere soon.'

'How long will we have to stay here?' asked Sasha.

'How long is a piece of string?' said Martin. He sat down on the chair and picked up the remote control. 'Do as John says and sit down. You make a lovely picture, but a lousy window.' Martin craned his neck around Sasha to look at the TV, aiming the remote control in its direction.

'In answer to your question,' said John, methodically closing the wooden-slatted window blinds. 'The quicker you give us all the information we want, the quicker we can sort out getting you and your family on the Witness Protection Scheme officially.'

'I want my family in Russia flown here before I talk. I want to know they are safe. My son needs medical treatment. He doesn't have time to wait months and months. I want it arranged now.' Sasha paced back and forth in front of the fireplace.

John could see the desperation on the Russian's face. The man wasn't thinking of himself in all of this, he was thinking of his young son. Was this what Tina had seen? Is this what made her want to help the man who had deceived her in the cruellest way? John knew how much Tina loved her own son, and it was beginning to dawn on him that her compassion reached far and wide, it spanned the raging sea of lies and connected in another continent with a seriously ill child, simply because of the blood ties between the two young boys. She had an amazing gift of empathy. However, it was out of her hands now, Tina had put her trust in him, she had handed the baton to John and he knew it was down to him to take it across the finish line, just as he had promised to do so for Neil.

'I'll see what I can do,' said John. The Russian stopped pacing and looked right back at John. He gave a small nod and seated himself on the sofa.

Chapter 36

Three days he had been holed up in the house at De Beauvoir Square and they were still not much closer to securing the deal with Sasha.

'What is taking so long?' Sasha asked for what seemed to John the one-hundredth time that day. 'Where are my wife and son?'

John bit down the urge to ask him which one he meant and instead fixed the Russian with a long, hard stare. The atmosphere between the two men had reached a stalemate state of tension. John watched Sasha wrestle with his reactions, keeping them in check, the desire to flare up finally losing the battle.

Sasha spoke again.

'You think I do not care about Tina, that what I did cannot be justified.'

John shrugged. 'Your words, not mine. Born of a guilty conscience, some might say.'

'Ah, John, you think you are far superior to me, what is it you say? Oh yes, you think you have the moral high ground.' Sasha gave a laugh. 'You and I, John, we are not that very different. We both tell Tina lies. We have both hidden the truth from her.'

'Don't even begin to compare us,' said John. He got up from where he was sitting and walked across to the window, tipping the blind to inspect the square. All looked normal. He wished Martin would get his arse here soon. He really didn't want to listen to what Sasha had to say, but sadly he had no choice.

'Remember, I know your lies,' said Sasha. 'The ones you told Tina, for a start.'

John spun on his heel and faced Sasha.

'What the fuck does that mean?'

'You know exactly what I mean. You haven't told her the whole truth and that, in my book, is the same as telling a lie.'

'Give it a rest,' said John, letting out a deep sigh. 'I'm not in the mood for riddles.'

'I know what really happened that day of the robbery.' Sasha stood up and walked over to John, standing inches away.

The words were like a blow to his thorax. John fought to stop himself from doubling over as he felt the air thud to the back of his lungs. He drew fresh oxygen in through his nose, inhaling deeply to dilate his airways once more.

'Leave it.' he said. The words hissed out like steam from a burst pipe.

John could feel Sasha's breath on his face as the Russian spoke. 'I wonder what Tina's reaction would be if she knew what you did. In fact, I wonder what your colleagues would think. If you do not fix it so that my wife and son are flown over to the UK within the next two days, then I may have to start sharing my information. After all, that is what you persuaded me to do back then. Perhaps, I should resume my role of informer.'

And there it was, the killer blow, this time hitting him in the larynx. Any verbal response lost in a constricted windpipe. John grabbed Sasha's shirt and hurled him towards the mantelpiece above the fireplace.

'You keep your mouth shut,' grunted John.

Sasha crashed into the mahogany mantelpiece, sending a small carriage clock smashing down onto the hearth. The copper coal bucket, a makeshift rubbish bin, was kicked over as Sasha struggled to regain his footing. The noise brought Martin rushing down the stairs, where he had been in the bathroom studying the newspaper.

'Hey! John! Stop!' Martin strode across the room and pulled the two grappling men apart. He shoved Sasha in the chest, propelling him into the fireside armchair. 'Sit the fuck down, you.' He turned to John. 'What the hell's going on?'

John put his hands up in surrender and moved away from Martin. 'It's okay. Nothing.' He took another couple of steps backwards and adjusted his shirt. 'It's okay,' he repeated.

Martin looked from one man to the other. 'Let's keep it that way, eh? John, why don't you get some fresh air? Me and Sasha here, we've got a game of poker to finish from last night.'

Sasha leaned back in the chair, placing his hands on each knee. 'You will be sorry. I hold all the ace cards.' He looked meaningfully at John.

John snatched up his jacket. He needed to get out of here. He felt suffocated, the air in the room dry and thin, the temperature stifling. John pushed through the living-room door out into the narrow hallway, a lightheaded feeling made him stagger for a moment and he ricocheted off the wall. Yanking the front door open he stumbled over the threshold, out onto the terracotta path. Using the gate pier to rest against, John leaned forward allowing the blood to rush to his head. He took long, deep breaths. The oxygen saturating his lungs, his breathing became more controlled.

Shit. That was a bad one. He hadn't had a turn like that in a long time. It was something that happened a lot after the shooting incident and it had taken a couple of years for the attacks to ease. He thought they were a thing of the past, but clearly he was wrong. Maybe it was seeing Sasha again. The dreams had started to become more unsettling, verging now, he would say, on nightmares.

Tentatively, he turned his thoughts to the events that had haunted him for so long. Neil hadn't meant to be there. It was supposed to be just John and Sasha. John had chased Sasha. He had to make it look realistic. Neither man wanted to give their agreement away to the other side or to their own, for that matter.

197

John could remember clearly the conversation he had with Sasha.

'*What the hell happened?*' he shouted at Sasha. '*You said there were no guns. It would be a smash and grab. What are you doing here?*' *He was out of breath from chasing Sasha. He had sent Neil off in the other direction, hoping to keep him out of it. John needed to speak to Sasha alone.*

'*They changed their plan. They didn't tell me, but they said I had to be a look out. They were getting suspicious. Pavel had to prove I wasn't a grass.*' *Sasha was insistent.* '*I cannot speak to you. If they see me I am a dead man. I do not want any more to do with this. Our deal is off.*'

Sasha turned to go. John swiped his gun from his holster, levelling it at the Russian. '*You're not going anywhere. Our deal is very much on.*'

Sasha eyed the gun in John's hand. He looked at John, staring him in the eye. '*I have a wife who is pregnant. I cannot be a part of this.*'

'*You should have thought about that before you started slipping the money through the till.*' *John uncurled and curled his fingers around the butt of the gun. He had no desire to shoot Sasha, but if he had to, he would. Sasha was too valuable an asset to be allowed to walk away.* '*Besides, if you walk, it could mean your wife gets to hear about what you've been up to. Or worse, the Porboski gang.*'

'*She does not know anything about this. It would break her heart,*' *said Sasha.* '*She does not know anything and I want it to stay that way.*'

'*Don't make me the bearer of bad news.*' *It was a below-the-belt threat, but John was willing to use all possible leverage at his disposal. Sasha Bolotnikov was not walking away. John had spent far too many hours turning Sasha, despite the lack of conviction from his DI that this would result in anything. John wasn't about to lose here. He remained poker-faced, his eyes boring into Sasha.*

'*You are threatening to tell my wife? You would stoop that low?*'

John nodded. '*There's still time for you all to make a new life. Free from this. Free from violence and crime. It will only be a matter of time before you are pulled in too deep.'*

He paused while the words sank in.

'You mean witness protection? A new life?' Sasha gave a derisory laugh and shook his head. 'I do not think so.'

John knew he had to dig deeper. And fast. He didn't have much time before someone found them. 'Do you want to watch your child growing up from behind prison bars? Do you want to subject your wife to queuing up with the other wives and girlfriends, their kids in tow? How degrading will that be? She'll be subject to all the low-life, other prisoners will get you to ask her to smuggle stuff in. All this, of course, if she stays with you.'

'All right. Stop.' Sasha's shoulders slumped. 'I do not have any choice, do I?'

'Not really. Not if you love your wife.' John lowered his gun and replaced it safely into his holster.

John didn't see the fist coming. The first thing he knew was the crack as Sasha's right hand connected with his jaw.

'Bastard.' Sasha's voice was a mixture of anger and sadness.

John staggered backwards, regained his balance and threw a punch back at Sasha, catching him with an upper cut to the stomach. Sasha doubled up from the blow but, without straightening, charged towards John. He threw his arms around John's waist, burying his shoulder under John's ribs. Both men stumbled back.

At that moment the sound of running feet on the concrete echoed behind them.

'John!' It was Neil's voice. The security fencing rattled as Neil shook it, trapped on the outside of the building site. 'Oi! Armed police!'

Sasha paused and turned his head to look towards where the voice was coming from. John felt Sasha's hold relax slightly and seized the moment. With a two-handed shove, he threw the Russian to the ground.

'There's a gap just down there!' shouted John, pointing towards the far end of the fencing.

Neil ran the twenty metres or so to the opening, his gun drawn, *and aimed at Sasha. John pulled Sasha to his feet by the scruff on his jacket collar.*

'You've got exactly five seconds to make your mind up or I'm throwing you to the lions and that goes for your wife and baby too.'

John pulled himself up short from revisiting the moments that played out after Neil reached them. He didn't want to go there. Not today. He looked at the safe house. He didn't fancy going back in there just yet. He decided to take a walk around the square.

Walking into the middle of De Beauvoir Square he passed through the brick pillars that marked one of the four entrances to the circular-shaped gardens. The laurel hedges and mature trees shielded the tranquil setting from the Edwardian houses that surrounded it. John breathed deeply and slowly as he meandered along the pathway.

He had been shut up in that house for too long with Sasha. Cabin fever was definitely setting in. It frustrated him that Sasha was being so stubborn about not giving any more information until he had confirmation that his Russian wife and son were on their way to the UK. Unfortunately, relations between the UK and Russian governments weren't at their best and their Soviet counterparts had got wind of what John's department was planning. They had an interest in the business activities of the Bolotnikovs and Porboskis, it seemed, and were themselves keen to speak to Sasha and Pavel. The sins of their grandfather coming back to haunt the brothers. John wasn't convinced the Russians really had any hard evidence on the Bolotnikovs, but were merely hedging their bets and being bloody awkward. Although John couldn't ignore a small nagging thought at the back of his mind that was becoming more insistent. What if the Russians were stalling for time in the hope of finding Sasha? A bit of a curve ball, but it certainly had potential.

After three slow circuits of the gardens and ten minutes sitting on one of the benches contemplating, John felt back in full control. He pulled out his phone and brought up his boss' number. He needed to put more pressure on getting the Russian side of things sorted out. It was taking too long and making John uneasy. The longer they were in one place, the more vulnerable they became, with the chances of being found ever increasing. If the Russians were going to launch an attempt to bring Sasha home, now was the ideal time.

John walked back into the safe house. Martin and Sasha were still playing poker, the pile of notes much bigger on Martin's side of the table.

'He cheats,' said Sasha, not looking up from the cards in his hand. 'I swear he has the cards marked.'

'You're simply a bad loser,' replied Martin. 'I don't cheat, I'm a member of Her Majesty's Constabulary.'

'My point exactly.' Sasha threw his cards face up on to the table. 'I do not want to play any more.'

'And you, my son, have just proved my point,' said Martin scooping up his winnings. 'A bad loser.'

'Now, now, children,' said John. 'Anyway, don't go getting too comfortable there.' He nodded in Sasha's direction. 'We're on the move soon.'

Martin looked up in surprise. 'We are?'

'Just a small relocation. I'm getting itchy feet here,' said John. He looked at Martin, who nodded. John didn't need to spell it out.

'When? Where? What about Rozalina?' Sasha got to his feet. 'I do not like this. You are playing games with me.'

'It's on a need-to-know basis and you don't need to know.' John tipped his head briefly towards the kitchen and Martin followed him out.

'What's the score then?' asked Martin.

'Tomorrow afternoon we're off to Battersea. Got a new pad there. We've been hanging around here for far too long, it's making me twitchy.'

'How do you mean?'

'The Sovs. They might want their boy back home.'

Martin considered this for a moment. 'Okay, I'll head back to the office and catch up on the paperwork. Do a bit of housekeeping and check out our new pad. Make sure it's all ready for tomorrow.'

'Good idea.'

'You okay here with our house guest for the night or do you want me to take over?'

'No, I'll be okay. We'll be ready and waiting for you tomorrow lunch time.'

'Right you are.' Martin looked at John. 'Look, mate, I know you've got a bee in your bonnet about getting the wife and kid over from Russia, but we can crack him without having to do that.'

John felt his jaw tighten. He knew what Martin was saying made sense, but he had a deal with Sasha; with Rozalina and Nikolay safe in the UK, Sasha would keep his mouth shut about the shooting incident.

'I've made a deal with him. I'm not going back on it,' said John.

'All you need to do is remind him what will happen if he doesn't co-operate. You know, if the Russians get hold of him, be it the Porboski lot or the police, he won't be seen again for a long time, if ever. He's got too much to lose to mess us about.'

'As I said, I'm not backing out of the deal.'

'Okay, have it your way.' Martin turned to leave, pausing in the kitchen doorway. 'What's he got on you?'

'That doesn't even deserve an answer,' said John. He matched Martin's gaze with his own. Now wasn't the time to give anything away.

Chapter 37

Tina had spent the last three days torn between waiting for John to contact her, as he had said he would, and wanting to contact him herself. She had barely been able to eat, such were her anxiety levels. It was as much as she could do to get up and take Dimitri to school.

John had arranged for a police car to make regular patrols of the road and to call at her door regularly to make sure she was okay. He was concerned about more Russians turning up.

Tina had phoned in sick to work, blaming a stomach bug and then a migraine. She wasn't sure if they believed her, but at that moment she didn't really care. Fay had left a message on her answer phone asking her if everything was all right, did she want Fay to pop round and help with Dimitri? Tina had managed to fob her off and assure her that Pam was there helping.

Tina knew there would be no way she could function at work. So many questions still swirled in her mind, but the one that she kept coming back to she had no answer for. What exactly had Sasha meant when he said she couldn't trust everyone close to her? Was he just referring to himself or did he include John? Small shoots of doubt had taken root. She knew not everything added up with John, yet she couldn't put her finger on anything specific. There was a small side of him that she didn't know. She studied the text she had prepared to John asking him if he was okay. Did she want to send it? Her thumb hovered over the send icon before returning to the text message. She added two words. *Ring me*. This time she did push the send button.

'Mummy,' said Dimitri, coming to sit beside her on the sofa. 'When is John coming back?'

'I don't know,' she replied, as evenly as she could.

'I like John,' said Dimitri, picking fluff from his jumper and rolling it around into a ball in the palm of his hand. 'I wish he was here.'

Tina went to answer, but the words caught in her throat. She wished he was here too, despite what Sasha had said, John was fast becoming her point of anchor. In her stormy life, after being tossed around like a small sailboat in an ocean of grief, John had guided her to a safe cove and she had weighed anchor.

'I need to see Tina,' said Sasha.

John's body tensed involuntarily. Sasha with Tina, not a prospect he particularly liked. 'No can do.'

They were sitting in the living room of De Beauvoir Square. It was dark outside and neither man was really concentrating on the football match playing on the TV.

'If I cannot see her, I need to speak to her,' persisted Sasha.

John let out a sigh. 'What for? You've had plenty of opportunity to say what you need to say to her.'

'I appreciate your desire to protect her, but I want to say my goodbyes.'

'Your goodbyes?'

'If I am to help you and give you the information you need, then I am sure I will not get a chance to see her again. If you are moving me to another house, how do I know where that will be and when it will happen? For all I know, this may be my last chance to speak to her. Ever.'

'I'll pass on a message.'

'No.' Sasha shifted to the edge of his chair. 'I understand that you care about her and I am grateful. I know you will look after her. I have come to understand that from now on my life will change in such a way that I will never have the chance to speak to her again. I will never have the chance to say goodbye to her and my son. I want her to know that I am sorry. I want her to hear it from my own mouth. I want her to forgive me. This I cannot do through a message.'

John was silent for a long time as he considered Sasha's request. If it was up to him, he wouldn't let Sasha have any contact with Tina again, but he knew that Tina might not appreciate this line of thought.

'You can speak to her on the phone. One phone call and that's it. Understood?'

'Thank you.'

The phone trilled next to her, making Tina jump. She glanced at the clock, it was gone ten. Tina picked up her mobile.

'John Calling' flashed across the screen.

Tina's stomach turned one way and then back again. She had sent the text message four hours ago and was just about to give up hope of him replying, making the excuse that he was probably busy with work, although she knew that a simple text to say he would call later wouldn't have been too difficult.

Tina accepted the call.

'Hello.'

'Hi, it's John. How are you?'

'Okay. I think. You?'

'About the same.' A slight pause before John spoke again. 'I'm phoning because Sasha wants to speak to you.' Tina acknowledged the small feeling of deflation that John wasn't calling to speak to her, but this was knocked into touch by the spike of anxiety that Sasha did. 'Tina? You still there? Did you hear me?'

'Yes, sorry. Okay, I'll speak to him.' Another pause – Tina sensed

John was still there. 'John?'

'I haven't forgotten you,' he said. 'It's just now is not the right time.' This time the pause that came was accompanied by the sound of the phone being passed from one person to another.

Sasha's voice was low and tender. 'Kak pozhivaesh?'

'I've been better.'

'I am sorry. I wanted to see you to speak to you in person, but it is not possible.'

'What did you want?'

'It is difficult.'

Tina sensed that Sasha wanted to say something but couldn't – either because he just didn't know how to express himself or possibly because John was there.

'Is it difficult to talk? Is John there?'

'Yes, as I said, it is difficult.'

She listened as Sasha put his hand over the receiver and heard his muffled voice asking John for some privacy.

'Still a little difficult,' he said to her after a moment. 'I wish I could see you to talk to you in person. Do you remember that time when we first met and we went for a walk on the wobbly bridge?'

Tina thought for a moment. 'The wobbly bridge? Do you mean in London – the Millennium Bridge?'

'Yes, that is right.'

'What about it?'

'Do you remember where we went after that?'

Tina cast her mind back. It was a Sunday – they hadn't been seeing each other for very long. They had decided to have a day as tourists. The London Eye, a walk along the South Bank, across the bridge and then to the cathedral.

'We went to St Paul's,' she said.

'That is right, we went to the cathedral. When you go again tomorrow at midday, think of me and I shall be with you.'

'I'm not going tomorrow. Why are you saying that?'

'So, you see Tina, I am truly sorry. I only wish I could see you in person. I wish I could hold Dimitri for the first and last time.'

Sasha's voice was louder, his tone had changed and he wasn't making sense.

Tina's mind went into overdrive as she fought to catch up with Sasha in this verbal jigsaw. Finally, the pieces began slotting into place.

Chapter 38

John had stood in the kitchen while Sasha made his phone call. He had tried loitering to overhear the conversation, to try and glean any bits of information, but Sasha had made a point of asking him to leave.

John couldn't catch what Sasha was saying, the Russian had closed the living-room door and talking in hushed tones. Something about a wobbly bridge was said, but John wasn't sure what they were talking about. He couldn't ignore the suspicious feeling hanging in the air. He didn't know whether this was from years of being in the police force or whether his senses were in tune. What John overheard hadn't sounded like much of an apology.

After a few minutes, John strained to listen but couldn't hear Sasha's voice any more. The TV had been turned on so it was safe to assume the call had ended.

John had remained wary for the rest of the evening, certain the Sasha was up to something, but the Russian had proved the perfect house guest. Now today they were sitting in the living room watching some God-awful daytime programme, like an old married couple who had nothing to do with their time.

As the closing credits rolled over on the latest dreary antique programme, Sasha stretched and got up from the sofa.

'I need a glass of water,' he said.

'Sit yourself down. I'll do it.' John watched Sasha hesitate before taking a seat by the window. There was a look in Sasha's eye that John didn't like it. Sasha's foot was twitching rapidly up and down. Something was definitely amiss. 'You okay?'

'Yes, of course,' said Sasha. His shoulders slumped and he rested his elbows on his knees. 'Actually, not really. I do not feel well. I had a bad night's sleep. I was thinking about Tina a lot.'

John thought about pressing Sasha for more information, but decided against it. He didn't really want to know what had gone on between the two of them. The phrase 'rubbing salt into wounds' sprang to mind.

John went out to the kitchen and filled a plastic disposable cup with cold water, but couldn't help wondering about Tina, despite not wishing to. He wondered whether she hadn't been as forgiving as Sasha had hoped. Perhaps that was why he looked flushed and unsettled.

As John went down the hallway back towards the living room, he noticed the door was pushed slightly to. His skin goose bumped and a small shiver ran down his spine. Something wasn't right, he was sure he had left the door wide open.

A shadow passed across the gap under the door just as John went to push it open, but it was a moment before John registered this as he took in the sight of the empty chair where Sasha had been sitting.

A sudden movement from behind him, which John sensed rather than saw, caught him off guard. He was momentarily aware of an excruciatingly sharp pain penetrating his skull before being engulfed in darkness.

It was the cold wetness he was first aware of; distant, like a patch of sea mist rolling in and wrapping itself around his body.

The musty smell and scratchy feel of the nylon carpet against his face came second.

John went to move his head to inspect the damp feeling on his stomach, but the pain this action triggered felt as if his skull had been cracked open like a hard-boiled egg.

He let out a groan as a muggy sensation swirled around his brain and he resisted the urge to move his head for a moment. The room came into focus, but disappeared into a fuzzy blur. John closed his eyes and opened them again. This time, when the room came into focus it stayed that way. He blinked several times to identify his surroundings – the floor of the safe house.

This time, when he moved his head he did so tentatively; he looked down towards his stomach, moving his hand to the wet spot on his shirt before bringing his fingertips up to his line of vision. He was relieved to see it wasn't blood. He remembered the glass of water he had been carrying. It was then he remembered Sasha. *Shit.*

John moved his head, ignoring the pain that had now turned to a heavy throb, and brought himself up onto his hands and knees. He looked around the room. No sign of Sasha, but his phone was lying underneath the coffee table. It must have landed there when he fell.

John got to his feet, unsteady at first, and retrieved his phone, noticing his wallet lying open on the sofa. He picked it up and inspected the contents. His cards were still there, but the cash of about forty pounds was gone. His next thought was his car. Grabbing his jacket he located the keys in the pocket.

'Sasha! Are you here?' John proceeded to check through the house, although he already knew it was a pointless exercise. Sasha hadn't been stupid enough to take John's phone or car, both easily traceable by the tracker systems installed. Just taking the cash, he couldn't be traced.

Shit. Where the hell could he be?

John splashed some cold water over his face and soaking a tea towel held it to the back of his head, while he gathered his thoughts. He needed to think clearly and recall the events of the last hour.

He looked at his phone. Sasha had used it to call Tina. Checking the time of the call against the time now, John estimated that he had been out for about five minutes. Not good. Sasha's had made his call about twenty minutes ago. John was sure Sasha doing a runner was related to the call.

He phoned Tina. Her phone rang out to voicemail. He hung up and tried again. Voicemail a second time.

'Tina, it's me, John. I need to speak to you as soon as possible. Call when you get this message. It's urgent.'

As he hung up, it crossed his mind that if Sasha's disappearance was related to his phone call to Tina, then it was probably unlikely that Tina would return John's call.

He could kick himself now that he hadn't insisted on staying in the room while Sasha had phoned her. He got up and soaked the tea towel with some fresh cold water and placed it on the back of his head again. At least he wasn't bleeding.

He thought back to Sasha's side of the telephone conversation. What he heard amounted to nothing. Just a wobbly bridge. A day out. The cathedral.

John adjusted the tea towel on the back of his head, seeking out a colder piece of cloth.

He needed to ring Martin and let him know what had happened. As he waited for Martin to answer his phone, the thought struck him with a weight equal to the blow to the back of his head. Why the hell hadn't he worked it out before?

Martin answered his phone. John was already grabbing his jacket and keys, heading out of the door.

'Sasha's done a runner. Don't ask questions, I'll explain later. Meet me at St Paul's Cathedral. Now.'

He jumped in his car and started the engine.

'I'm stuck in traffic on the other side of the river.'

'Get there as soon as you can.'

'What's going on?'

John didn't bother to answer, he cut the call, threw his phone onto the passenger seat, shoved the gear stick into first position and lead-footed the accelerator.

Chapter 39

Tina readjusted her hold on Dimitri's hand. Her palm felt damp with sweat and the little boy's hand was in danger of slipping through her fingers.

'Where are we going now?' asked Dimitri, as he broke into a small run to keep up with his mother.

Tina looked across the River Thames. 'You see that foot bridge there?' She pointed towards the Millennium Bridge. 'We are going for a walk over it and then St Paul's Cathedral on the other side.'

They ascended the metal steps up to the bridge. Tina hurried Dimitri along. 'Now can you see that big building in front of us with the big dome, the big round roof? Yes? Well, that is St Paul's Cathedral.'

'Can we go to the top?' said Dimitri.

'I don't see why not. We can go up to the Whispering Gallery.'

'What's that?'

'It's like a big balcony that goes all the way around the dome and if you whisper against the wall, your whisper travels round the walls and can be heard on the other side. It's like magic.' Tina smiled at the look of excitement on Dimitri's face.

'Like magic?' he said.

'Yes, like magic.' Tina glanced over her shoulder as they hurried along the bridge, an action she had been performing every few minutes since they had left home that morning. She had made certain the local police had done their routine drive-by before she left the house that morning. She was sure, at any minute now, John would turn up or she would feel a hand on her shoulder and someone telling her she was under arrest for aiding and abetting.

She looked down at Dimitri. 'Before we do that, though, mummy is going to speak to her friend. He's going to be there.'

'Is he coming up in the whispering place with us?'

'I don't know. He might do.' Tina let go of Dimitri's hand for a moment while she wiped the damp palm on the side of her jacket. The sound of the bells at St Paul's rang out, marking the middle of the day. Taking his hand once more, she picked up the pace. 'Come on, we're late.'

As they crossed the road and hurried round to the front of St Paul's, Tina realised that she hadn't agreed an exact meeting spot with Sasha. She scanned the paved area at the front, her gaze travelled up the stones steps, sweeping from left to right, trying to spot Sasha amongst the sea of visitors. She manoeuvred herself and Dimitri to the steps and climbed to the top, all the time looking for Sasha.

She reached the top step and turned to look out at the area below her. She sensed him before she saw him. Behind her. She turned and there he was, moving out of the shadows of the huge doorway.

He paused, not quite in full daylight. He beckoned her towards him.

'Tina, I knew you would come,' said Sasha. He gave her a brief hug and then looked down at Dimitri by her side. The tension immediately left his face, the frown lines dissolved as the muscles relaxed and softened his features. 'Dimitri.' It was a whisper. Sasha dropped to one knee, his hands gentle as they held the boy's shoulders.

'Dimitri,' said Tina, hoping she sounded natural. 'This is mummy's friend. Sasha.'

Sasha held out his hand. 'Hello, Dimitri. It is a pleasure to meet you.'

Tina watched as her son, their son, looked at the outstretched hand. He glanced up at Tina, who nodded encouragingly, before shaking hands with Sasha. It broke Tina's heart. Father and son greeting each other in this way. It just shouldn't be. There should be hugs and kisses, smiles and laughter, not this formal, unfamiliar meeting of two strangers. She could see the tears fill Sasha's eyes as he stood up and looked at her. He went to speak, but the words seemed to stick in his throat. He looked out across the square for a moment, regaining his composure.

'Come inside. It is safer. We need to talk,' said Sasha finally.

'Are we going to the whispering place now?' asked Dimitri as they made their way in through the side door, Sasha paying for full access to the cathedral with the cash from his pocket.

'Yes, we'll make our way there now. It's over there on the right,' said Tina finally releasing her son's hand and letting him skip ahead. 'What's going on, Sasha?' she said as they walked towards the staircase for the Whispering Gallery.

'I do not have much time,' said Sasha, his voice low. 'I am not supposed to be here and I am sure John will be here any time now.'

'Where is he? Is he okay?' said Tina, suddenly alarmed.

'He will be okay. Maybe have a little headache, but that is all.'

'Sasha! What did you do?'

'Sshhhh. I do not want to attract attention. He will be okay. I needed to get out on my own. He would not let me speak to you.' He placed his hand on Tina's arm. 'I need your help.'

'It depends what you want me to do,' said Tina. She took Sasha's hand from her arm, with every intention of letting it drop away, but as she touched him her mind was flooded with a morass of memories and feelings. She gripped his arm to steady herself. Sasha tucked her hand into the crook of his elbow and placed his other hand over hers.

'Come. I will explain.'

Dimitri, still ahead of them, was jumping up the stone stairs that led to the Whispering Gallery. 'One!' Jump. 'Two!' Jump. 'Three!' Jump.

Tina, her arm still linked with Sasha's, followed their son, the progress was slow but it gave Sasha chance to speak.

'It is my son, Nikolay.'

'Your other son.' Tina couldn't help correcting him.

Sasha sighed and closed his eyes momentarily. 'Yes, my other son. He needs this operation. I do not think the police are really going to bring him over to the UK. They are taking far too long. They are making excuses every day, always blaming inter-country relations and red tape. I cannot wait. Nikolay cannot wait.'

'What do you want me to do?'

'I need you to get the money I hid. It is in a safe-deposit box.' Sasha looked behind him and then to each side. 'You have the key for the box. You must get the money and send it to my wife … Rozalina.'

He cut Tina to the core. Sasha talking about his son and his wife. They should be her and Dimitri. Another woman and another child had taken their place.

'Please Tina, I am begging you. For Nikolay, a child. He is only two years old.'

'But if the police have agreed to help you, why do you need me to do this?'

'Because they are playing games. I do not trust them. They want information from me, but I do not believe they are going to bring Rozalina and Nikolay over to the UK.'

'One hundred!' announced Dimitri as he came to a halt halfway up the staircase. His face was pink from the exertion, the jumping long since abandoned in favour of a customary approach to steps.

Tina herself was beginning to wilt. 'Well done, darling,' she said, allowing herself the opportunity to pause for breath. She had a vague recollection of reading a sign that said something about over 250 steps to the Whispering Gallery. 'Come on, let's keep going.'

'One... Two... Three... Four...' Dimitri recommenced his counting.

Sasha raised an eyebrow in amusement at Tina and, taking her hand in his, continued the climb.

'Will you do it?' he asked, without looking at her.

'I don't know.' It was an honest answer. Tina didn't know whether you could or should. It was, after all, illegal money. Blood money. It had the death of John's colleague on it. 'If I do this, then I am not only handling stolen money but, more importantly, I am part of the murder of that police officer.'

'That was not meant to happen. I swear to you on the life of my son.' He paused before adding, 'both my sons.'

'What exactly happened that day?' It was something that had plagued her. Something terrible must have gone wrong, otherwise why would John have reacted so badly to her questioning? He had overacted and it was so out of character for him, she had never dared ask him again. And what of the nightmares he had? She was convinced these were to do with the robbery, but again he refused to discuss them.

'You mean you do not know?' Sasha stopped on the steps and turned to look at her.

Tina shook her head. 'Not really. Tell me.'

Sasha took her arm once more and began climbing the steps. 'Come.'

Finally they reached the Whispering Gallery. Tina looked down over the railings at the black-and-white-tiled floor more than ninety feet beneath her. She gripped onto the black iron railings and looked up at the domed ceiling above her. Rectangles of light shone through the panes of glass, which stood like soldiers around the edge of the dome. Above that the painted ceiling gave an illusion of continued architecture. Illusions. Lies and untruths. She was surrounded by them. Was she ever going to find out the truth about what happened that day?

'Mummy!' Dimitri's voice broke her thoughts. He was tugging

216

at her sleeve. 'Show me the whispering magic.'

'Okay. I'll sit here and you go along to the end there, as far as that doorway and then put your mouth close to the wall and whisper something to me.' Tina sat on the stone seat that curved its way around the wall of the balcony.

'I'll take you,' said Sasha. He held out his hand to Dimitri. Tina watched as father and son walked around the ledge, hand in hand. She felt her heart break yet again.

Tina placed her ear to the cold Portland stone. The little whisper from her son floated round. 'Hello, Mummy.' She smiled and placed her mouth to the wall, waiting for Dimitri, under instruction from Sasha, to rest his ear against his end of the wall.

'Hello, darling. Can you hear me?'

'Yes!' called out Dimitri, forgetting to whisper against the wall. Tina and Sasha exchanged a look and laughed. For a moment it put the broken pieces of her heart back together. She could buy into the illusion that they were just a normal family enjoying a day out. What a bittersweet moment; one that wouldn't … couldn't … be repeated again. The trick of the eye splintered into tiny fragments, dissolving into dust mites that swarmed in the light from the windows above.

Tina leaned the side of her head back against the wall, waiting for Dimitri to speak, but instead he sat on the stone seat, sliding his bottom from left to right. She closed her eyes to the sadness that was beginning to overwhelm her.

'We have a wonderful son. You have made me very proud.' The words scuttled round the wall to Tina's ear. Her eyes snapped open and she looked across at Sasha. In his eyes she saw a sadness as deep as the drop below her.

A tear sprang from nowhere and cascaded down her cheek. She put her lips to the wall and waited for Sasha to do the same with his ear.

'You have missed so much.' More tears fell, one after the other and she swallowed down a sob. 'All I ever wanted was for us to be a family, but I was robbed of that. Never at any point did I ever suspect it was you who was responsible for committing that crime against us.'

She brushed the tears away from her face and stood up. 'Let's go outside,' she called over to Dimitri. He jumped up and ran over to her. 'We have to go up this tiny spiral staircase now,' said Tina as she ducked through the opening in the wall and, despite the ache in her legs from the first flight, moved swiftly up the stone steps. She needed fresh air. Lots of it.

The breeze was stronger and colder up on the terraced area. Tina looked out at the London skyline. She could see the Millennium Bridge they had crossed earlier and, walking round towards the front of the cathedral, the London Eye came into focus.

'Can we go on the big wheel?' said Dimitri, coming to stand by her side. He peered through the balustrades.

'If we have time,' said Tina. This seemed to satisfy Dimitri and now, seemingly underwhelmed by the view of the city, he crouched down to inspect an ant scurrying around on the floor.

Sasha came and stood beside her. He spoke without looking at her. 'I was a police informer. I was being blackmailed. If I didn't co-operate, they were going to tell Porboski I was a snitch. My life, your life, would have been in danger. I had to agree.'

'Who exactly was blackmailing you?' She asked the question, although she knew the answer.

'The police. I told you.'

'No. I mean, who in the police was blackmailing you?'

'It does not matter.'

Tina made a scoffing noise. 'Well, I admire your loyalty, but I'm not really sure who you are trying to protect. If you're saving me the upset, don't bother. If you're saving him, again, don't bother. I can guess. In fact, I can more than guess. I know for a fact.' She turned to look at him. 'It was John, wasn't it?'

Sasha didn't reply, but the lack of any form of denial was the confirmation she needed. Another betrayal. It cut deep like a knife.

'I am sorry,' said Sasha.

'What happened on the day of the shooting? What went so badly wrong that it caused you to disappear from my life? Why couldn't you take me with you?'

Sasha exhaled deeply. 'It was Pavel who shot the police officer. I was there. I was party to that. I could have stayed and taken John's offer of witness protection but I panicked. Before I could think properly, Pavel was dragging me away. He shot John too.'

An invisible band tightened itself around Tina's waist, squeezing her diaphragm against her rib cage. She had seen the scar on John's shoulder. He had said it was a war wound, but hadn't gone into any detail. Something else he had refused to talk about. Now she knew why.

'You could still have sent for me. We could have started a new life together in Russia. I would have gone to the ends of the earth to be with you.' Tina looked down at Dimitri, who was now crawling along the concrete terrace, tracking the ant's progress.

'Believe me, I wanted to but, as I said, an English-speaking woman in Russia … we would have been found in no time.'

'I would have learnt to speak Russian. We could have lived in the middle of nowhere. We could have made it work.' She was clutching at straws. Scenarios that would never have worked. She knew that. Deep down, Tina knew it would have been impossible.

'I loved you, with all my heart,' said Sasha.

'I loved you too,' said Tina. 'So very much.'

Sasha pulled her into his arms. She allowed herself to sink into the folds of his jacket and, closing her eyes, gave herself permission to imagine, just for one tiny moment, that all was well in the world. Sasha held her tight.

'I wish things had been different.' He kissed the top of her head. 'But … but, they are not. I have Rozalina and Nikolay. As much as I regret what happened, how can I regret what I have now? I need you to help me, Tina. Please, say you can.'

Tina looked away at Dimitri and then back again at Sasha.

How could she refuse to help his son? Not only Sasha's son, but the half-brother of her own son.

'What do you want me to do?'

Chapter 40

John let out a sigh of relief as he exited yet another heavy spot of traffic on Queen Victoria Street. A blue light for the car would have saved him a good ten minutes, but the undercover BMW had no such luxury. A black cab tooted him as he cut right into Cannon Street. John accelerated through onto St Paul's Churchyard and, throwing the wheel right, pulled up onto the apron of the small opening that was only accessible on state occasions. Today, as most days, a heavy linked chain spanned the entrance, the pedestrians having to jump back out of the way of the vehicle.

John leaped out of his car and strode onto the grey block-paved concourse, scanning the area, looking for either Tina or Sasha. A quick look round the statue of Queen Anne that stood outside the west entrance proved pointless, so John headed towards the steps, closing in on the twelve great pillars of Portland stone that marked the entrance to the cathedral.

He was only at the top of the first flight of steps when, straight in front of him, exiting the main doors, came Tina, Dimitri and Sasha.

The Bolotnikovs spotted him at the same time. They stopped in their tracks, too, their eyes fixed on John. Sasha leaned into Tina and spoke to her. She nodded and, staying where she was, watched Sasha make his way down the top flight of steps to John.

'I knew you would come. I am sorry about the bang to your head,' he said standing in front of John.

'Apology accepted. Shame I can't return the favour.'

'I wanted to say goodbye to my son.'

John nodded and looked up towards Tina. She was holding Dimitri's hand, gazing down at them both. She looked tired and dejected, yet strong and beautiful all at the same time. All he wanted to do was to take her home, wrap her in his arms and look after her, to take her away from all this grief and heartbreak. He also knew it was impossible, for he was just as much a cause of her distress as anyone else was. If not more.

The sound of a motorbike's engine revving somewhere behind him brought John back from his thoughts. Something wasn't right.

'John.' Sasha's voice was urgent, his face one of alarm as he looked beyond John's shoulder. John looked round. The motorbike clearly wasn't just passing along in the traffic. It was here on the concourse. A rider and a pillion. The passenger was getting off the bike, his crash helmet still on, the visor down. John could tell from the cupped hand, held at the passenger's side, that he was concealing something. John had momentarily allowed himself to be distracted and had missed the warning signal by a second. And it was in that second that their advantage had been dented.

Sasha must have realised too. 'Look after Tina and Dimitri. You owe me.' With that he was half-running, half-walking away to the north side of the cathedral.

'Sasha!' John shouted, but his voice was lost amongst the tourists. He looked back at the advancing motorcyclist, then up at Tina and Dimitri. His gut contorted at the sight that met his eyes.

Tina was staring at him intently, fear transmitting from her eyes. Her bottom lip trembled and she was visibly shaking as her hand held tightly onto Dimitri's. Behind her stood another leather-clad motorcyclist. This time an open-faced crash helmet, but with a bandana pulled up over his nose, covering all but his eyes. His hand was at Dimitri's neck, John couldn't be sure, but he thought a knife lay behind the leather gloved fingers.

John's blood ran ice-cold. He couldn't risk chasing Sasha and there was no way he could attempt to get anywhere near the guy to try and disarm him. It was too risky.

Where the fuck was Martin?

The pillion passenger was now at John's side.

'You chose well,' he said in a heavy Russian accent. 'You will do well to remain where you are for a little longer.'

John had no choice. He toyed with the idea of reaching for his gun, but dismissed it almost instantly. He couldn't fire it through the crowds of people. He wouldn't be able to fire it at the man standing behind Dimitri, not with the split-second advantage he would have to aim and be sure of hitting his target and no one else. No, the knife would be in Dimitri before he could even take aim. He looked back at the motorcyclist, who had now turned the bike to face the way he had come, the engine silent.

John's only hope was Martin. The reality was he had no hope, not unless Martin suddenly materialised out of nowhere at that exact moment. He looked up at Tina, held her gaze and although he knew she couldn't hear him, he said the words out loud to reassure her.

'Stay calm. You're doing great.'

It felt like he had been standing there for an eternity, when in fact he knew it was only a matter of minutes. The starting of the motorbike engine behind him caught his attention. The pillion passenger jumped on the back and the bike sped off across the paved courtyard and into the London traffic, heading towards New Bridge Street.

John span round and looked up at Tina. She was crouched down, cuddling Dimitri in her arms. No sign of the other motorcyclist. John took the steps two at a time, skidding to a halt in front of Tina and her son.

'You okay? Promise? Just stay here. Don't move. Martin will be along soon.'

223

John raced down and across the steps of the cathedral and round the north side where Sasha had gone. He ran through the gates and into St Paul's churchyard itself.

There, sitting on the bench was Sasha. John slowed to catch his breath. Relief that he had found Sasha, though, was quickly replaced by an unnerving sensation that something wasn't right. Sasha didn't move.

John crouched down in front of Sasha. The Russian raised his eyes but not his head. His hand was round the handle of a blade, which protruded from his chest. He went to speak but it was a gurgle of air bubbling in blood. John could hear a sucking noise coming from the wound; a sure sign that the blade had punctured the lung.

John grabbed his mobile and called for an ambulance.

'Lean back against the bench, Sasha,' said John, leaving his phone on the bench, the operator still on the end of the line. John ripped off his jacket and padded it around the blade. He knew any attempt to remove it could prove fatal, if it wasn't already.

A couple of passing pedestrians had stopped. One woman screamed. A man came over to offer his help. Suddenly, in a matter of seconds, a crowd had gathered around them.

Despite John's instructions to stay put, Tina found herself running after him, Dimitri running along by her side, hand in hand.

She had felt frightened and vulnerable up on the steps – she needed to be with John. She needed to know that Sasha was safe.

As she clattered across the flagstone and into St Paul's churchyard, she saw a crowd gathered around one of the benches. Her heart flipped and her legs suddenly felt heavy. Through a gap she could see John leaning over someone. She knew it was Sasha.

Pushing through, the sight that confronted her made her gasp. She pulled Dimitri to her, trying to shield his eyes. John was holding what looked like his jacket to Sasha's chest, his fingers coated red with blood. Sasha looked pale, colour drained from his face.

'Oh, my God!' she gasped. She dropped to the bench beside Sasha, putting her arm around his shoulders. 'Do something, John, please.'

She was aware of another woman leading Dimitri to one side. She could hear the woman chatting to her son, obviously distracting him and for that Tina was grateful.

'The ambulance will be here any minute,' said John.

Tina looked at Sasha, his lips were beginning to take on a blue tint, his breathing was more like a gurgle and the blood was already soaking through the makeshift dressing John's jacket had provided. Sasha's eyes rolled, his head flopped forwards.

'Sasha! Sasha! Open your eyes!' Tina tapped his face with her fingers. It seemed to have the desired effect. Sasha's head came up and he tried to focus his eyes on Tina.

'Look … after … boys,' rasped Sasha.

'Don't try to speak,' said John.

'Promise … me,' said Sasha.

Tina nodded. Her eyes filled with tears once more. 'I promise, Sasha. I promise I will. Both of them. Dimitri and Nikolay.'

Sasha moved his hand to his jacket pocket. Even such a small action seemed exhausting for him. Strength, like blood, was seeping from him.

Tina looked down. His finger pointed to his pocket. Tina delved into the pocket, pulling out a stuffed toy; Billy the Bear. The toy that had gone missing from Dimitri's room, the toy Sasha had bought for his unborn child; Sasha's only connection to the son he was never able to know.

A tear seeped from the corner of Sasha's eye. Tina began to cry too. Not big dramatic sobs, but gentle heart-breaking tears. They had said they loved one another back in the cathedral, but both knew that was in another time and place. Not in a cold London church yard with blood blooming red across a white shirt, colour draining from their faces, one as death beckoned and the other as heartbreak approached for a second time. She was losing Sasha all over again, this time there would be no return.

Chapter 41

The ride back to Sussex in John's BMW was heavy with silence. Tina was sitting in the back with Dimitri as John drove them. Neither said anything. Tina wasn't sure she could. She couldn't quite believe what had happened. She wasn't supposed to have her son's life threatened and to see her husband die from a knife wound. Things like this didn't happen to normal, everyday people like her.

Thankfully, Dimitri didn't seem to be badly affected by it. He had asked if the man they had met was going to be okay and Tina had to gently explain that the doctors hadn't been able to help him and that he had gone to heaven. Dimitri had nodded and then switched subjects, asking if Tina could read his pirate story as it was his favourite bedtime book. She had gladly obliged, hoping it would distract her, if only for a few minutes.

Tina had stayed with Dimitri until he had drifted off to sleep. She stroked his head, moving small strands of hair from his eyes. Tonight he looked even more like his father.

His father? She couldn't really call Sasha his father. The hour at St Paul's Cathedral today didn't qualify Sasha to fulfil that definition. In fact, John had spent more time with Dimitri doing fatherly things. John was so natural with Dimitri, there seemed a genuine bond between boy and man, but she couldn't help wonder how much of that was real and how much was for his job. The notion that John had betrayed her son, an innocent child, made her stomach clench.

Having now put Dimitri to bed, Tina came downstairs. John was sitting in the living room, Rascal was stretched out on the sofa next to him, thoroughly enjoying the belly-rub John was administering.

'He's gone straight to sleep,' said Tina. She sat down in the armchair.

'That's good,' said John. He stopped stroking Rascal and sat forward on the sofa. 'How are you?'

'Honest answer? I don't really know.' Tina rubbed her face with both hands. 'I feel I should be some sort of physical and emotional wreck, but I don't actually feel anything. I'm not sure that's a good way to be.'

'You're probably in a bit of shock.'

'What was your real reason for getting involved with me?' Tina watched John's reaction. Clearly taken aback and caught off-guard, he did well to compose himself almost immediately.

'When I first came here, it was with the sole purpose of finding out what you knew.'

'Thank you for being honest.' His words, though soft and gentle, may just as well have been a blade slicing through her skin. An image of Sasha slumped in St Paul's skittered before her. She shook her head to dispel the thought.

'But ...' John looked at her. 'But, within a short space of time, another reason was jostling for my attention. You, yourself. I came here purely to get information, but I became involved not so much because I wanted to, but because I couldn't help it.'

If his previous answer had caused a wound, then this answer provided the bandage. But still the injury was painful.

'You were blackmailing Sasha. You threatened to tell me about him. You threatened to tell the Porboski gang about him. You caused all this. You brought all this on my family. Because of you, Dimitri grew up without a father. I thought I was a widow. You

228

were responsible.'

'You're wrong, Tina. Very wrong.' John's words were said with force. She looked at him, waiting for him to continue. 'Sasha is responsible for part of this.'

'You forced him into an untenable position. He had no choice but to comply.'

'I never forced him to launder that money. I never forced him to agree to be a look out for the robbery. I never …'

'Carry on, you never what?' Tina jumped to her feet. 'Tell what you never did. What happened that night?'

'Just leave it.'

'No, I won't leave it. Why can't you tell me the truth? Why don't you practise what you preach for once?' The anger swelled inside her. She was on the verge of losing control. Rascal must have sensed this too as he sprung to his feet with an angry meow, jumped to the floor and trotted out of the room.

'Tina, please. Sit down. I don't want to argue.' John remained seated.

Tina walked over to the window, trying to regain control. The sun-catcher of the boat hung from the sash window. It looked dull, without any light streaming in from behind in. She ran her finger around the edge and traced over the sparkly gems glued onto the blue sea glass. A present from Sasha on their honeymoon in the Lake District.

She felt the anger subside and a deep sadness take over.

'There are certain things I can't tell you. It would compromise my position.'

'That sounds like an excuse to me.' She turned to look at him once more. 'I know there's something you're not telling me. Is it to do with your nightmares?' There, she had said it – a question that had burned within her. She studied his face for a reaction. He dropped his eyes before looking back at her.

'I saw one of my best friends shot. I tried to stem the blood flow, but it was impossible. I had been shot too. My phone stamped on.

I couldn't even call for an ambulance. I had to leave him while I ran to get help. I had to make a split decision. I knew if I released the pressure to his wound, he would just bleed out. I also knew that staying, applying what pressure I could with my one good hand, was only a short-term solution.'

Tina dropped to her knees in front of John, resting her hands on his. 'You were in a Catch Twenty-Two position. You couldn't win. It wasn't your fault.'

John took his hands away and rubbed his eyes. 'It haunts me. It's always there, like some demon on my shoulder.'

'Is there anything else?'

'What did Sasha want to meet you for?' The change in direction threw her. John was back to his controlled business-like self. She stood up, returning to her position by the window.

'To say goodbye … and to see Dimitri.' She comforted herself with the thought that this was the truth, if only part of it.

'And?'

'And nothing.' Rascal returned to the room and rubbed his arched back against her leg. She bent down and scooped the cat up. 'Hello, boy.' She nuzzled her face into his fur. 'Do you want feeding? Come on, then.'

Avoiding any form of eye contact with John, Tina left the room for the kitchen. She wasn't surprised when John followed.

'Did Sasha mention Pavel at all?' said John leaning against the doorframe.

'No.' Tina kept her back to him. It was easier to lie if she didn't look at him. She rummaged around in the cupboard seeking out a tin of cat food.

'What about the money?'

Tina felt her body stiffen. She hoped it had escaped John's notice. 'I don't know anything about that.' She took a tin from the shelf and peeled back the lid.

'I thought he might ask you to get it for him, seeing as that's what he was here for. I figured if he could get it himself he would

230

have done. For whatever reasons, he needed you to help him.'

Tina forked the meaty jelly into the cat bowl. Her hand was shaking as she placed the bowl onto the floor. She watched Rascal sniff at the offering before crouching down to eat. She had to word her next sentence carefully. 'I didn't think the police would still be bothered about it.'

'It's all part of the case and, besides, it does actually belong to someone. If we ignored it, we wouldn't be doing our job properly.'

Tina rinsed the fork under the tap. 'What about if someone found it?'

'If they didn't hand it in, then they would be in trouble for potential money-laundering, handling stolen money.' John pushed himself off the doorframe and walked over to the breakfast bar. He rested his forearms on the shiny, black surface. 'Aiding and abetting, even.'

Tina placed the fork in the dishwasher and faced him across the worktop. 'So you can't just forget about it?'

'Turn a blind eye, you mean?' He paused and when he spoke again, his voice was soft. 'No, I can't.'

'I understand.' She studied John's face. He didn't believe her, she was sure. How she hated lying to him. She was painfully aware that she was doing exactly what she had hated John doing to her. But she had promised Sasha she would help Nikolay. Sasha had given his life trying to help his son. She couldn't let either of them down.

'What happens to Sasha's body now?' she asked.

'I wanted to speak to you about that. Repatriation could prove difficult as, legally, a valid passport is needed to send the body home. Sasha, of course, hadn't come into the country under his own name. He came in on a false passport.'

'What's the alternative?' she asked.

'He could be cremated here in the UK and the casket sent out to Russia. Technically, you are next of kin, it's up to you,' said John. 'You've got a few days to decide while we gather the coroner's report and death certificate.'

231

'Okay, thank you. What do you think has happened to Pavel?' she asked.

'We don't know. We've had a report that he's already left the country,' said John. 'We're waiting for confirmation.'

'Will I be safe?'

'We've put the word out that we've got the money. The Russians won't bother with you any more. The money was the draw for everyone, Sasha, Pavel and the Russians. If they all think it's out of play, there's no reason for them to come for you. I'll hang around for a few more days, just to make sure.'

Tina nodded. She wanted to ask what would happen next between them, but she had something to do before then. She had unfinished business. A promise to fulfil.

Chapter 42

The trains were running to schedule as Tina arrived at Brighton station. She was in good time for her appointment. She double-checked her directions and headed down the hill towards the city centre. It was a beautiful morning; she could smell the salty sea air and feel the coastal breeze tickling her neck. Her heart tugged as she thought of the last time she was here and what had brought her here today.

She hadn't known she would be coming here so soon after the events at St Paul's, but two days on and John had explained he had to go up to London, something to do with the two Russians and their initial court hearings. It had only given her a few hours' notice, but that had been all she needed to make arrangements.

The small private bank was innocuous from the outside. In fact, it looked more like an office building than a financial institution. Tina checked the plaque on the wall and pressed the small brass buzzer next to it. A tiny click alerted her to the automatic door lock being lifted. She pushed against the white, panelled door and stepped into a small reception area, where a member of staff greeted her, asking her to take a seat.

Within a few minutes, the lift doors on the other side of the reception area opened and a tall suited gentleman exited.

'Hello, Mrs Bolotnikov,' he said, extending a hand to her. 'I'm

Mr Thomas. Branch Manager.'

Tina shook hands. She was surprised that the branch manager himself should greet her. Sasha must have been a valued customer. It sat uncomfortably with her. 'Highly valued' in the banking world usually meant high net worth. In Sasha's case, this meant laundered money. She shrugged the thought away, replacing it with that of Nikolay. She was doing this for a young boy who needed lifesaving treatment, which could only be paid for by this means. It eased her conscience. Just.

Tina followed Mr Thomas into a small interview room situated on the other side of the lift doors.

'I do need to go through some security checks, if that's all right with you, Mrs Bolotnikov?'

'Of course.' She wouldn't have expected anything else. Sasha had told her it would be very straightforward, there were no trick questions or answers. She would know all the right responses, for they were the truth. The only thing she needed to remember was the password.

She handed over her passport as photographic identification. Mr Thomas tapped away at the touch-screen computer in front of him, recording her passport number.

'Can you confirm you mother's maiden name, please?'

'Morris.'

'Mr Bolotnikov's date of birth and full name?'

Tina answered the questions duly, each time Mr Thomas nodding and tapping at the screen.

'Finally, can you confirm password one?'

'Windermere.'

'And password two?'

'Pier. As in Brighton Pier.'

'Thank you.' Mr Thomas looked up from the monitor. 'I'm pleased to say that you've passed all the security checks. Everything is in order. Can I take this opportunity to offer you my condolences? It is with sadness that we meet. Your late husband made provisions that you would only come here to collect the safe-deposit contents in the event of his death. I was, of course, hoping this meeting would never take place.'

'Thank you,' said Tina.

'I trust you have the key with you,' said Mr Thomas. 'We only issued the one key.'

'Yes, I have it right here.' Tina took the silver key from her purse. The key to Sasha's heart. God, had she been so naïve to believe all his lies? She hated that she now had such conflicting feelings about him. Before he came back she only ever had love and respect for him. Now her emotions swung back and forth like a pendulum.

Tina followed Mr Thomas through a series of corridors, CCTV tracking their every step. Finally, they reached the vaulted strong room. A security guard was there to meet them. Tina was escorted into a room about the size of an average bedroom. Three walls were lined with drawers of varying sizes; smaller letter-sized drawers to her left, gradually increasing in size until the ones on her right were the size of a small suitcase. A table and two chairs occupied the middle of the room.

Mr Thomas pointed out drawer number eighty-six. 'That's yours there, Mrs Bolotnikov. We will leave you in private now. If you need anything, please ring the bell here.' He pointed to a doorbell on the wall next to the door. 'Likewise, when you've finished, ring it and we will let you out.'

Tina waited for the two gentlemen to leave and closed the door behind them. She ignored the claustrophobic sensation of being shut into a small space with her only way out dependent on someone else opening the door.

She put her bag on the table and approached box eighty-six. Turning the key, the door opened with ease. Tina's hands shook as she reach in and pulled out a cardboard shoebox. Men's shoes. Size 10. Sasha's size. A picture of a pair of desert boots was printed on the end of the box. She remembered the boots well. He had worn them a lot.

The box felt heavier than she had expected. Holding it with two hands, she gave it a small shake, but there was no sound or feeling of movement.

Tina placed the box on the table. The lid had been taped down and, using the edge of the key, she sliced around the lip of the box. She wiggled the lid free. She knew there was going to be cash in the box, Sasha had told her so.

Pink and purple bundles of notes filled the box, an elastic band keeping each one neatly in place. She ran her fingers across the money, pushing thoughts of its origin from her mind. She focused on the picture she had seen of Nikolay. A small innocent boy. If this money could be used to save his life then neither Sasha nor the police officer would have died pointlessly. She had to make something good come out of something bad.

Tina began taking the bundles of notes from the box, transferring them in to the rucksack she had brought with her. She didn't count the money, but estimated each bundle contained around five thousand pounds. She would wait until she got home to count it properly and check it matched Sasha's figure. There was no CCTV in the room, for which she was grateful. She didn't want to imagine what she must look like as she stuffed bundle after bundle into her bag.

As she cleared the last layer of money from the shoebox, she noticed a postcard sitting in the bottom. A scene of a small sailboat bobbing on a lake surrounded by countryside. She didn't need to read the back to know where the picture had been taken.

Lake Windermere. She and Sasha had honeymooned in the Lake District. They had had their first lunch as Mr and Mrs Bolotnikov at a restaurant overlooking the lake. Her hand shook as she reached in to pick it up. Sasha had left this for her. She turned it over. The black biro words had been penned by Sasha.

And the sun's rays reflected back from the water like gems of tears.

She read it again. It made no sense. Maybe something had got lost in translation? She went to put the card into the rucksack, but changed her mind and placed it in her handbag instead. She would look at it when she had more time.

Five minutes later she pressed the internal buzzer to signal she was ready to leave. All she had to do now was to deposit the cash into the Swiss bank account of the clinic, where, Sasha assured her, they would ask no questions whatsoever. He had specifically told her not to do a bank-to-bank transfer. He didn't want a paper trail. Once the money hit the account, the clinic would contact Rozalina direct and organise everything from their end. She was relieved she wouldn't have to have any direct dealings with Rozalina herself. Tina wasn't sure either wife would be able to cope with that, especially now Sasha had died.

Stepping out onto the pavement, Tina breathed a sigh of relief. She adjusted the strap of the rucksack to a more comfortable position on her shoulders. The sun had managed to shake off the clouds and the rays momentarily blinded her. She fished in her handbag for her sunglasses.

As she put them on a hand caught hold of her arm. Fingers gripped around her elbow.

'Hello, Tina.'

Chapter 43

Tina felt sick to the pit of her stomach. She thought she had been so careful. She was sure she hadn't been followed and, yet, here he was, right by her side. She attempted to shrug John's hand from her arm, but he wasn't letting go.

'I could just scream and cause a scene,' she said, not breaking her stride.

'Then I would just have to arrest you officially,' said John, keeping step with her. 'You could make it a whole lot easier by simply getting into the car.'

'No thanks. I'd rather walk.'

'You won't mind if I walk with you, then.'

'As a matter of fact, I would mind. A lot.' Tina continued striding down Queen's Street. The seafront was directly ahead and she knew anytime now the pier would come into sight. An overwhelming feeling of despair flooded her, drowning her hopes. Tears filled her eyes. She had got so close. She was going to fail. She couldn't quite give up yet. She stopped walking and turned to face him. 'Please, John. Don't do this.'

'I'm sorry.' He looked genuinely upset. 'If there was any other way …'

'There is. You can let me go. Pretend you missed me.'

John shook his head. 'I can't do that.' His voice was tender yet firm. He lifted his hand to her face and wiped away an errant tear from her cheek.

She tried once more. 'Please? I'm begging you. Look the other way, just for a few seconds.'

'Tina. Don't do this.'

'No! You don't do this.' She reined in a shout, aware they were drawing attention to themselves. She went to move, to test his resolve. He gripped her with both hands.

'It's blood money, Tina. It has Neil's blood on it and now it has Sasha's blood on it. I can't let it go. Or you.'

For a moment she wondered what those last words meant. She didn't have time to consider them fully. 'The money, it's not for me or for the Porboski gang. It's for Sasha's son. He needs medical treatment. Urgently.'

'I know. I do know that,' said John. 'It doesn't make any difference.'

'You're a cold-hearted bastard, John Nightingale.' Tina wanted to slap him. How could he be so indifferent? 'Your job really does come before everything else, doesn't it? Even the life of a child.' John said nothing. His silence enraged her all the more. She grappled the rucksack from her back and shoved it into his chest. 'Here. Have it. You can now add Nikolay's blood to the list.'

It had been a week now since John had followed Tina to Brighton. He had guessed she had a plan to collect the money. She had a motive. She was determined. It was so easy to read her.

He wished now, more than ever before, that his job hadn't once again intruded into her personal life. He had already lost his wife to the job. Divorce in his line of work was almost a foregone conclusion. Now it seemed it was killing any chance he had with Tina.

'You still pissed off?' Martin's voice came across the desk.

'Mind your own business,' he said. John picked up a file and pretended to study it, although none of the words were actually registering.

'Why don't you simply go and see her?' said Martin. 'She might have calmed down by now.'

'As I said, mind you own.'

'Have it your own way,' said Martin, hooking his feet up onto the desk as he sank back into his chair. 'I suppose that means you would rather I went and saw the lovely Mrs B to find out what she wanted to do with the body?'

John shot his partner a look. 'What's that?'

Martin sat up again, a big grin spread across his face. 'Aha, that got your attention, didn't it?' He picked up a piece of paper and passed it over the desk to John. 'Coroner's report all done. The body can be released for burial, cremation or repatriation. That is if she wants to ship it off to Russia. If she does, she needs to get the undertakers to embalm it and issue a certificate.'

'Yeah, all right, spare me the detail. I know the score.' John felt irritated. Martin had certainly hit a nerve. 'I'll go and see her myself.'

'Thought you might,' said Martin, who made no attempt to hide the smug look on his face.

Adam came out from Brogan's office and called over to John.

'Boss wants to see you two.'

John exchanged a look with Martin, who shrugged. 'Don't ask me.'

'Better go and see what's up, then,' said John leading the way.

Brogan was sitting at his desk, paperwork spread in front of him. John noticed a picture of Pavel Bolotnikov on a report sheet.

'You wanted to see us, Sir.'

'Yes, come in. Sit down.' Brogan waited while the two officers seated themselves on the opposite side of the desk. 'Need to close this Porboski case as soon as. We haven't got much time. If we're going to do anything, we need to do it now.'

'Sir?' said John. He felt his blood pump a little faster around his body. This was what he had been waiting for. He had put his proposal to his superior the day before. Now it looked like it was going to be given the go-ahead.

'How's your Russian?' said Brogan.

John resisted the urge to pump his fist in the air and shout 'Yes!' Instead he replied with the calm voice of the professional he was. 'Good enough.'

'Mummy! There's someone at the door.'

Tina heard Dimitri call up the stairs to her. She had just got in from work and was changing out of her uniform. 'Okay. I'm coming down.' She pulled on her jeans and hurried out onto the landing, fastening them as she went.

'Mummy, it's John!' The delight in her son's voice was apparent. 'I saw him out of the window.' She heard the chain on the door being slid out of position and jangle as it swung free.

'Don't open the door!' she called down the stairs. John was here. Her heart bobbed like a yoyo to her stomach, then to her throat and back into place. She hadn't heard from him all week and, although she was still angry and hurt, she couldn't deny that she had missed him too.

She hurried down the stairs, reaching the half landing as she heard the door open and Dimitri shouting in delight at their visitor.

'Hey there, little man,' said John. 'How are you?'

Tina reached the bottom of the stairs and held onto the door. Seeing John standing on the doorstep, ruffling her son's head, who had gripped John's waist in a hug, was almost too much to bear.

'Hello, John,' she said. Suddenly she felt shy and unsure. His face was giving nothing away. In fact, he was looking very business-like. 'Is this an official visit?'

'Yes.'

'You'd better come in.' Tina prized Dimitri away. 'Come on, let John in.'

'Can we play football in the garden?' said Dimitri. 'Have you caught any bad men?'

John gave a laugh. 'I'm a bit tired today, I don't think I'll be able to play football, I've been catching too many bad men and I'm all worn out.'

'Hmm.' Dimitri folded his arm, sticking out his bottom lip.

'Leave John alone for a moment,' said Tina. 'He's just finished work and needs to talk to Mummy. Go back and watch the TV for a little while.'

'I'll see you before I go,' said John. 'Be a good lad for your mum.'

Reluctantly Dimitri scuffed his way back to the living room.

Tina took John into the kitchen, using the few seconds to try and get a grip on her feelings. John had said he was here on official business, not pleasure. He obviously didn't care about her as much as she thought he had. She had hoped to hear from him sooner to say he had changed his mind about the money or that he wasn't handing all of it in. She had so wanted him to do something to quash the opinion he had forced her to make about him last week. What she wouldn't give for him not to be the cold-hearted bastard who had taken away the only hope of a sick child.

'How have you been?' said John.

'It doesn't really matter does it? What was it you wanted to speak to me about?' She wasn't going to let him think that everything was okay between them. That would be far too convenient for him.

'It matters to me.'

She swallowed hard, straightening up. She did wonder who she was trying to kid more with her act of indifference. 'Well, it shouldn't. Can we get to the point?'

'The coroner's report has been completed, which means, as Sasha's next of kin, you get to decide what to do with the body.'

'I have actually thought about this.' Tina paused to maintain her composure. 'Sasha wasn't my husband. He hadn't been for a long time. My husband died five years ago. He needs to go back to Russia so his family, his mother, his wife can all grieve for him. They can bury him and have a grave to go to. It's how it should be.'

She heard the wobble in her voice. It had been a hard decision, but she knew it was the right one.

'Would you like us to arrange that for you? Only, without a passport it's not so straightforward. We can liaise with the Russian embassy and make all the necessary arrangements.'

'Thank you. I'd appreciate that. As I'm sure the Bolotnikovs will.' Tina drew a deep breath. 'Does Rozalina know about me?'

'She will need to be informed.'

'I thought about asking you not to tell her, but then I decided she should know. Not because I want to even the score and upset her or get some sort of revenge kick from it, but because her son, Nikolay, has a half-brother. They should know about each other.'

John nodded. 'I understand. For what it's worth, I agree with you.' John took a small brown envelope from his pocket. 'I thought you might like to keep this. To show Dimitri one day.'

Tina took the envelope and, looking inside, slipped out a small photograph. It was of Nikolay. It was the one Sasha had kept in his wallet.

'Thank you. I can't bear the thought that this is the only picture Dimitri will have.'

'There's every chance there will be more.'

'How is there?' The spark of anger ignited itself once more. 'You saw to that.'

'I'm trying to convince my bosses to honour the deal, even though Sasha's dead.'

'What?'

'I'm putting as much pressure as I can on my boss to arrange for Sasha's son to be treated in Switzerland.'

'You are?' She could barely believe it. She watched John nod. 'When will you know?'

'I'm not sure. In the next week or two, I hope.'

Tears blurred her vision and she blinked hard to stop them falling. 'Thank you.'

'See, I'm not such a cold-hearted bastard,' said John.

She had misjudged him and, for once, she was glad she had got it wrong. 'I'm sorry. I shouldn't have said that.'

'Don't worry. I've been called worse.' John shifted on his feet.

'Would you like a cup of coffee?' Tina was relieved. The olive branch had been accepted.

'Can I ask you something?' said John as he sat down at the table.

'Depends what it is,' said Tina. The disquiet that had receded over the past week was back, small ripples of anxiety reaching out to her, lapping at her heels.

'Why did Sasha put the money in the safe deposit? He went to a lot of trouble, laying the way. He gave you that key a long time before he had to disappear. He must have been planning something.'

'I don't know all the details, he briefly told me at St Paul's that day. The money in the safe deposit, he had been gradually laundering it through the business. It wasn't his money. It was the Porboski money and it was coming to him via Pavel. Sasha didn't know this at first and by the time he did, it was too late. He was already implicated. Pavel never told him the truth.'

'And he couldn't exactly report his brother, I suppose,' said John.

'No, he couldn't. If he did, then Pavel would be in danger as Sasha would himself. Pavel made it clear to him that the danger would extend to me as well.'

'Nice brother.'

'You could say that,' said Tina. 'Sasha was a man who got dragged into all of this by his brother. It wasn't until he had been in Russia a few days that Pavel told him Neil had died. Up until then Sasha always thought there was a way back.' Tina could feel the tears building up again. She looked at John. He had gone quite pale.

He stood up and made for the back door. 'Need some fresh air,' he muttered as he grappled with the door handle.

Chapter 44

John almost tripped over the threshold as he staggered into the back garden. He tried desperately to ignore the memories of the fateful day.

'John!' It was Neil's voice. *The security fencing rattled as Neil shook it, trapped on the outside of the building site. 'Oi! Armed police!'*

Sasha paused and turned his head to look towards where the voice was coming from. John felt a slight relax in Sasha's hold and seized the moment. With a two-handed shove, he threw the Russian to the ground.

'There's a gap just down there!' *shouted John, pointing towards the far end of the fencing.*

Neil ran the twenty metres or so to the opening, his gun drawn and aimed at Sasha. John pulled Sasha to his feet by the scruff of his jacket collar.

'You've got exactly five seconds to make your mind up, or I'm throwing you to the lions and that goes for your wife and baby too.'

The first shot rang out and screamed past John's ear. What the hell was Neil playing at shooting at him? In the next second he realised that it couldn't have been Neil who fired, the shot had come from the other direction. His pushed Sasha to the ground and simultaneously threw himself into the dust, drawing his gun at the same time.

The third shot came from Neil's gun; the bullet whistling above

245

John, missing its target on the other side.

The fourth shot made contact. John yelled in pain as a searing heat bore into the flesh of his shoulder. He dropped his gun as he writhed in pain. It was only for a second or two but it was long enough.

Neil shouted his name, distracted momentarily. It was all the distraction needed. Pavel Bolotnikov stepped out from behind a concrete pillar and aimed his gun straight at Neil. The semi-automatic pistol sent three rounds to its intended target.

John shook his head, he gasped for breath, throwing his head up to the sky above him. The red blood seemed to stain his vision, everything around him looked crimson.

'John! John. It's okay. Whatever it is, it's okay. I'm here.'

He could hear Tina's voice to his left. He turned his head towards her. Her face blurred in front of him. He forced himself to fix on her eyes and listen to her soothing voice of reassurance. Gradually, the distortion faded, the red paled to pink and then washed away to white. It took a supreme effort of concentration on his part, but finally the world around him came back.

He rested his hands on his knees, dipping his head. He felt Tina's hand on his back, firm yet gentle, small circular movements of reassurance.

'I'm okay,' he said, straightening himself up. 'Really, I'm fine now.' The look on her face told him she probably didn't believe him.

'Let's sit here,' she said, guiding him towards the garden bench. 'What happened that day, John? What is it that tortures you so much?'

John sat down on the bench. His automatic reaction, one honed by years of practice, was to brush the incident off. To put it down to feeling unwell or a hangover or having eaten something that didn't agree with him. He had told the lie so many times, for so long, he almost believed it himself. It was far easier than having to face up to the real cause.

Something today stopped him. He realised that he had to tell the truth sooner or later. Tina deserved to know what happened that day. She needed to know for her own peace of mind, so that there were no longer any unanswered questions stopping her from moving on. She also needed to know so that she knew everything about him. If he didn't confess, then there would always be a secret between them.

It was a gamble, an ember of hope. She might never want to see him again, but he knew they had no future while there was a secret between them.

She looked expectantly at him. Pale-blue eyes rested on him. Her face, as always, so easy to read, so open; no shutters hiding her thoughts and feelings.

She listened as he relayed the events of that day to her. Patiently she sat next to him. Her hand a constant reassuring touch, moving from his back and to his head. He felt her body wince as he came to the part where he had chased and cornered Sasha. There was a deep sigh of sadness as he recounted the scuffle. A shake of the head, despair and resignation filtering across her face, emphasised by a dull pain in her eyes. And finally, a sharp intake of breath at Pavel firing the gun. Then her whole body stiffened as she learned of Pavel and Sasha taking flight.

'I'm sorry,' said John. 'Truly, I am.'

She gripped his hand harder. 'What are you sorry for? You were doing your job. I understand that. I may not like what you have to do or how you have to do it, but I do understand it comes with the territory.'

'If I hadn't pushed Sasha into becoming an informer, then he and I would never have been at that building site having that conversation. Neil would never have been there and Pavel wouldn't have been either. You were right when you said I put Sasha in an untenable position.'

'But you were also right when you said that ultimately, Sasha was responsible. He made the wrong choice at the very outset. I can see that now. I was wrong blaming you.'

'You're a very understanding woman, do you know that?' Not for the first time, the breadth of her compassion and understanding, amazed him. 'If I can bring Pavel in and charge him for murder, then I can at least have some sort of closure. I can give his wife some feeling of justice.'

'Is it justice or forgiveness you're looking for?'

God, she was perceptive.

'Truthfully? Both.' He paused before he spoke again. 'From Neil's wife … and …' He couldn't finish the sentence. It was too much to ask. She didn't deserve to be put on the spot like that.

'And from me.' A statement, not a question.

He gave a small nod, forcing himself to look her in the eyes. He needed to see what she was really thinking, what she was feeling. Her look could say so much more than her words. He saw his answer before he heard it.

'I forgive you. I really do.' She held him and he felt like a child. He clung to her, a sob escaping his throat. 'I understand the reasons behind the … the deceit. And I'm trying really hard, so very hard, to accept it. But, I do forgive you, John.'

At the sound of the back door opening and Dimitri's voice calling out to his mother, John and Tina pulled apart. John drew his forefinger and thumb together under his eyes to remove any trace of tears.

Dimitri stood in front of them. He cocked his head sideways looking at John.

'Your eyes are all red,' he said.

'Hay fever,' said John, then stopped. 'Actually, that's not quite true. I was feeling a bit sad, but I'm okay now.'

'Were you crying?'

John exchanged a look with Tina, a small smile of compassion rested on her mouth. John turned his attention back to Dimitri. 'Yes, I was. Only a little, but your Mummy made me feel better.' He forced a smile of reassurance.

'Mummy gave me a plaster when I was sad and hurt myself.'

'I needed a hug.'

'Okay.' Dimitri seemed satisfied. 'Can we play football now?'

'Yeah, sure.' John smiled at the boy. He was glad he had been honest with him. Kids could be very accepting, this one, clearly, inheriting the trait from his mother. 'There is one thing I wanted to say, while we are all here.' He put a hand out to draw Dimitri further into them. The five-year-old sat himself on John's knee. 'I have to go away for a couple of weeks. It's to do with work, but when I get back, I'd like to come and see you both again. If that's okay?'

'Work? A couple of weeks?' Tina said, a look of alarm crossed her face. 'A new case?'

John sighed. He wanted to be honest with her, but this was work and at this stage he couldn't. He looked apologetically at Tina.

'Sorry, I shouldn't have asked.' She waved her hand as if clearing the air of the question hanging between them.

Dimitri jumped up. 'Let's play football!' He ran across the grass to the shed. 'I'll get the ball. You be in goal, John.'

'Go on, John. Get in goal,' said Tina, a smile tipped the corners of her mouth. 'Do as you're told.'

John jogged across the grass to where Dimitri was now waiting with the blue plastic football. His steps may have been light, but his heart was heavy. She hadn't answered his question. Perhaps he had misjudged it all?

Chapter 45

Tina stood at the kitchen window watching John and Dimitri play football. The look of pleasure on her son's face warmed her heart. The two of them looked so happy and natural together, it was a mutual friendship. Having a male role model was good for Dimitri. She acknowledged that John wasn't perfect, but then she wasn't naïve enough to believe that there was such thing as perfect. She might have done once upon a time, but not any more. Perfect was overrated. Good, happy, content were worth just as much; they were honest. Perfect wasn't.

She thought of Rozalina and Nikolay and wondered what the future held for them. Relying on John's boss organising the money wasn't ideal but it was the only option. She picked up the photograph John had given her of Nikolay and took it into the living room. She wanted to keep it safe. One day she would show it to Dimitri and explain about his half-brother.

Tina opened the back of the photo frame with a picture of her and Sasha and tucked Nikolay behind them. A symbolic gesture of merging the two lives of Sasha, she decided. She went to put the frame back on the mantelpiece, but hesitated. Instead she placed it on the bookcase in the fireplace recess. No longer the focal point of her life. Another symbolic gesture.

As she turned away, the sun emerged from behind a cloud. It

streamed in through the window and the sun-catcher, spreading a shimmering sea of colours across the room. Sparkles of silver bounced off the mirror above the fireplace. The words Sasha had written on the postcard of Windermere came back to her.

And the sun's rays reflected back from the water like gems of tears.

'You look miles away.'

She turned at John's voice and smiled at him. 'Do I? Mind wandering, that's all.'

'Sure?'

She hesitated. So far she hadn't mentioned the second postcard, more because she had forgotten about it than a deliberate omission. She thought about leaving it that way, but immediately corrected herself. No more secrets.

'In the safe-deposit box … there was something else.'

John raised his eyebrows. 'Do I want to know about this?'

'It was a postcard.'

'Another one? Any cryptic messages this time?'

'Don't joke.' She scanned the room for her handbag, locating it on the armchair. She paused with her hand in her bag. 'Where's Dimitri?'

'He's now burying his ball in the sand pit. Apparently, I need to practise my goal-keeping skills as it makes it too easy for him.' John gave a grin. 'That will teach me to go easy on him.'

Tina laughed. 'Nothing to do with you actually being rubbish in goal, then?'

'Certainly not.'

The conversation came to a halt. Tina looked at John, his smile distracted her. He spoke first. 'Are you going to stand there all day with your hand in your bag or is there something you wanted to show me. You know, like a postcard?'

'Oh, what? Sorry. Yes, here.' She retrieved the card and handed it over to John. 'I've no idea what he means, but I was simply standing here and the light from the sun-catcher caught my eye and it reminded me of the postcard.'

John looked up at the window. 'What's the connection?'

'The card, it's of Lake Windermere. We went there on our honeymoon.' She turned to the window as well. 'We bought the sun-catcher in a little gift shop there.'

She watched John re-read the card. 'And it doesn't mean anything to you, what's written here?'

Tina shook her head. 'Nothing. Absolutely nothing.'

'Gems of tears. That's an odd expression. I don't think I've heard that before.'

'Neither have I, but sometimes words and expressions used to get a bit lost in translation with Sasha. He might have misquoted something he'd once heard or read.'

John looked thoughtful. He studied the card for a third time and then went over to the window. Tina watched him lift the sun-catcher down and inspect it thoroughly.

'It's only a cheap gift. It's not worth anything,' she said.

John seemed to spend a long time examining the glass trinket. He glanced up from under his eyelashes and raised an eyebrow.

'What?' said Tina.

John didn't reply. He held the sun-catcher up to the window, the light once more streamed through the coloured glass. He turned it over and back again, then tucking the postcard under his arm he picked with his finger at the glass stones glued to the blue glass.

'Has this ever been broken and repaired?' he asked.

Tina came to stand beside him, looking over his shoulder as he ran his finger over the glass.

'No, not that I'm aware of.'

'And nothing looks different about it to how it looked when you first bought it?'

'Not that I remember. We used to have it on the wall behind the counter at the deli. When I moved here I packed it away and forgot about it for a long time. It wasn't until I was going through some boxes about a year ago that I found it and hung it up.'

John nodded. He read from the card again. 'And the sun's rays reflected back from the water like gems of tears.' He looked at her. 'You don't get it, do you?'

'No.' She felt frustrated. 'You obviously do, but then you are the detective.'

'Gems of tears,' said John. 'What are gems?'

'Precious stones.'

'Such as …'

'Diamonds, rubies, sapphires … come on, John.'

'Tears. You cry when you are sad. Tears can look like little gemstones. I'm thinking diamonds.' He ran his finger along the glittering stones glued to the sun catcher.

Tina's hand shook as John passed it to her. 'You think these are diamonds?'

'Remember, I said that money was taken during the robbery?' He paused while Tina nodded. 'Well, initially it was thought that other items were stolen as well. Like jewellery and precious stones. However, they were never listed on the final report. The victims of the crime decided not to admit to having anything else stolen other than money. Probably because they had come by those things in a dubious manner themselves or had no proof of officially owning them.'

Tina looked up at John. 'But there were and somehow Sasha ended up with them?'

John shrugged. 'Your guess is as good as mine.'

Tina pushed the sun-catcher to John. 'You'll be wanting this to hand in too, like the money.'

John took a step back. 'I can't do that. There's no proof that that's where they came from. They weren't reported missing so, therefore, can't be returned. They belong to you.'

'They do?' Tina's mind rushed ahead. 'So, if they are technically mine, then, technically, I can do what I like with them.'

John smiled. 'Whatever you like.'

'I can sell them?'

'If that's what you want to do. And, if it helps, I know someone who would be happy to take them off your hands.'

'You do?'

'Yeah. A guy called Baz. He lives in Ireland now but he used to own a café in London.'

'And he will buy diamonds?'

'He's got contacts. I've known him a long time. In a professional capacity.'

'I think this may be one occasion where I don't really want to know the whole truth.'

'I think you may be right.'

Tina looked down at the sun-catcher. The excitement of the discovery faded and a warm feeling of realisation took its place. 'I can help Nikolay after all.'

John's phone vibrated and sounded out, the ring tone breaking the silence that had fallen between them. He pulled it from his pocket, looking at the screen.

'Sorry, I need to take this.'

Tina went down to the kitchen to give him some privacy and to check on Dimitri.

His dark head was bent as he knelt in the sandpit, happily pushing a plastic seaside spade into the sand, withdrawing a scoop and letting the yellow grains cascade over the football.

She turned as John came in to the kitchen.

'Look, I need to get off. Work,' he said. He went out into the garden and again Tina looked on from the window. She watched John crouch down next to Dimitri. They appeared to be chatting, before John ruffled her son's hair and made his way back into the kitchen. 'Let me know if you want me to arrange someone to look at those diamonds.'

'Can you take them with you now and sort it before you go away?' She didn't want to waste any time. 'I want to get it sorted as soon as possible and then you can tell your boss not to worry. I don't suppose they will argue with you, seeing as they aren't keen on the idea anyway.' She wrapped the sun-catcher in kitchen towel and handed it over to John. 'I'll text you over the bank details of the clinic. You can pay the money straight in. If there's any left over, send it to Rozalina. She doesn't have to know it's from me. You can tell her it's from Sasha.'

'Nothing else?'

Tina considered for a moment. 'Actually, if she asks, tell her the truth. If it was me, I'd want to know.'

John leaned forward and gave her a kiss on the head. 'Take care of yourself, Tina.'

A sudden feeling of panic swamped her. He was going. Possibly forever. She hadn't answered his question earlier. 'John, wait.' She put her hand on his arm. 'You be careful too. Ring me.'

'I can't, I'll be working.'

'No, I mean when you get back. Call me. I'd like to see you again.'

He studied her, his eyes measuring every inch of her face, every ounce of her body language analysed. 'You sure?'

'Positive.'

Chapter 46

The next two weeks dragged. Tina mentally crossed each day off in her mind. She was looking forward to John coming home so they could make a fresh start of their relationship. One that would be free of the past and free of secrets.

By the fifteenth day, she had still not heard anything from him. She had even taken to checking her phone by calling it from the house phone, just to make sure it was working properly.

'How are you today, pet?' asked Mr Cooper as she came into the living room with a plate of shepherd's pie she had made earlier that day.

'I'm fine,' she said, raising her voice several decibels to be heard. She smiled in confirmation.

Mr Cooper looked over his glasses at her. 'You look as if you have the weight of the world on your shoulders. Is it that young man of yours?'

'Of course not,' said Tina, secretly marvelling at the elderly gentleman's perception. He might be deaf, but there was nothing wrong with his eyesight. He took the tray from her and placed it on his lap, looking up at her with an expression that clearly said he didn't believe her. She sighed and sat down on the footstall. 'Okay, I confess. It is John.'

'I may be old, but I'm not stupid,' said Mr Cooper, following his comment up with a chuckle. 'I was young once myself, you know. Now, what's the problem?'

'He's working away and I was hoping he would be back by now.'

'Be patient, pet. He'll call you as soon as he can. He hasn't long been back in the country.'

'What?' Tina frowned. How would Mr Cooper know that John had been working abroad?

'John Nightingale, isn't it?'

'Yes, but …'

'On the news this morning, he was.' Mr Cooper picked up his fork and turned his dinner plate around a fraction to a more desirable position.

'John was on the news? I don't understand.' Tina swung round to look at Mr Cooper's television, as if by some miracle the news programme would appear. Instead a BBC2 quiz show greeted her. She looked at her watch. It was six twenty-five. The news would be all but over now. She looked back at Mr Cooper for further explanation. He was just putting a forkful of mash potato into this mouth. She willed him to eat quickly. As soon as she saw him swallow, she launched her next question. 'What did the news say?'

'I don't really know. I couldn't hear everything. Something about an arrest and it being a big coup for the serious crime squad. Some Russian bloke.' Mr Cooper returned to his dinner.

Tina rose to her feet, the need to get home and search through the news channels and trawl the internet for any scrap of information was overwhelming.

'I've got to go now, Mr Cooper,' she said. 'Lock your back door.'

'Bye, pet,' said Mr Cooper without looking up. 'Don't fret. The news will be back on again at nine o'clock.'

Tina burst through the kitchen door, flinging it closed behind her.

'Dimitri!' she hurried through to the living room and grabbed the remote control. 'Mummy quickly wants to check something, do you mind?' She was already calling up the menu.

Dimitri protested, but his voice was somewhere in the background, her mind not focusing on his response. 'I won't be long,' she muttered, immersed in searching the news channels.

The weather. A protest in London. Sports round-up. Fighting in the Middle East. A Royal official visit. Everything but an important arrest or even a sniff of John. She let out a long sigh. Flicked to the final channel available. More weather.

Admitting defeat, she reinstated Dimitri's programme and picked up her laptop.

She should have made this her first port of call. There on the homepage was the story.

RUSSIAN ANGER AT ARREST OF MOORGATE COP KILLER

International relations with Russia have become strained in a war of words over the arrest of a Russian citizen, who the Met believe is responsible for the fatal shooting of Police Officer Neil Edwards during the fumbled Moorgate bank heist five years ago. Another police officer was shot and injured that day.

The Russian Embassy is accusing the British Government of launching a covert operation to enter Russia and kidnap one of their citizens. The Home Secretary has strenuously denied all allegations.

'Our suspect was arrested on British ground under British law. The arrest has been carried out to the letter of the law, as I would expect it to be.'

Russia and the UK have no bilateral extradition treaty. Although Russia signed up to the European Convention on Extradition in 1996, it exempted itself from agreeing to send a Russian citizen to another country or state for prosecution. The Russian government has, in the past, stated that it would consider extradition of one of its citizens, but only in exchange for other Russian nationals held under arrest in the UK. The Home Office has always refused to trade nationals, stating that the Russians would be tried in their homeland for crimes against the government and could not, therefore, expect a fair trial.

Today's arrest comes after a five-year-long investigation into the criminal activities of the Porboski gang, who were reportedly responsible for organised crime across the capital. The Met, however, are making no further comment on the arrest.

There was a picture of the iconic Scotland Yard sign, but that was all. Tina read the online article again. There was no direct mention of either John or Pavel. She wondered if Mr Cooper had got it wrong about John. She would have to make sure she watched the news this evening.

Tina was seated in front of the TV long before the ten o'clock news. She patiently watched the hands of the clock climb their way to the hour and the opening music sound out across the room. Gareth Hughes greeted viewers, and against the backdrop of music, short VT images announced the headlines.

A tornado in America. A NHS hospital scandal. A product release by Apple.

Tina fidgeted in her seat and her patience was rewarded.

'Russia accuses Britain of kidnapping one of its citizens in the wake of the arrest of a suspect charged in connection with the killing of police officer Neil Edwards during the Moorgate bank robbery five years ago.'

Tina studied the news footage. It showed a car pulling into what looked like some sort of police compound in darkness, accompanied by two police outriders, their blue lights flashing. No sign of John.

She sat glued to the seat, willing the news reports to pass quickly, until they got to the Moorgate robbery item. The Welsh lilt of the news presenter seemed to dance across the room, repeating what Tina had already learned, really providing no more information. It showed a picture of Neil Edwards in his police uniform and a clip from five years ago of the scene cornered off after the shooting. Then it skipped back to the present day and the footage of the cars pulling into the compound. Tina sat on her knees in front of the screen, not unlike Dimitri did when he was watching something really exciting, and then she saw John. He was exiting the unmarked car and as he turned to open the rear door, she caught a good look of his face. She pressed the pause button. It was definitely John. Full marks to Mr Cooper for spotting him.

Tina watched the rest of the report and then spent the next ten minutes replaying it, purely to get a glimpse of John. The footage had cut back to the studio before the occupant in the rear of the car had been revealed. She didn't need to see. She knew who it was. She was glad for John's sake.

Maybe now he could forgive himself.

Chapter 47

John looked through the two-way glass into the holding room where Pavel Bolotnikov sat on a plastic chair in the middle of the empty space.

John had been wrestling with his feelings ever since they had arrived at the high-security unit. They weren't taking any risks with interviewing Pavel at a police station, there was too much of a chance that someone would want to either attempt to rescue him or, more likely, silence him.

John hadn't had time to consider his own emotions when they picked Pavel up in Russia. Too much was at stake to take his eye off the job in hand. Entering the country covertly, without attracting the attention of the Russian authorities, was one thing – kidnapping and extracting one of its citizens from right under their noses was another. If they had been caught they were, to all intents and purposes, on their own. Imprisonment, interrogation and, possibly, even death the only thing to look forward to. The Home Office's official line was that the British Government wasn't sanctioning any extradition operations, a line they were maintaining after the successful bid to bring Pavel back to the UK for trial.

Now, in the cold light of day, John wasn't experiencing the feelings of euphoria that he had anticipated. The past five years had been leading up to this moment and now that it was here, it wasn't that it was an anti-climax, but more of accomplishment. A job well done. The anger no longer burned, the hatred had been quelled. It surprised him. He was also left with something else he couldn't quite identify. Peace? Was that what he felt? Had he finally got justice for Neil? Maybe not justice, that would come when he saw Pavel sentenced. He hoped the courts wouldn't be too easy on him in light of the deal now on the table.

The door behind John opened and he turned to see Martin coming in.

'So, the bastard is going to deal, then?' He stood beside John.

'Looks that way.'

'How do you feel about that?'

'He'll still be put away for a long time. There's no way they'll be too lenient with someone who has killed a police officer.' John turned his back on the glass.

'True. Plus you won't have to go in the witness box and have your identity hidden and all that shit.'

John gave a shrug. 'Not that I'm particularly bothered having to do that. In fact, it would be my pleasure. But, as you so eloquently put it, it saves all that shit.'

'Fancy a pint?' said Martin, his hand resting on the door handle. 'You can show off your war wound to the lads.'

John touched the cut above his eyebrow. A wound courtesy of Pavel expressing his disagreement at being bundled into a car.

'Yeah, only the one, though,' said John. 'I've got someone to see.'

'That wouldn't be a certain Russian widow would it?'

'Need-to-know basis, mate,' said John, giving his friend a nudge in the back. There was also another widow he needed to speak to and Martin definitely didn't need to know that.

It was a bit of a shitty thing to do; keep watch on Hannah's house until her boyfriend went out, but John didn't want a confrontation with the guy. It would only upset Hannah and that was exactly what he wanted to avoid.

262

He waited a few minutes to make sure the boyfriend was well on his journey before knocking on the white UPVC door of the semi-detached house.

He could see Hannah's figure approach the door through the glass. She opened the door and, on seeing John, closed it immediately. John resisted the urge to put his foot over the threshold. It wouldn't be a smart move.

'Go away, John. I don't want to speak to you.'

'Please, Hannah, give me a couple of minutes.'

'If you don't go away, I'll get Ben. He's in the back garden.'

John pressed his mouth close to the doorframe. 'I've just watched him drive off to squash or badminton, or whatever it is he's doing with a racquet and gym bag.'

The door opened a fraction. Hannah glared at him through the two-inch gap. 'You have two minutes, starting now.'

'Can I at least come in?'

'Ten seconds gone already.'

She wasn't budging. 'Okay, here goes. Pavel Bolotnikov was arrested and charged with Neil's murder last night. He wants to deal information to shorten his sentence. The powers that be have agreed, but we are still going to be pushing for a harsh jail term.'

'Is that it? I saw it on the news last night. I'm not stupid, I worked it out myself.' There was a slight wobble in her voice.

'I also wanted to say sorry.' John paused. 'Sorry for creating a situation that put Neil in danger. Sorry for not being able to save him.' He hesitated once more as he too heard his own voice crack a fraction. 'And I'm sorry for giving you hassle about your new boyfriend. You deserve to be happy.'

Hannah opened the door wider. 'He's a good man, John,' she said. 'He loves me and adores Ella. We love him. He makes us happy. He makes us a family again.' She reached out and put her hand on John's arm. 'It doesn't mean that we don't love Neil any more. I know you miss him and this thing has been eating you up. We all miss him too – every day – but we can't live in limbo.

And you shouldn't either.'

John took Hannah's hand in his. 'I'm glad you're happy. Really I am.'

'I don't suppose me telling you that you're not to blame is something you haven't been told before. Go easy on yourself.'

John returned the small smile she offered. 'Yeah, thanks. You too.' John let her hand fall away.

'Goodbye, John.'

He turned away and heard the soft click of the door locking shut as he walked back down the path.

Standing in the park, watching Dimitri enjoy the challenges of balancing along a wooden log, Tina zipped up her jacket. The once-gentle breeze of autumn had defected over to winter, lacing its touch with icy-tipped fingers. She made a mental note to dig out their gloves and hats as she wiggled her fingers into her pockets to warm them up.

Dimitri didn't seem to notice, his attention far too focused on the task, as he shuffled along the log, his arms outstretched.

'Look at me, Mummy!'

'Very good,' she called back.

It was two days since she had seen the news item and still no word from John. Perhaps she hadn't made it clear enough that she wanted to see him again. Maybe he had got cold feet. Or worse … perhaps now he had achieved his goal of arresting Pavel, he didn't actually want her any more, despite what he had said when he left.

Something made her turn around; a sixth sense sort of feeling. She was alone in the park with Dimitri, the lateness of the afternoon, coupled with the cooler weather, deterring others from venturing out.

She shivered, aware that it wasn't because of the cold. She turned a full three hundred and sixty degrees. Empty.

'Mummy!' Dimitri's excited voice snapped her eyes directly onto her son.

He was waving at something behind him. Tina looked on. Her heart dive-bombed to her stomach and rebounded straight back up, taking her breath from her lungs.

'John.' Her voice a whisper that only she could hear. He'd come back.

He raised his hand and waved, before breaking into a jog and with a hand on the fence to the play area, hopped over the barrier. Dimitri ran towards him and John's firm hands immediately lifted the boy up, spinning him around in the air.

'Hey there, little fella,' said John, putting him back down. 'How are you?'

'Can we play football?'

John gave an exaggerated look around the play area. 'I'd love to, but I can't see a football or a goal post.'

'Come to our house. Play in our garden,' said Dimitri, jumping up and down on the spot.

'I'd love to come to your house.' He looked over at Tina. 'That's if your mummy doesn't mind.'

Tina knew the grin that had involuntarily plastered itself across her face already told John the answer to that one.